Fight to the Finish

They dropped their gun belts to fight it out another way. Buck Surratt knew his adversary had the strength of a rock-crusher. There was immense power in those ropy shoulder muscles, the girth of his neck, those thick wrists and fists, giving his arms the look of heavy-knobbed clubs. And yet Surratt goaded him, and so Bill Head threw himself across the room toward him. Surratt's mind told him he had made another mistake. Head slammed terrifically into him and threw him against the wall. His skull struck the boards, his brain roared. Head's fists were like axes chopping into his temples, driving daylight and memory out of him. Strength left his legs entirely, and thus blinded and stunned and momentarily helpless, he reached for Head's waist and caught it to weather the storm . . .

But that wasn't to be the end of it . . .

① A Signet Brand Western

SIGNET Westerns For Your Enjoyment

Trail Smoke

ERNEST HAYCOX

A SIGNET BOOK

NEW AMERICAN LIBRARY

TIMES MIRROR

SIGNET TRADEMARK REG. U.S. PAT. OFF. AND FOREIGN COUNTRIES
REGISTERED TRADEMARK—MARCA REGISTRADA
HECHO EN CHICAGO, U.S.A.

SIGNET, SIGNET CLASSICS, MENTOR, PLUME, MERIDIAN AND NAL
BOOKS *are published by The New American Library, Inc.,*
1633 Broadway, New York, New York 10019

FIRST SIGNET PRINTING, JANUARY, 1974

5 6 7 8 9 10 11 12 13

PRINTED IN THE UNITED STATES OF AMERICA

Chapter One

MAN ALONE

Forty hours of steady riding brought Buck Surratt across the wide desert to these foothills. The road at once left this burning plain and followed a canyon's rising tangents into broken masses of ravine and butte and deep green sweeps of pine. Far away and high up the Gray Bull peaks reared their stony shoulders.

A long training in trouble turned him aside from that canyon road. Bearing to the left, he climbed the ridge and reached its summit and there, with the invitation of the pines directly ahead of him, he paused to scan his back trail. His high, flat body became still and all the restlessness of his nature flowed into a hard, prolonged attention. The sun had dipped against the western horizon, and its edge seemed to burst and spill a golden lava across the earth; that final light laid a clear flame on the far mountains over there. Emptiness and a smoky heat haze filled the flat, tawny desert lying between. Buck Surratt's glance explored every detail of it, the whole picture engraving itself on his retentive memory. Afterwards his eyes turned to the green tangle of the hills. Up there was coolness and isolation—and anonymity for a man. And because these were the things he sought beyond all other things, he lifted his reins gladly and passed into the timber. . . .

At dark he sat on his heels with a pipe clenched between his teeth, watching the livid coals of his campfire burn a ruby hole through the felted shadows of the forest. Water ran sibilantly along the bottom of a ravine on his left; a damp, earthy smell rose from that black depth. The voice of the forest and its mysteries pulsed around him, softened by a small cool wind flowing off the Gray Bull peaks. Out of this deep solitude came the air-borne call of wildness, intangible, yet striking definitely through him. His shoulders swayed a little, he cocked his head to listen,

5

and the pressure around the corners of his long lips relaxed and smoothed away the taut, dry bitterness that had so long been there. The firelight struck up a bright flash in his eyes. A windless chuckle disturbed his chest and his inscrutable, sun-darkened cheeks broke to a faint smiling. He was still smiling when he rolled the blankets around him and fell asleep, the presence of that wild mystery invoking a swift response in his wire-tough body. It eased and nourished him, though he did not know why. There was some ancient familiarity here he didn't understand. The last thing he heard was the patient stir of the pony around its picket rope. . . .

The shot ripped a ragged hole through the stillness, its sound near enough to strike physically against him. Wakened, he remained a motionless moment in his blankets, keen to the possibilities of the night, hearing the echoes of the shot break and run down the corridors of these hills and die out remotely. His fire was dead and a thin, damp fog lay along the ground, with the curdled blackness of early morning condensed in the sky. The shot, he decided, had come from the canyon on his left. Down there brush began to break before a traveling body. He lifted his head from the saddle and reached beneath it and pulled his gun from the holster; and kicked aside his blankets, rolling quietly away. He got up and stood behind a tree. His horse blew out a gusty breath.

Somebody crashed up the side of the canyon without regard for secrecy. He heard the sound of a quirt slashing down and the reaching grunts of a pony. The rider came straight on, broke through the last brush and reached the little clearing. The pony stopped, and the breathing of animal and rider rasped heavily across the black; the pony was turning around and around, without control, and the rider's shape seemed to sway and almost fall from the saddle. An odd groan came out of the rider, very thin and very high. After that he wheeled and went away at a reckless gallop, bound east into the deeper mystery of the hills.

Buck Surratt remained by the tree until the last fugitive murmur had faded in the distance, then came back to his blankets and packed and lighted his pipe. He crouched down, pulling a blanket over his shoulders. There was no additional rumor in the canyon, no signal of life or pursuit. He lifted his watch to the pipe bowl and blew up the tobacco coals, and by that dim glow he registered the time. Ten minutes after two of a chilly morning. He replaced the watch and lay down in the blankets, supported on an elbow, his thinking sharp and taciturn and wary. There was, he understood, no more sleep for him. That one shot had destroyed all his security; his nearness to it had enmeshed him in whatever trouble was to follow. So considering, he debated his course and at half-past three, with a dim band of light beginning to break above the Gray Bull peaks, he rose and went down that slope whence the fugitive had come. At the bottom he distinguished a small clearing and a line rider's log cabin. The door was open and a saddled pony stood near by. He came up to the door, listening for sounds that never arrived. Presently he went in.

Twenty minutes later he climbed back up the canyon, breathing hard, the pipe clenched more tightly between his teeth. All his motions were swift and decided. He saddled and caught up his blankets; and then did a strange thing. Until this point in his journeyings he had worn his gun. Now he put gun and holster and belt in the blanket roll and lashed it behind the saddle. A little beyond four o'clock, with full daylight breaking, he rode eastward away from his camp.

The pony prints of the fugitive were increasingly clear to him, and at one point he got down and paid them a slow, enigmatic attention. He went on then, following the trail continuously upward, with his mind sticking hard to the central fact of the night gone. The trees broke away in front of a small mountain meadow turned amber by summer's heat; beyond the meadow the trail coursed out to a point and from that point he saw the road again, looping its way along the bottom of the rocky canyon. Beyond the road the country continued to rise in green waves toward the Gray Bull peaks. Turning to resume the trail, he found a rider poised at the edge of the trees. The man put both his hands on the saddle horn. He said, without inflection: "Mornin'."

There was in Buck Surratt the sudden leap of a wicked flame, but it made no change on that sun-darkened, wind-ruddied face; it did not disturb the enigmatic, faintly wistful gravity. He held himself straight, poised for whatever unexpected turn might come, and the powder-gray surfaces of his eyes bit into the opposite rider and absorbed all significance. The man was small and gray-haired, and his shoulders sloped from the years he had obviously spent punching cattle for thirty dollars a month. The corners of Buck Surratt's mouth relaxed imperceptibly.

He said, "Mornin'," in the same brief tone.

The small man allowed indifference to shade his talk. "Camp around here last night?"

"Back on the ridge."

The puncher's nose twitched briefly. "Hear a shot?"

"I heard it."

The puncher said, "Where——?" and definitely closed his mouth. He stared at Buck Surratt with a narrower interest. It was as though he threw up a guard and retreated from what he suddenly saw in Surratt. His glance fell to Buck Surratt's beltless waistline and remained there, showing wonder. "Well," he said, "I guess it's none of my business."

"That was my thought likewise," Buck Surratt mused. "So I rode on."

Silence fell, polite and discreet. Sunlight definitely reached over the Gray Bull peaks, slanting immaculate golden splinters across a flawless sky. The color of day stepped up one full octave. The puncher lifted a hand casually to his shirt pocket and got out his cigarette dust and rolled a smoke. He licked the cylinder with his tongue; his eyes were bright beneath the shading brim of his hat.

"Looking for a job?"

"That pegs my situation."

"I judged so, from the desert dust you're packin'. Go see Bill Head in Morgantown."

"Why Bill Head?"

"If you want a job," the puncher softly added.

Curiosity stirred Buck Surratt. He said: "I'm a great hand to pick my outfits."

The puncher's small shoulders lifted and fell. "That may be. But if you work, Head's the man you work for."

"Nobody else?"

"I doubt it," suggested the puncher. His words had a dry rustle; remote speculation gleamed in his calico-blue glance. "Morgantown's three miles. Cut down to the road." He picked up his reins and slowly rode a circle around Buck Surratt. There was a caginess here Surratt clearly identified. Matching the gesture he put his horse in motion and passed into the trees. He wasn't impolite enough to look behind him, but at the next sharp turn of the trail he caught a glimpse of the puncher's pony sliding into the far brush. A little beyond that point the trail swung down from the ridge to the road.

A stage came careening around a high bend of that

road, four horses running freely and a great boil of dust behind. The squealing of the brake blocks and the rattle of doubletree chains broke dissonantly across the dreaming peace of the morning and lingered long after the stage had rumbled out of sight beyond a farther curve. On the road, Buck Surratt took the lifting grade at a walk, his head bowed against the dust hanging heavy in the warming atmosphere.

To either side of him the canyon walls ran upward to distant vantage points, arousing in him a restless dissatisfaction at his exposure. It was a protective instinct he could not forget; and strengthening that feeling was the memory of the friendless reserve of the puncher on the ridge. There was a tension here that had its roots in some background of which he knew nothing. Once, looking behind, he caught a view of the distant desert all asmoke with its own glaring yellow heat.

At nine o'clock, hungry and alert, he rounded a final high bend of the canyon and came upon Morgantown.

It sat narrowly within the walls of the canyon, its single street bending between front-flared wooden buildings that held about them a beaten, long-settled look. The sidewalks were shaded by overhanging, second-story porches and trees grew intermittently up from the dust. Alleys ran back from this street, and down the alleys he observed houses clinging to the steep canyon walls. A woman in a blue dress and a white shirtwaist came out of one of these alleys, to look fully at him and to turn into a store whose sign read: "Annette Carvel, Dressmaker." Farther on, a saloon's ornate and varicolored windows set up a little blaze in the slanting sun. Beyond that, at the intersection of another alley, stood a new brick building with high, gingerbread cornices. Up in its central arch an inscription said: "William Head, 1887." A few horses stood three-footed at the hitching racks and a few people moved with unhurried leisure beneath the shade of the overhanging porches. All these things Buck Surratt absorbed with that insistent need for detail which forever drew his eyes to the stray motions of the world and to the subtle changes of men's expressions. At the stable beyond the bank he left his horse and quartered over to a restaurant he had noted.

He ate without haste and came again to the street, packing and lighting his pipe. The town seemed livelier than before. One rider came down from the hills into the upper end of the street at a canter and wheeled before a group of men standing there. The girl in the white shirt-waist appeared at the doorway of the dressmaking shop and rested a round white arm against the wood. Her eyes were on him deliberately, with a faint insistence that carried over the interval and stirred him. He saw then that she was young, and that her lips were full and curving and red across a face made graphic by some warm, frank curiosity lying within. Her hair was black. Even in the shadows there it was shining and turning her forehead and her cheeks whiter, more expressive. He dropped his glance, for something came from her to him and touched him with embarrassment. A man behind him said:

"Come up to the office a minute."

There was a short civilness in the tone, nothing more. Surratt turned without hurry to look down on the broad bulk of a man whose long and gray mustaches made a half-moon pattern along a face purely unemotional, plainly dogged. Surratt's attention remained on him steadily. A softness ran on with his talk. "Whose office?"

The older man's eyes dropped to Surratt's unbelted waistline and lifted with a freshening interest. "My name's Tom Bolderbuck," he said. "Marshal of the town." His glance deepened, and a reserve and a faint courtesy rubbed the edges of his command. He stepped half a pace backward. Two thin lines started across the pink swell of his forehead. "Some gentlemen up the street want to see you a minute in the jail office."

Behind a continued impassivity, Surratt's mind ran quick and knowing. There had been a shot deep in the hills and the invisible telegraph of cattle country had picked up that rumor of trouble and carried it on. He had a part to play here, as he had known since the crash of that bullet had wakened him. He said, "Sure," and moved his high, alert body up the walk, the marshal tramping at his side.

A man at the hotel doorway wheeled and stared. The group collected farther up the street had disappeared through a doorway, but the rider who had come so rapidly into town still stood by his horse. Surratt saw the pony's flanks stained with sweat; his glance came up to the puncher and recognized him to be the thin fellow he had met on the trail. The man's eyes were fixedly on him, deliberately without recognition, remotely hostile. Bolderbuck said, "Go ahead," and Surratt bowed his neck and passed into the jail office.

In the semidarkness he saw the forms of men standing along a far wall. They were waiting for him and in the room was a feeling of challenge. It sent a rapid warning all through his flat muscles.

A voice said, in a swift, attacking way: "You camped on Soapstone Ridge last night?"

"A ridge near the road," replied Buck Surratt. "I'm not acquainted with its name."

"You heard a shot?"

"Yes."

"Know anything about it?"

"No."

"Where's your gun?"

"Packed in my blanket roll, on my horse."

Stillness came on, broken only by a curt murmur that sent Bolderbuck immediately out of the jail office. Surratt's eyes, better accustomed to the darkness here, saw five men posted beyond a table, watching him across a bottomless gulf of suspicion. They were all past middle age, except for the one who had done the talking. He was young, as young as Surratt, and he stood a halfbeam above them, with a muscular swell to chest and arm and neck that was impressive. He had a round face, whose bold and lively features gave it a handsomeness that was faintly heavy and very sure. He was a yellow-haired man, with lips long and heavy and controlled.

He laid out his question in the manner of a man who would not be denied, who never had been denied. "Where do you come from?"

"West of the desert."

"Whereabouts, I said."

Buck Surratt's shoulders shifted. His voice rode a steady tone. "Who are you, my friend?"

The man stared at Surratt, displeased. "My name's Bill Head. I still want to know where you're from."

"I have told you," Buck Surratt remarked softly, "as much of that as it is necessary for you to know."

A sudden tide of ruddy color washed across Bill Head's round, self-certain face. Temper flashed in his eyes and pressed arrogance into his full lips. "The hell you say. I don't like saddle bums talking that way to me."

There was a man at the end of the group in a blue serge suit that fit him loosely. He seemed deferent in this company, oppressed by it. He said a dry, cautious word to

11

Buck Surratt: "You're in a ticklish situation, my boy. Answer the question and——"

Bill Head cut him off. "I'll do the talking, Sheriff."

It stilled the sheriff. Looking at him in curiosity, Buck Surratt saw how he accepted that rebuke without resentment—and filed the man's character in the back of his mind.

"What are you doing up here?" insisted Head.

"Just traveling."

The marshal, Bolderbuck, came back into the office. He said in his matter-of-fact voice: "It's there all right." A small interval of tight silence came on again and Surratt's eyes memorized that scene to its smallest detail. The sheriff was a nonentity in a blue serge suit, the marshal an unimaginative errand boy. It was the other four lined up side by side against the wall who had the power here. He saw them in brief clearness; the old man with the transparent skin and mild eyes who chewed silently on his tobacco quid and listened, the fat-bodied one whose skin was dusky as that of an Indian, the long and bony and sharp-nosed one who nodded at each spurt of talk—and this Bill Head who seemed to rule them.

Bill Head asked: "Want a job?"

But there was an interruption. Somebody came into the office and stood slightly behind Buck Surratt, and then the whole atmosphere of the place changed. There had been suspicion and unfriendliness rolling against him. Now it seemed to change direction and strike beyond him, against the newcomer, with a greater and more resentful effect. Deeply curious, Buck Surratt looked around and saw the man—tall and lean and restless—smiling back at that obvious dislike with an ironic twist of his mouth. He was redheaded and excessively freckled, and his eyes were almost green against a sandy complexion.

Bill Head spoke bluntly enough. "This is a private meeting, Torveen."

"So I heard," agreed Torveen. His talk reached Bill Head with a cool and malicious effect. Bill Head's glance burned out his distrust, yet he had nothing more to say to the man. Buck Surratt remembered that, and found this Torveen's glance to be appraisingly and shrewdly on him. Bill Head repeated his question.

"You want a job?"

Surratt said: "Who with?"

"Maybe I'll give you a job."

12

"I'll think about it."

Bill Head's solid chin stretched forward. "Wait a minute, mister. You're too fast with your answers entirely. Maybe you've got only two things to do—take the job or go to jail."

Surratt said softly: "Why?"

"Because you were entirely too damned close to that shot last night. I propose to find out more than you've told me."

"I'll still think about it," Surratt drawled. There was, then, nothing to break the force of their general scrutiny. They were tearing him apart with their thoughts; their minds were fencing him in with the events of the night. He reached for his tobacco and packed his pipe. He scratched a match on the table and wiggled it across the bowl. His features had nothing to tell them; but his glance crossed to Bill Head and remained there narrowly. He turned without comment and walked from the room.

Below the jail office he stopped and considered the stable across the street, where his horse was. But he understood he could not ride away now and so went on, past the white porch of the hotel and beneath the shade of the overhanging board awnings. There were many people collecting in town, and the smell of trouble definitely lay along the street. He knew it and he understood it, this Buck Surratt who was somewhat of a specialist in trouble. It keyed him up. He came to a stand on the edge of the walk, pipestem bitten securely between his teeth, his mind alive.

A rider—a girl—ran out of the upper trees into town at a steady canter, lifting the thick dust behind her. Buck Surratt looked that way incuriously; and then was curious. She was dressed in a man's blue levi pants and a man's brown cotton shirt, open at the neck. She rode the saddle in a way that was good to see, her shoulders swinging, her body full of grace. Turning in at the rack across the street she dropped to the ground with one careless jump and went across the walk toward the door of the dressmaking shop, calling in a quick and even-pitched voice: "Annette." Surratt got one brief view of her face before she disappeared inside; she had looked back and her attention struck him and noticed him, and then the brim of her wide hat hid her expression.

Without directly watching, he saw Torveen come along the walk at a lazy stroll. Somebody said: "Hello, Sam."

Torveen's answer was plain and, as it had been in the jail office, cheerfully ironic. "Don't speak to pariahs like me, Spud." He stopped beside Surratt. He teetered his boots on the edge of the walk and looked out into the yellow dust, his eyes half shut. He said indifferently: "You been offered one job, friend. I'll offer you another."

"What kind of a job?"

"A job," said Torveen laconically.

Surratt murmured: "I rode into this damned country to keep out of trouble."

Torveen murmured: "That's your hard luck." He was grinning, his lips thin and crooked. Some deviltry in his thoughts kept sparkling through his eyes.

"Thanks for the offer, but I guess not," said Surratt. "Who's that girl?"

Torveen chuckled. "You're an observin' scoundrel. Which girl? Annette? Or the one which just came in? She's Judith Cameron. You saw her daddy in the jail office—the benevolent-appearin' old pirate with the white mustache and tobacco chaw. I thought you were tryin' to keep out of trouble."

He turned his head quickly, toward the upper end of town. Following suit, Buck Surratt saw a file of riders coming down with a pack horse. There was a burden, rolled in canvas, lashed across the pack horse. Surratt's lips tightened; the pipe shifted between his teeth. He said: "Who've they got?"

Torveen turned and stared at him, for once not smiling. "It's the man that was killed last night in the hills." Surratt saw speculation flickering in those green eyes. "Leslie Head—Bill Head's brother. Maybe a lot of things are plainer to you now."

The two women had come from the dressmaking shop. They stood in front of the doorway, staring up the street. He saw the drawn expression on Annette Carvel's cheeks and the enormous soberness of the other girl, Judith Cameron. She felt Surratt's glance, and looked abruptly at him; and turned her eyes away again. Surratt removed his pipe; he bowed his head and remained in this studying attitude. He said: "I'll take the job—for reasons of my own."

Torveen's grin freshened across the brick-red skin. "I got reasons of my own for askin' you. So we're even. Get your horse and ride up the road three miles till you see a fence. Turn in there." But after a minute he added dryly: "That is, if you can leave town. There may be some argument about that."

Surratt left him, quartering over to the stable. He paid the hostler and went back and got his pony. But he stood a moment by it before mounting, staring at the blanket roll. It had been pawed apart, and the end of his gun belt hung out. He withdrew the gun belt and strapped it on, and lifted the revolver and spun the cylinder before replacing it. In the saddle he sat motionless, his head bowed a little. His lips made a faintly downward semicircle and his breathing deepened. He turned and rode from the stable.

Bill Head had walked down the street with the others. They were halted by the hotel now, a circle of townsmen forming around them. Sam Torveen loitered against a near-by porch post and seemed indifferent to the scene. Bolderbuck noticed Surratt and broke from the circle, walking over and waving his hands negatively. "You'll have to get down——"

Surratt brushed by, riding toward the circle. He slipped from the saddle and walked on to where Bill Head stood. Bill Head had been watching, his big shoulders reared. Surratt's cheeks were thin and his voice slashed against Head with a queer, exciting effect:

"I believe it was your suggestion that sent the marshal down to paw over my blanket roll and look at my gun. Is that right?"

Bill Head showed a sultry surprise. "Certainly."

Buck Surratt's body kinked at the waist. It threw his torso ahead of his hips. He stood this way, stiffly, with both arms hanging straight down. A man behind Bill Head suddenly pushed himself to one side—an obvious move that agitated and shifted the other townsmen. Head looked around, scowling at this change; and then his glance whipped back to Surratt, his attention rigid and full with what he saw. All the group turned dead still.

"I am warning you," said Buck Surratt. His talk struck the silence recklessly, flattening and swelling. "Never touch my things again. Do you understand? Never touch them again."

He took a backward step and got into the saddle; and turned and went trotting up the street. Nobody spoke. Sam Torveen, with his shoulders against the porch post, was silently laughing. Judith Cameron saw him doing this and looked at Bill Head with a deepening wonder, and then watched Buck Surratt rise at the head of the canyon

15

and turn beyond the bend of the road and disappear. Bill Head's cheeks were locked in a flushed, angry confusion. Annette Carvel at once whispered to Judith: "Who is he—who is that new, good-looking man?"

Chapter Two

SAM TORVEEN

He rode out of Morgantown at a short trot, as deliberate in retreat as he had been in attack. But when he turned the first bend of the road he set his horse to a fast, reaching canter and held it.

The road kept winding and climbing, with lesser roads angling off at intervals to ranches hidden somewhere behind the trees. Now and then, up an occasional vista, he got a brief view of the Gray Bull peaks, but otherwise his roving glance struck against the solid green wall of the forest. The day was fresh and still, with the fragrance of pine resin strong in it. All the details of this mountain world were vivid and pleasant. They fed his senses in a way that was strange to him, fulfilling a hunger he did not understand, covering him with a comfort and a familiarity even as his regretting thoughts dwelt on the scene in Morgantown. He had crossed the desert to find ease and rest—the deep desire of his life; yet the echoes of that night bullet had laid an ancient pattern of trouble over these hills, and he was trapped in the pattern. The ways of a man's life, he thought wistfully, always caught up with him.

Around the next quick bend of the road he came upon a man riding loosely and sleepily, the fatness of his body jiggling to the motion of the horse. A black-brimmed stetson slanted over his features and hid them until the sound of Surratt's nearing pony roused him. He hauled himself back in the saddle then and hoisted his shoulders. His eyes were a sparkling black, set close to a gigantic nose that brought the rest of his face to a point. He stopped immediately, and Surratt, following suit, saw some kind of an emotion ripple through this vast hulk and straighten the loose lines of a pendulous mouth. Surratt dropped his hands on the saddle horn. Severe and motionless he

17

watched the man scan him and identify him. He said then:

"You never saw me before, Blackjack. And I don't know you. Do you get it?"

The man's lips spread and became loose again. He folded both arms across his bully chest and seemed to struggle darkly with his confused thoughts. His eyes dropped from Surratt, and that was all. Surratt went by him. Three hundred yards up the slope he saw a fence and a road paralleling it. This he followed, passing into the semidarkness of the pines, into a thick warm silence. Five minutes later the trees dropped away and left him on the edge of a rolling basin surrounded by timber and ridges. A creek slashed its way through the meadow, glistening under the sunlight; across the creek stood a ranch house, long and low and gray, surrounded by the customary clutter of sheds and corrals of cattle land. Surratt went over a plank bridge, lifting a hollow signal of arrival, and circled the house. A dark little man sat on the edge of the porch oiling a rifle. He looked up with the sharpest and briefest of glances, and returned his attention to the gun. Surratt dismounted.

The man's head instantly lifted again. He said, uncharitably: "Anybody invite you to light here?"

"Torveen's place?"

"Yeah."

Surratt shrugged his shoulders. He walked to an empty box and overturned it and sat down; he got out his pipe and loaded it. But his nerves were alert, keened by the suspecting unfriendliness of that other man's attention. He was beyond forty, Surratt judged, and gray at the temples; there was a thinness of body and temper about him, a wicked excitability. Something struck Surratt on his left side then, something that had weight but no physical substance. He got a match out of his pocket and lighted it, his glance sliding quickly along the porch. A sort of an ell ran back from the left corner of the house, with four doors opening into what he judged to be kitchen and bunkroom. His eyes went along the ell and reached a window and stopped. Behind the window was the attentive face of a young man, pallid and prematurely etched by lines of violence.

Surratt ground the burnt match into his palm, creating a sooty disk there. He pulled smoke into his lungs, his lips lengthened and tightened. The feel of this place was bad. It rubbed his fur the wrong way, it kept plucking at his senses, it cocked his muscles. A horse scudded out of the trees. Looking up, he saw Sam Torveen wheel around the house and step to the ground. The little man on the porch rose immediately. He stared at Torveen.

"You know this fella?"

"Sure," said Torveen.

The man's wire-edged features snapped to anger. He said something under his voice and picked up his gun and went scowling through a doorway, into the ell.

Torveen's grin streaked angularly across his sandy cheeks. "You may like Nick Perrigo," he said carelessly. "Or you may not. He's my foreman. Come inside." The restlessness of this redheaded man sent him across the porch at a high stride. Soberly following, Buck Surratt came into a long bare room cluttered with the gear of a cattleman. There was a bunk at one end, and a fireplace, and a desk with a tally book and a pad of writing paper on it, and two chairs. The windows had wooden shutters that closed from the inside; a stand containing four rifles stood near the bunk. Torveen dropped into a chair. He hooked a leg over the chair's arm and began swinging it. The greenness of his eyes was brighter and there was the stronger impression of a controlled rashness playing behind that color.

"Want a drink?"

"No."

"You've heard my name mentioned. I don't know yours."

"Buck Surratt."

Sam Torveen bent forward. "What was the idea of that play against Bill Head?"

Surratt said, gently: "Just to freeze things up long enough for me to get out of town."

"Supposin' the play hadn't worked?"

"It worked."

"Supposin' it hadn't?" insisted Torveen.

"I never figure more than one step ahead at a time," murmured Surratt.

"The hell you don't," countered Torveen. "You're half a mile ahead of yourself, every foot of the way. I been laughin' to myself ever since—the way you framed that." His grin was hard and cheerful. "You're trapped in town but you walk up to Bill Head, give him hell, and ride off before he can get unsnarled from his surprise. If he was a man quick on the recoil you couldn't of made that play

19

stick, friend Buck. But you pegged him as bein' slow. I take off my hat to you."

Surratt's mind reviewed the scene in Morgantown methodically. There was a need in him for information, as there always was. "Who's Bill Head?"

"He runs the Crow Track for his old man, who's a cripple. It's a big jag of land, north of here, up in the hills."

"There was a dark, heavy fellow standing beside him."

"Dutch Kersom, another old-timer with plenty of cattle. I already named you Ab Cameron. The fourth fellow, the one with the bony face, was Hank Peyrolles. They'll account for eighty per cent of the beef in this section."

"The sheriff's not a proud man," reflected Surratt, "and the marshal just does what he's told."

Torveen chuckled broadly. "You're figgerin' again." But his eyes were curious. "Why did you ride into Morgantown, instead of goin' back to the desert? You must of known that shot would get you in trouble."

Surratt looked at Torveen steadily. Torveen shook his head and made a dry observation. "I'm not sayin' you did the shootin', Surratt. I meant that you're a stranger and you're pulled into it."

"Where would I run?"

Torveen remarked, very quietly: "So you're here, for reasons of your own. The pay is thirty a month."

"If I stay."

Torveen had a poker expression on his roan cheeks. "You came for a reason. It still holds good, doesn't it?"

"Yes," said Surratt. But his thoughts were on Nick Perrigo and the pallid face in the window, and his mind balanced evenly, with no decision. He could not resolve the puzzle. The reflection of it crept faintly into the studying soberness of his cheeks.

Slack in his chair, Torveen watched this out of his jade eyes. "Your head," he murmured, "never stops working. You got this ranch sized up and there's somethin' about it you don't cotton to."

"That's right."

Torveen shifted his body. The smile left him, the corners of his mouth stiffened. Inscrutably patient, Surratt searched the sandy cheeks of this Torveen, seeking some solid bottom behind the surface recklessness, beyond the skeptical glint of deviltry. He could not help it. All the hard training of his years had disciplined him to silence, to patience, to a perpetual vigilance against the trickeries of

20

men. Faintly, he saw something now. Torveen's cheeks relaxed and a strain showed itself and his tone became ragged. He said: "If you stay, you'll find out for yourself. I need help, friend Buck, but I'll tell you no more—and I'm not askin' you to stay."

A steel triangle on the porch began to beat harsh sound across the day. It was noon, it was dinnertime. Boots scraped the porch boards and there was a rider coming in from the meadow. Torveen said, "Let's eat," and rose and led the way to the porch. He ducked through a door of the ell, into a dining room. Coming in, Surratt found three men already at the table and an enormous Chinaman standing against the wall. Then a fourth man entered and took his place, staring at Surratt with one brief, curious glance. Surratt sat down, silently reversing his capsized plate. Torveen said to the crew in his casual touch-and-go voice: "The name of the new member is Buck Surratt. Wang, if you don't quit puttin' so damn many eggshells in the coffee I'm going to throw a plate at you."

The Chinaman didn't stir and didn't show a change of expression. Torveen reared his head, obviously irritated. "I meant that," he grunted. But he covered the irritation instantly, nodding his head at the individuals in the crew as he named them for Surratt. "You know Perrigo, the gentle soul. The kid there is Ferd Bowie. Good-lookin' gander near you uses a title called Chunk Osbrook. It may be his real name, I don't know. Last man there answers to Ed."

They looked briefly at him without acknowledgment. For his part, Surratt went imperturbably on with his eating. But his mind registered them with a camera clarity and their faces told him things they hadn't intended to tell. This Ed was an easy-going misfit in a crowd that had a jarring, explosive note. Perrigo sat stirring his coffee with a bitter and unpleasant concentration on his dry, drawn features. The kid—Ferd Bowie—was bony and peaked. He still had an adolescent down on his cheeks, but there was a sallow savagery all about his look that told Buck Surratt of wickedness too early learned. Chunk Osbrook lifted a pair of ink-black eyes and seemed to measure Surratt for weight and reach. He was blunt and solid and proud of his strength, and Surratt understood then he would never be satisfied until he had demonstrated it. Buck Surratt suddenly remembered another man in his past who had been like that.

21

They ate out their hunger and left the room. More leisurely, Surratt listened to their idle palavering on the porch. When he was through he went out there and packed his pipe and glanced through the soft bright heat of the meadow, not noticing them. The talk had stopped with his appearance and the silence was a morose, alien thing. Torveen stood in the doorway of the main house, indifferent and minutely smiling, as though he were removed from this animosity and impartial to it. But Surratt detected the irony of that man's glance.

He tried another match on his pipe and clenched it between his teeth. Stepping off the porch he walked over to his pony and unlashed the blanket roll. The stillness behind him was hard and continuing, and he had no need to turn to see how closely they were watching him. He strolled back to the ell and went along it to the end door. Inside, he saw a dozen double-decked bunks surrounding a stove and a table and four home-made chairs. Heat and stale smoke and the horsy smell of men's clothes lay thick through the room. He dropped his roll on an empty bunk and walked back to the porch.

Nick Perrigo sat on the porch edge, his back bent far forward, his hands on his knees. He glowered at the dust; the nerve-ridden thinness of his face sharpened. He said idly: "Chunk, you left your tobacco in the bunkroom."

Chunk Osbrook rose with a jerk, as though released from enforced waiting. His spurs dragged along the porch. Not looking that way, Surratt heard him strike the flat of his hand against the building wall and go into the bunkroom.

There was a quality of expectancy flowing out from this crew that fanned across Surratt's cheeks; it was an intangible thing other men might not have felt. But for him, trained in the shadings of trouble, it registered on receptive senses and ticked a coolness along his nerves. In the bunkroom something fell to the floor. He turned then and stared at these men. They were looking away from him, motionless against the sunlight—and waiting. There was, he thought regretfully, nothing new in this pattern; it was the pattern of his life and all the running in the world would not help him. He walked back to the bunkroom door and went in.

It was his blanket roll on the floor, thrown there by Chunk Osbrook. The man stood backed up against the table, his feet braced apart. A slow, deep breathing lifted

22

and lowered the heavy arch of his chest; and his eyes were round and bright and greedy. He said:

"Your junk was in my way."

Surratt walked around the table. The space was narrow and he had to pull his shoulders aside to avoid brushing Osbrook. He went on around. Osbrook made a swift wheel and sudden doubt shaded the glitter of his desire. The table lay between them. Surratt put his hands at the edge of the table, gripping it. His thoughts were dismal then, darkened by the going of a hope. The ways of a man's life always caught up with him. Somewhere was peace but not for him; and this chore had to be done. There wasn't any emotion in his voice.

"The boys wouldn't want to miss this, Chunk."

The sweep of his hands carried the table up against Chunk Osbrook's taut frame and destroyed the rush the man was set to make. Osbrook flung the table aside with a lunge of his arm. Rage came out of Buck Surratt in a gust of breathing and turned his face white. He threw himself against Osbrook, the point of his shoulder driving Osbrook across the floor to the doorway. Osbrook struck against the casing and ripped up a jabbing blow that caught Surratt wickedly in the belly. They fought and heaved and wrestled around the doorway, using their knees and their elbows. But Surratt dislodged Osbrook from the casing and drove him to the edge of the porch. Osbrook fell off backwards, landing on a shoulder.

Surratt jumped down to the dust and leaped aside. Osbrook, on his knees, made a dive for Surratt's legs and missed. He rolled on and lunged up to his feet—and charged, his knees driving him, his shoulders low and crouched. Surratt met him savagely. He broke up that lowering, bull-like rush. He sheered away those flogging arms and reached Osbrook's turning temple with one sledging smash. It exploded through the man's head and he saw Osbrook's eyes mirror the streaked craziness it produced. It took the power out of Osbrook's fists; they sagged and struck without aim, and then Surratt crashed his temple again and sent him down into the dust. Osbrook was blind, he was half knocked out, but the attacking instinct still held him together and he reared back on his knees and made another grab for Surratt's legs. Surratt kicked the man's hands aside and tramped a half circle around Osbrook. He reached down and got Osbrook around the neck, hauling him up that way. There wasn't any pity in him as he battered that broad and dogged face at will. Osbrook's lips began to drip and spread formlessly, and when he fell he rolled a little and his hands reached vainly for Surratt; and then he was through, his legs squirming involuntarily.

Surratt walked backwards; he turned. The crew hadn't stirred. They didn't stir now, but the color of Ferd Bowie's eyes was deep and hating, and the wildness of his disappointment burned bright spots on his starved, consumptive cheeks. Nick Perrigo stared at his feet, bitter and biding his time. The other man, Ed, rested his body on the building wall and seemed afraid of all this. Sam Torveen remained in the doorway, an obscure smile on his face; he was behind the crew and they didn't see him raise a hand toward Surratt in a half-saluting manner.

There were three of them here, Surratt understood, who respected nothing but the whip—Perrigo and Bowie and Chunk Osbrook. Pity or generosity they didn't know. He cast a quick look behind him to where Osbrook had risen uncertainly. He looked back to the porch again, the temper in him still pitched to kill.

He said: "Is that all—or is there some more?"

They had nothing to say. He hadn't felt Osbrook's blows and hadn't been aware of being struck. But suddenly his body began to hurt where those blows had landed.

Twilight flowed across the meadow in indigo ripples, and somewhere in the depths of the hills a coyote's howl thickened the land's deep loneliness. A faint wind came off the Gray Bull peaks and rustled through the trees like the echoes of a distant waterfall. Abruptly it was dark, with the lights of the ranch laying rich yellow beams across soft blackness. Ferd Bowie's horse clacked over the creek bridge and Ferd Bowie wheeled into the yard. He said, "All right," and got down.

The crew made vague shapes on the porch. Somebody ticked a cigarette through the air, and when it fell its burning tip burst into a vivid spray of light. They had been waiting here, the sense of it very strong to Surratt—and now the waiting was done and they were rising along the porch. Sam Torveen's voice was keen and a little whipped-up. "Everybody inside." He turned into the big room, the others at his heels. Following, Surratt heard horses traveling down his road.

Torveen stood in the center of the room, his red hair ragged on his forehead. He was smiling again, crookedly.

24

"Some of them will come in and some will stay in the yard. Ed, you go stand at the corner of the house." He looked at Buck Surratt, that glinting amusement strong in his eyes. "You came up here for reasons of your own, friend Buck. The reasons are about to appear." He moved around the room, closing the wooden shutters against the windows and dropping the bars across them. He returned to the table, caught up the lamp and placed it in a corner of the room where its light would not make a background. Perrigo and Bowie and Chunk Osbrook had posted themselves around this room, making dark and studied shapes. The oncoming men boomed across the plank bridge. They were in the yard presently—and halted. A voice that was familiar to Surratt hailed the house.

"Torveen. I want to see you."

Torveen reached the doorway. He stopped there. He seemed to be suppressing laughter. "Come in, Bill." A boot began scraping behind Surratt, and he stared around and saw the kid, Ferd Bowie, waving a little. He said: "Stop that, kid." The kid's glance burned wickedly on him. Torveen had taken a few deliberate back steps into the room; and now men filed in and made a sober, alert rank there. He recognized Bill Head and the sheriff. The others were strange to him.

Bill Head's ruddy face veered and his eyes found Surratt. The angry memory of Morgantown wrote itself across the man's bold features. He said to Surratt: "Get your belongings. You're going to Morgantown."

Torveen laid his electric grin on Head. He said: "You offered this man a job today. What for, Bill?"

"To keep my eyes on him," grunted Head.

"He's got a job here—and I'll keep my eyes on him."

"No," grunted Head. "He's bein' arrested."

Torveen turned his attention to the sheriff. "You got a warrant, Ranier?"

"Yeah."

Surratt spoke quietly. "What for?"

"The killin' of a man named Leslie Head," said Ranier.

Silent laughter showed across Torveen's eyes. "Tear up the warrant, Sheriff."

Bill Head swung and threw his shoulders forward. "What?"

"He ain't goin'."

The breathing of these men filled the room. Lamplight disturbed and stained their expressions. The shadow of violence lay here. The sheriff's body was stiff and crooked. Bill Head seemed to be rummaging his mind. Surratt thought that his first impressions had been right; the man was slow on the bounce. But it was to be seen now that he had an implacable stubbornness.

"That's bad, Torveen."

Torveen said, almost idly: "I stand back of my men. You should have known that before you came. You might have guessed a warrant would do you no good. There is no way of getting Surratt except by takin' him. You think you want to take him, Ranier?"

Sweat glinted along the sheriff's forehead. His eyes turned and begged Head for an answer. Behind Surratt the kid's feet were restlessly shuffling again.

Head said definitely: "No. We'll leave the gunplay alone. It isn't necessary." He directed his talk at Surratt. "Better consider this and ride into Morgantown tomorrow. You're in a trap. If I don't see you in town twelve hours from now it's open season on you, wherever you're found."

"That's plain," said Torveen cheerfully.

Head's face showed the sting of the remark. It was flushed and irritated. "You better take a long look at your own hole card, Sam. Come on."

They filed out. Motionless, Surratt listened to them mount and ride away. Nobody spoke until the echo of their departure had died beyond the trees. Ed came across the porch then and put his head through the doorway. Torveen said: "You plant yourself on the bridge, Ed, and stay till you're relieved."

It broke up the party. Ed disappeared, and Perrigo led Osbrook and the kid out of the room. Torveen turned on Surratt. He had ceased to smile.

"Your reason for comin' up here was to get yourself some protection you saw you were goin' to need. Well, I gave you the protection. That's my part of the bargain. But call it quits if you want. I'll not hold you from ridin' away."

Surratt murmured: "I don't welsh on my debts."

"I didn't think you would," drawled Torveen. "Well, I told you I had my reasons, too. You'll discover them soon enough. As for the crew I've got, you know their kind. But I'm in a fight and I can't be nice about my choice of men." He stopped, framing some further explanation. Surratt saw it die. Torveen only added: "What you have to

26

do to those boys is your business, not mine. I guess you've figured that already, so I don't have to warn you."

Surratt turned to the porch. He went along it, stepping into the bunkroom. Osbrook was lying on one bunk, Perrigo on another. The kid sat up to the table, playing solitaire in moody silence. None of them looked directly at him, yet as he unrolled his blankets and pulled off his clothes he felt the effect of a sidewise, covert scrutiny. He rolled into the bunk and put a palm over his eyes and stared above him, slowly balancing the help they had given him against the unqualified hatred they bore him. There was the thread of motive running through this contradiction, but he could not ferret it out. They were men who answered only to the whip: they did not understand softness. He knew then he had something to do here.

He turned his head toward the kid and spoke bluntly, ungently. "Kill that light, kid."

Ferd Bowie's head jerked. The sullen hatred that was so strong in him poured across the room. He burst out: "What the hell did you come here for?"

Surratt reared from his blankets. He put a hand on the edge of the bed. "If I come over there, runt, I'll spank you dry. Put out the light."

The kid kicked back his chair, rising. There was a violent agony of choice printed on his sallow cheeks. Nick Perrigo remained still on his bunk and looked at this scene with a bright, scheming attention. But the kid blew out the light and stamped from the room. Presently Surratt heard Perrigo get up and call Osbrook. They went out. A door slammed down the porch. In a moment he heard their voices rising and quarreling with the fainter voice of Torveen.

Something was plain enough to Surratt then. Torveen hired them because he needed them. But it appeared they had gotten beyond his control. Maybe this was why Torveen had offered him the job. He considered it slowly. But he was tired, and there was a sharp regret in him for the ways of life he could not escape and the hope of something he could not name and could never reach; and presently he fell asleep.

Chapter Three

GIRL WITH THE
YELLOW HAIR

Surratt swung into his saddle. "I'm going to have a look at this country."

Torveen murmured idly: "That's all right."

Morning swelled across the meadow in warm full waves of sunlight. Surratt's horse pitched gently around the yard, strong with the desire to travel, but Surratt was watching Nick Perrigo, who remained so still and dissenting by the bunkroom door. There was a challenge in this man, rising from some obscure purpose. And then Surratt let the pony go, lining out over a meadow still sparkling with night's dew.

The sky was flawlessly blue, and a piny smell lay thick and pleasant in this upland air. Five hundred yards beyond he reached the trees and passed into them, following the climbing curves of a broad trail. He looked back at this point to find what he had expected he might find; a rider cut away from the ranch house and trotted over the meadow at a different angle, soon disappearing.

But the morning laid its ease upon Surratt and he was smiling in a way that relieved the gray sharpness of his smoky eyes, and his glance traveled the quiet brown corridors of these hills with an eagerness long unknown to him. He passed the scar of a woodcutter's camp, thereupon falling into an ancient corduroy road. The day was turning hot, a faint drone of the forest's minute life disturbing this shadowy stillness. A bird's scarlet wings flashed out sudden brilliance across the trail. Impelled by the restless vigor of his body, he kept climbing, and two hours later came to a bald knob high on a ridge where two roads crossed and an ancient signboard pointed northward, reading: "Carson's Ford." He went on out into the clearing—and stopped.

Eastward the timber rose in continuous green folds. But

elsewhere, from this high vantage point, the hill country lay clearly visible under the gold streamers of the sun. Far to the west the desert rolled on beneath its own sultry flashing—on to copper and blue horizons. Nearer, crowded against the trees, the housetops of Morgantown made a rectangular pattern against the tawny earth. He caught all this in one sweep, and turned then to look directly below him. He had climbed the southern side of the ridge and saw at his feet a valley running away from the north slope of the ridge. Narrow and summer-yellow, it lay between stiff-pitched hill walls, with fences setting off its surface in square design and one long ranch house sitting in the center of it, surrounded by outbuildings. A river cut a black-green serpentine course down the valley's middle, crossed by a bridge; on the road beside the river were the lifting dust puffs of some stray rider. He considered the picture with a definite approval, and then looked regretfully to the high east, where the Gray Bull peaks marked the boundary of some far country. There was a feeling in him to be on his way, to run with the days and leave his campfires behind him, one by one, until the rash and foot-loose mood in him turned cold. But even as he thought of it, he remembered his obligation to Sam Torveen and turned back to the trees.

A woman sat on a roan mare and waited for him, just inside the trees. When he came up to her and stopped—because she barred his way—he saw that her eyes, gray as his own, were direct and strong with interest. She wore the same clothes he had seen on her the morning before in Morgantown, a man's denim overalls stuffed into boots, a man's wool shirt loose across a firm and rounded chest. She held her hat across the saddle horn, and deep-yellow hair ran faintly lawless back from features as serene and fair as he had ever seen on a woman. Restlessness swayed her a little.

He said, "Good mornin', Miss Cameron," and lifted his stetson.

There was a smile lying behind the contour of her lips. "I wondered if you'd remember me."

"Why not?"

She said: "Well, you had your mind full of other things yesterday morning."

"My name," he told her quietly, "is Buck Surratt."

"I was about to ask you," she murmured.

He said: "What is that valley down there?"

"It belongs to my people."

"What's beyond the ridge?"

"Another valley, where the Peyrolles run." Her head turned and indicated the timbered masses in the higher east. "If you ride that way you'll run into Head country. Martin Head. Bill's father." She looked at him with a more direct interest. "Leslie Head's father also—the boy that was shot near your campfire the other night."

He said: "My campfire was out."

Her chin lifted with a certain resoluteness. Her voice at the moment had the candid directness of a man. "I came here to talk to you about that."

"How'd you know I'd be here?"

"I've been following you ever since you left Sam Torveen's place."

Admiration was strong in him. She had a poise and a serenity. Good breeding defined all the regular features of her face and made them expressive and stirring. He kept his peace, waiting for her to go on.

"Were you curious about that shot, Buck?"

He reached for his pipe and packed it and lighted it. He swept a gust of good smoke into his lungs. His mind was on the question, but he noticed the sudden gravity on her smooth cheeks. He said finally: "I did a little looking around."

"You went down to the cabin?"

"Yes."

"Inside?"

He said, "Yes," again, very slowly.

Her question was rapid and concerned: "Did you find something in that cabin, Buck? Something you put in your pocket and carried away?"

Her hands, he observed, were long and slender and supple; and she held them quietly folded on the saddle horn. A slanting beam of sunlight reached through the trees to accent the yellow luster in her hair; and that rich color deepened the ivory tints of her skin. But there was something breaking through the rough man's clothing she wore—the fire of a womanliness that touched him and fed his senses powerfully. It played tricks with him, unsettling the cool run of his thoughts, disturbing his ease. He had known many women, but not the kind of a woman this tall, graceful girl was.

She said: "Give it to me, Buck."

A slow wistfulness got into his answer. "Many people have trusted me."

She straightened. Her words came back almost impulsively—and quite direct. "I trust you, if that is what you want me to do."

"What kind of a man was this Leslie Head?"

Her face was in the bright sunlight, but her thinking cast a shadow across it. It wasn't fear he viewed there; it was the memory of a thing bitter and unpleasant. She murmured: "Speak no evil of the dead, Buck."

"He had enemies?"

"He had no friends."

The need to have things clear made him go on. "Did he live in that cabin?"

"No. Up at the Head ranch."

"What would he be doing in the cabin, then—at night?"

Her eyes remained on him, but she didn't speak and it was Surratt who broke that long stillness. He relighted his pipe. His head inclined toward the road running up to the Gray Bull peaks. His words were faintly regretting. "For a fellow like me the world is wide and all trails lead over the hill. I should be riding now, for if I stay here the answer will be the same answer as always. A man carries his fortune with him. It is like printed instructions written on his chest, for everybody to see."

She said gently: "Then why do you stay?"

He said: "Sam Torveen did me a favor."

The softness, the melody of her voice was enormously stirring. She was a woman, full of hidden riches for some man who one day would capture the fidelity that was in her and command the high loyalty of her heart. For that man, Surratt thought sadly, there would be no more trails beckoning. She was the end of that man's trail.

She said : "You pay your debts, don't you?"

"If I didn't there'd be no pride in me, and I'd be a miserable man without pride. It is a thing my kind has to have—since we have nothing else."

"I thought it was that way," she told him. "I thought so in Morgantown, when you stood against Bill Head." She lifted her arms and the round curves of her body changed. "Sam Torveen's all right. You may doubt his crew, but Sam's——" She thought about the proper word and afterwards looked at him with a small surprise. "He's like you. You are a pair, except that he keeps the world away with

31

a smile—and you keep the world away with a poker face."

"I like him," said Surratt.

"You're a pair," she repeated softly. She scanned the green corridors of the forest with a quick glance. She dropped her voice. "Bill Head's called for a meeting of the big ranchers tonight, up at his house. Sam will want to know that."

"I'll tell him. As for the other thing——"

"I said I trusted you," she interrupted. "Let it go like that."

He nodded and pointed his horse back down the trail. But her voice came abruptly after him, turning him back. She came on until she was beside him once more. Interest was strong in her and she studied this man with a strange emotion. His high, square torso made an alert shape against the shadows of the trees; there was a tough and resilient vigor all about him, a hard physical power to his body. Discipline lay along the pressed lines of his broad mouth, but a rash and reckless will was in his eyes, struggling against the discipline. She saw it. His head, she decided, would never betray him, for it was cool and introspective. But a latent storminess, a subdued capacity for terrific gusts of feeling, made him dangerous to others and to himself. It was his heart that someday would betray him. These were the things she thought in that little interval; and she wished he might smile as Sam Torveen smiled.

She said: "I think your own eyes have warned you. But there are many things about this country you don't know. And you have made Bill Head your enemy. Bill is not a forgiving man. You ought to remember that."

"I'll remember it, Miss Cameron."

"My name," she told him quietly, "is Judith."

"Yes," he said, "I know. There was a woman in the Bible by that name. I've often thought of her."

Her glance dropped and color came strongly to her cheeks. She swung the pony with a long, graceful dip of her body and cantered down the trail. He watched her until she vanished round a lower bend, and then turned homeward.

He rode idly, the picture of her departure so vivid in his mind that some of his customary riding vigilance deserted him. When he reached the woodcutter's camp he pulled himself reluctantly from his thinking and chose another route by which to descend the slope. An increased heat lay trapped underneath these trees, and the midday's sultry stillness was a thick substance all around him. "The rights of other men," he said softly, "are not my rights. When I have paid my bill to Torveen I ride away from here." And he was wrapped in the somberness of that thought when the reaching crash of a shot threw his pony back on its haunches and whipped him forward in the saddle.

He had not been struck, but there was deep in his head the long-planned reaction to just such a contingency as this. It came to him now like a boxer's instinctive defense. Rolling on forward across the saddle horn, he capsized and fell to the soft humus soil and turned over and over until he crouched at the base of a pine. His horse stood fast. The echoes of the shot went rolling and ricocheting down the slope; it died out in little fragments and eddies.

He lay with his head turned upslope, keening the hot twilight of the trees. The sound had struck at him from his right side, and therefore his eyes went to the higher ground, across the brown roll of hummock and stump and deadfall. A mule deer came scudding along the trail, its tail lifted, and plunged on to remote shelter. Surratt's eyes focused on the fan-shaped barricade made by the root system of a capsized pine; it was two hundred yards away, on the high side of the trail. He edged away from his protection and got to his knees and made a run for another tree. Whipped behind it, he studied the slope again. When he next moved—circling and bending as before—he kept his eyes to upheaved roots. He side-stepped and reached a breast-high deadfall. He crouched and ran with it, to the margin of the trail. Paused for one long moment, he finally made one long dive across the trail and dropped behind a stump. From this spot he had a glimpse of the rear of the fallen tree's roots and saw nothing. But there was a bowl where the roots once had been, and in this bowl a man might crouch. Surratt drew his gun then and broke for the adjacent pine. When he reached it he didn't stop, but walked deliberately toward the bowl. It was a strange thing. Perrigo sat on his heels in the bottom of this depression with a rifle across his knees. He saw Surratt coming, but he didn't make a further gesture.

Surratt walked down into it, coming against Perrigo. He was breathing a little from his run and sweat had reached his face; yet the stillness of Perrigo's attention, the bright

33

and malicious burning of the man's black eyes steadied the fresh, strong pulse of his anger and made him alert.

"You've got some bad habits, Nick," he grunted. "And this is one of them. I don't love a man that tries to get his turkey cold."

Perrigo said: "Don't make that mistake, mister. If I'd wanted to hit you I'd aimed at you."

"So maybe you're just trying to run a little scare into me?"

Perrigo got to his feet. He put the rifle butt on his toe and cupped a hand over the muzzle. His shortness made him tip his head to reach Surratt's measuring inspection; it seemed to heat the little man's wrath. He stepped backward. "I don't like strangers. I'm tellin' you."

"I understood that last night," Surratt told him dryly.

"I don't get why you rode up there and met the Cameron girl," growled Perrigo. "It didn't look like an accident to me."

"It bothers you?"

Perrigo said, with a wicked calm: "A lot of things bother me. I don't like you around. You know too much about that shot the other night." His eyes pointed on Surratt, as bitter and dangerous as the muzzles of a double-barreled shotgun. He whipped out his thin question. "What do you know about it?"

"You got an interest in the matter?" inquired Surratt.

Perrigo pressed his mouth together. His dry features betrayed a faint fear. Surratt saw that and marked it in his mind and spoke again, somewhat more agreeable. "I'd suggest we get along, for I'm staying on with Torveen awhile. But if we're not going to get along I want to know that, Nick. When a man declares open season on me I've got my own remedies. Two can play this tune."

"You smell like a Head rider to me," stated Perrigo.

"You're dead wrong. I braced him the other day, didn't I?"

"Men don't brace Bill Head like that," countered Perrigo. "They don't get away with it—not unless it's a faked scene."

"Do we get along or don't we?"

Perrigo blazed up. "The hell with you! You battered Chunk Osbrook's face out of joint and you laid your tongue on the kid. I'm warning you never to try that on me! I'm running that ranch for Torveen. I tolerate no man on the place that rides in front of me. I want that understood. If you stay, you take my orders. You get that?"

"No," said Surratt.

A quick reflex of temper sent Perrigo's arm forward with the muzzle of the gun. But he checked the impulse. Whiteness showed on his cheeks and made the blackness of his eyes more unreasoning. Violence shook him. "Then watch out for yourself!"

"I wanted it clear," Surratt murmured.

"You got it clear," cried Perrigo.

He climbed from the bowl, and Surratt watched him go up to a thick swirl of pine seedlings and pull out a horse standing there. The little man trotted to the trail and galloped away. Surratt went thoughtfully back to his own horse, following the slope down. He came upon the meadow and crossed it to the ranch house. The crew had gone, but Torveen sat in his office room, sprawled out in a chair, somehow deeply engaged with his thoughts and ruffled by them.

He said, with perceptible relief: "So you're back."

"Was there some doubt in your mind, Sam?"

Torveen shrugged his shoulders. "I couldn't blame you if you kept right on going away from here."

Surratt sought his pipe and packed it. "I am to tell you that Bill Head's called a meeting of ranchers at his place tonight."

"So you met Judith." Torveen shifted his back against the chair; he seemed at once irritable. "You get around, friend Buck. You sure do get around."

"Any objections?" asked Surratt dryly.

Torveen lifted his green and slantwise glance. He didn't like it. He showed his restless resentment. But then he got abruptly up. "Oh hell, Buck, let it ride. I'm nervous as a cat. I've no intention to rag a man like you."

Surratt smiled. "When did you have a good drink last?"

"If that helped any, I'd be drunk as a lord. So Bill's called a meeting?"

"You going?"

Something in the question reached Torveen's sense of humor. He grinned. "That wasn't why Judith sent the news along, Buck. No, we won't be there. We'll be somewhere else tonight." He drew a long breath; he turned sober again. "I guess you'll have the chance soon enough to find out what my hole card is. Stick with me, Buck. This is going to be tough."

35

Chapter Four

BUSINESS
AT NIGHT

This was night again and the crew was in the yard, waiting to go. A quick, cold wind flowed off the peaks; there was no moon. Torveen stood in the doorway of his office room, yellow light strongly shining against his roan cheeks. Posted at the foot of the porch, Surratt could make out the man's driving nervousness; there wasn't any fun in Torveen now and all his motions were swift and short. He drew a last long breath of smoke from his cigarette; he threw it out into the dust. His voice flattened.

"You got any questions, Buck?"

"That's all right," remarked Surratt very quietly.

"It may be—it may not be. But, God, you're cool about it! Well, let's go." Torveen jumped down from the porch and traveled over to his horse, Surratt following. The group whirled out of the yard, across the plank bridge and into the timber. At the main road Torveen turned eastward and led his men up the stiffening slope of the hills. They ran between the solid pines and through a covering blackness, with only a dim steel-blue strip of sky above. They crossed a covered bridge, booming deep echoes out into the night. They seemed to pass along the edge of a canyon, for Surratt could hear the rush of water down there, even above the steady flogging rhythm of pony hoofs. His horse was drawing for wind, but the pace kept on that way without break during the best part of half an hour; after that they walked a little way, surrounded by a dense blackness still—and presently broke into the long canter, again covering the miles.

They whirled suddenly out of the trees and pounded through a narrow gap. A steady, down-scouring wind met them in the face, with the chill of a higher elevation in it. There were a few short and stubby second-growth pines vaguely standing along this way, but these soon faded and they were riding across the face of a rocky slope, the black and abrupt bulk of one of the Gray Bull peaks running spirelike into the sky above them. Even without a moon the bare talus fields of this area reflected a tawny radium glow through the gloom. They plunged into a cold and damp mist cloud and rode sightlessly through its muffling substance. But somewhere along this stretch of road Surratt felt the grade level off and tip downward. He knew then they had crossed the pass.

Without warning, they were beyond the mist. Torveen spoke a slow order. Surratt piled into the rider ahead of him and reined up abruptly. The crew had stopped behind Torveen, whose body turned in the saddle, right and left. There was no talk, but the labored breathing of the horses reached out and disturbed the chilly dark. An opaque, triangular pattern just ahead seemed to mark the presence of a defile.

A voice came stolidly from the near-by rocks: "Torveen?"

"Yeah."

"Go ahead."

They passed into the defile and paced through it and emerged upon what seemed to be a meadow. Alert to all this, Surratt pulled up his chin and keened the night. And then he was relaxed and amused, and puzzled. His nostrils told him the mystery; and his ears told him. Another man walked vaguely into view, to challenge as the first man had done. A white, moving mass stirred along the earth, bleating up a confused, unmistakable sound. Here were sheep, the smell of them strong in the wind.

Torveen's voice came back, pitched to a high and driving restlessness. "You take the front, Nick. Rest of us scatter along the edges of this band. Stay on the road all the way back until we reach the turnoff to the upper meadow. Move along. Keep these woollies from straying. Push 'em, but not too fast. Come on."

Surratt went into the meadow, sheering off from the edge of the band. The sheep were already in motion, pressing through the defile into the road. Torveen had disappeared and the others had disappeared. Surratt turned and drifted. When he reached the road he flanked the sheep and sat loosely in his saddle. Torveen's voice came up from the rear. "Faster, Nick." Surratt saw the blurred white stream bulge and break from the road, just ahead; and he trotted that way and pressed the sheep back into the straggling column. His horse didn't like the work and shied away, but he squelched that with a few quick prods of his spur and went idle again, amused to the point of silent laughter. At twenty-five he had turned sheepherder, a job that all his cattle training had taught him to despise. There was humor in this situation for him, a kind of sardonic by-play on the swift turnings of his own life. Yet his quick mind reached beyond the humor of it and saw a reality that contained no reason for laughter. He knew then why Sam Torveen had wanted help and why Torveen had kept his silence until now.

Those pointed feet slicing into the pastures of cattle land meant somebody's blood. It had always been so. Somewhere in these hills lay a boundary line; imaginary, yet as broad and visible as a painted stripe. Beyond that line sheep could not go in peace and men could not herd sheep and live secure. This was a law that stood on no statute book, but it was a law nevertheless, and one that cattlemen would fight for more bitterly than any other. Buck Surratt's life had been with cattle and with cattle people, and he knew the iron steadfastness of the rule.

Long afterwards—deep in the midnight hours—they reached the heavy timber and crept in scuffling confusion across the covered bridge. The wind ran steady and cool, ruffing up the spurious waterfall sound in the treetops. Sky's blackness thickened, and the bleating of the sheep band ran the silence in plaintive ways. The bell on the leading wether tinkled gently back. Surratt was thinking that the smell of this night's traffic would reach Morgantown before day came and that the invisible telegraph would carry it to the remotest corner of the hills; he was thinking that, solemnly reflective, when Perrigo's voice reached him. "We turn."

Surratt remained at his station, but another of the crew galloped forward and began to curse in a slow, methodical fashion. The pale stream bent. It vanished from the road into the anonymous trees, going down some narrow trail. There was no room here for straying and so Surratt dropped back into the dusty rear, riding silently beside Torveen. Torveen said, wearily: "What's the time?"

Surratt pulled out his watch and struck a match. "Near one." The run of the hours surprised him.

"The longest night I'll ever put in," growled Torveen. In twenty minutes they were through the trees, into another meadow of those hills. The sheep faded across it and the

38

crew came trotting back, to collect around Torveen. He said: "Where's the herders?"

A man roved up, afoot. "Here."

"There's a cabin across the way. That's your headquarters. Sleep there, but don't be in it or around it by daylight. Camp out in the woods then—and keep your rifles with you. I'll come by after breakfast."

It was one of the two herders brought along with the sheep. He said in an unemotional, faintly Irish-burred voice: "Indeed, Mr. Torveen," and slowly dissolved into the dark. Torveen breathed a weary order. "We can go home." He led the way straight down the meadow and plunged into the trees, in a little while arriving at the ranch. Surratt turned out his pony and carried his saddle to the bunkroom. But he didn't stay there; he walked back along the porch, hearing Torveen speaking to Perrigo in the office.

"I don't expect trouble tonight. But you'll ride the timber and listen for it."

Perrigo came out, flicking a quick, black look at Surratt. He went over the yard to the darkness of the corral and Surratt heard him swearing at the horses off there. Afterwards Surratt went into the office. Torveen sat in his chair, his body slack and his usual cheerfulness entirely gone. The strain of the night had broken up his roan face, it had scratched dangerously across his nerves. The color of his glance was a pale green.

He said: "Well, you know my hole card now."

Surratt said, "Yes," imperturbably and got out his pipe. He walked to the fireplace and tapped the bowl sharply against the stones, and filled it and fired up his smoke. He turned to find Torveen's glance narrowly set upon him.

"Maybe you'll want to know why I didn't give you a hint before now," said Torveen. "Well, it was the idea of sheep. You're no sheepman, anybody can see. And I figured you might ride off. I don't like the damn blatting woollies myself."

Surratt drew a gust of smoke into his lungs and expelled it. He said: "Ever been in a gunfight, Sam?"

"No."

"I've had some experience along that line," Surratt murmured. "You will have some, soon enough."

"You get the idea here?"

"Sure. You're bringing sheep into cattle country. There's only one answer to that. Hell's got no wrath like the wrath of a stockman who sees woollies creepin' across cow territory. I see what's happened tonight, and I see what's going to happen. What puzzles me a little is your particular reason for bringin' this grief onto yourself."

Torveen straightened. He was entirely serious, momentarily drawn away from his worries. "Well, I'm still young, and a young fellow has ideas—and some ambition. I've been a two-bit cattleman ever since I took over this place from my dad. I don't cut any great figure against the old-timers like Martin Head or Cameron or Kersom or Hank Peyrolles. They were born and raised with beef and they can't see anything else. They don't know what's goin' on outside of these hills. They don't care. But I know what's goin' on. Sheep's a crop that goes well with cattle, and sheep are comin' in all around here. Hell, these hills are swell for sheep. The way for a man to build himself a big ranch is to run both. And sheep is the easiest way for a young fellow to start."

"And the easiest way to lose his ranch," suggested Surratt.

"I used to have friends in this country," commented Torveen irritably. "Then I started talkin' sheep—and I've got no friends now. You saw how those boys in the jail office regarded me. Well, they knew I was stubborn and would follow my ideas. So they scared off my crew. What I've got now is a bunch of men I'm not proud of. But they're tough and I need that kind. Perrigo used to ride for Head until he killed a fellow up there and had to leave. The kid is a maverick I don't trust. He's wicked with the gun and he's got no morals. Chunk Osbrook was fired off Ab Cameron's place and came to me. You see the reputation I got? Ed's the only hand of my old outfit that stuck." Torveen got up and prowled the room with a surge of temper. "To hell with the old-timers. We've brought in our sheep and the game's started. We'll stand on our stack and play it strong."

Surratt studied this redhaired, electric man. He softly suggested something. "You've got a good reason for wanting to build up the ranch and swing your weight with the rest."

Torveen said impatiently: "There's no law against bein' ambitious, friend Buck. I'm too young a man to be satisfied with a two-bit spread." But he quit talking a moment, and the roan color of his face began to surge down his neck. "Sure. I want a big outfit and the money that goes with it and the pride of walkin' like a man into Morgantown's bank. Ab Cameron can write his check for six figures on a piece of butcher paper and cash it anywhere in this state. That's what I want."

"The reason is clear to me," drawled Surratt.

It stirred Torveen's strange and moody temper. He was recklessly angry. "You're too sharp with your eyes, Buck. You see too much you shouldn't see in people."

"You object to that?" countered Surratt quietly.

Torveen said at once: "I did you a favor, but I won't hold you to it. You can ride any time."

Surratt removed his pipe. He laid it on the table and his tone prowled catlike across the room's quiet. "We'll consider you didn't say that, Sam."

Torveen reared his head and his shoulders. A willful heat sparkled across his green eyes. He wasn't, Surratt saw, a cool man; he was a fighter who could be baited into trouble. Yet even as he saw this and marked it for the future, he noticed Torveen's insistent sense of humor loosen the fighting streak along his mouth. Torveen grinned frankly. "Think of you and me talkin' like this! To hell with it, Buck."

"Sure," said Surratt, and smiled again. "To hell with it. We've got a little game of poker coming up and it won't be mild. Maybe I can help out, for this is a game I've played before." Then he added softly: "It will be strange to you, until you learn. And when you learn you'll be a different man, with a wisdom you'll wish you never had."

Torveen shook his head. "You're a tough one. A lot of livin' has run over your shoulders. But it is queer to me you smile so little and sometimes look so regrettin'." He shrugged his shoulders and abruptly changed the subject. "You pounded the whey out of Chunk Osbrook, and he's the kind of a boy that will mind you and respect you for the poundin'. It is not the same with the kid or Nick Perrigo. Maybe I don't need to tell you this—keep your guard up with them."

Surratt nodded and left the office, strolling back to the bunkroom. Perrigo was out on patrol and Ed stirred somewhere in the yard. Osbrook had turned into bed; the kid sat at the table playing solitaire. Pulling off his boots, Surratt saw the kid's eyes reach him and show once more that sullen, sallow flash of hatred, as wild and consistent as it had been the previous night. Surratt pulled the blanket over him and shaded his eyes, considering what he had to

41

do. The kid was like a dog reverted to wildness, cringing back from men but forever showing his teeth. He needed another slash of the whip. Surratt let his hand fall from his eyes. He rapped his order at the kid.

"Turn out that light, punk."

The kid put his elbows on the table and stared down, with a quick breath disturbing his narrow chest. Surratt slowly reared himself to an upright position; but he didn't have to speak again. The kid bent over the lamp and blew out the flame.

The sheep had entered the hills without trouble, but not without being observed. On a little bench near the pass, Judith Cameron stood in the dark and watched the pale blur of the herd fill the road and go bleating by. When they had disappeared she turned away and rode rapidly through the rugged folds of this upland country toward the Cameron ranch house. Lower down, near the covered bridge, another spectator held himself back in the brush and silently observed. And long after the sheep band had turned into the upper meadow Blackjack Smith remained in his covert and ruminated over its meaning, his big jaws biting into his tobacco chaw.

Chapter Five

A MAN'S
COLD WILL

Old Martin Head, who was master of Crow Track, sat on the west porch with a blanket covering his crippled legs while watching twilight fade across the land far below him. The lights of the Cameron ranch began to wink through a thickening cobalt air and the whitewashed house of the Peyrolles, in the valley beyond, slowly sank under darkness. Past the tangle of ravine and river and steep pine slope, the distant desert lay all blanketed in a faint silver mist. This world was at his feet, as he wanted it to be; for Martin Head had been raised in the Tennessee mountains and there was that strong instinct in him against low lands.

Just before the final dark closed in, Old Martin saw riders converge on the Cameron valley road and join and turn up toward Crow Track. He swung his shoulders a little, calling for his son. Bill Head came out and stood beside his father, saying nothing.

"Company's coming," said Martin. "Why?"

"I asked 'em," explained Bill Head. "That all right?"

Martin Head rolled back against the chair. Silence enveloped him and hid away his feelings and his thoughts. It did more than that—it definitely pushed his son away from any hope of affection. He gripped a cigar between his teeth, and above his high cheekbones two powerful eyes narrowed against the night with a kind of slit, Mongol passivity. A cropped black beard, like General Grant's, concealed all expression; he was engrossed in this colossal, brooding indifference when his neighbors rode up this hill.

They hailed him and came to the porch—Cameron and Dutch Kersom and Hank Peyrolles and Henry Ranier. Martin Head had known these men for a good many years. Yet he said, "Good evening, gentlemen," with the inflexible, courteous tone he used for all men of whatever degree. Bill

43

Head came forward then and got behind the chair and lifted it and carried his father into the living room. He put the chair beside the fireplace and stood back, not exerted enough to show it by deeper breathing. The visitors followed. Dutch Kersom, himself a burly man, spoke with a touch of admiration.

"You're a powerful brute, Bill."

Martin Head said, not looking at his son: "The bottle, Bill, and the glasses." Bill Head turned out of the room, leaving behind him stillness that wasn't comfortable. Pine knots on the fireplace hearth exploded, and the light swelled and rippled across the low ceiling, against the whitewashed walls. Out in the kitchen men were talking, and dishes clattered. Above the fireplace a cavalry carbine and a saber with a heavily ornamented hilt hung half crossed. Below the weapons was a lithograph of General Jeb Stuart, under whom Old Martin had ridden during the rebellion. There were no other pictures in the room, which was a measure of Martin Head's mind. Beauty Stuart was a bright memory to him and never would cease to be; and the Southern cause was still a thing Old Martin believed in with the hard and full partisanship of his nature. But of this he never spoke; for he had come to a period of life in which the spoken word could not cover all that he felt and remembered; and so, contemptuous of the paleness of sound against the bitter, turbulent brightness of things he carried in his head, he remained still. He had lost a son in the rebellion; and afterwards had created two sons to carry his name. His wife was dead and now one of his later sons was dead.

Bill Head returned with the whisky; and poured a drink for Old Martin, who waited until the rest had served themselves. He said then: "My son Leslie's funeral will be in Morgantown tomorrow. But do not bother to come. A dead man is dead, and the living have too much to do to waste time on sentimental ceremonies."

All, save Ab Cameron, downed the drink. Ab Cameron was fifty-five, but an old man in this rough country; he had a white and narrow and sad face, with a long mustache stained a little on the edges from tobacco; his hands were like those of a scholar, blue veins showing through transparent skin. His voice was soft, it was unassuming.

"It is a sad thing, Martin. God rest his soul."

But Martin Head's tone ran blunt and growling through

44

the room. "He lived in his own fashion—and died that way. In bed, with a bullet through his chest and his own gun belt hangin' on a peg, the other side of the shanty. No doubt he was thinkin' of a woman when he died, as he was always doing."

Bill Head said resentfully: "He was your son."

"I keep rememberin' that," growled Old Martin. "He was my son, but he was a worthless man."

The silence grew grayer. Peyrolles, who had a little more feeling for the amenities than the rest of them, changed the subject. "You wanted to see us, Martin?"

Old Martin's shoulders shrugged. "My son did. He seems to be running this show." He leaned back in the chair and wrapped his massive silence around him like a blanket.

Bill Head stepped forward, as though he wanted to free himself from the wide shadow his father made across that room. His body was a huge, straight column in the lamplight; color flushed his fair skin and a stubbornness lay along the forward throw of his chin, along the very broad lips. His eyes were light—and at this moment rather calculating as he faced these older owners.

"Ranier and I went up to Sam Torveen's last night to take this Surratt back to Morgantown. Torveen made an issue out of it. I didn't like the idea of a fight right there on his own doorstep, so we didn't get Surratt. That gives you an idea of Sam's frame of mind."

A little interval of absorbed reflection came to the room. Peyrolles smiled then in a tight, acid way. "The boy," he murmured, "wants to be tough with us, does he? Well, Sam Torveen's dad was a friend of mine, and I rode Sam in my saddle when he was a kid a good many times. But I do not take presumin' ways from any man, let alone this boy."

Dutch Kersom cocked his bullet-round head; not a great deal of emotion got through that swarthy skin. "What's he stickin' up for this newcomer Surratt for, I want to know?"

"Just one more maverick to add to that wild bunch he's got," said Peyrolles.

Ab Cameron's talk was uncertain. "I always used to like Sam. I always thought well of his family. As for the men he's got in his crew——"

"They stink, for a fact I say," stated Dutch Kersom.

"Certainly," agreed Bill Head. His eyes weighed these

45

people and he played their tempers with a dexterity born of understanding. "He needs them for the sheep he's bringing in."

"Sheep?" said Ab Cameron. "It's all talk. The lad wouldn't try it."

"You don't know Sam," remarked Bill Head.

Sheriff Ranier had remained thus far in the background. He spoke now. "Sam's stubborn. He don't change his mind."

"We will change friend Sam's mind," murmured Peyrolles, still showing that faint streak of acid smiling.

"If he tries it," added Dutch Kersom, unemotionally.

"He's got the sheep all right," said Bill Head, driving the information home in a quick tone. "They're up around the peaks, waiting to come in."

"Where?" jerked out Peyrolles.

"I can't find out. They've got a herder posted on the peak with a rifle and good eyesight. I don't want to get my men shot up. Not yet."

It was as though the wind swung around from west to east. The temperature of this room seemed to drop, and the air to become cold and furious. These men had been idly discussing a possibility they didn't believe would happen. Now they were faced with it, and now they changed with the suddenness of their kind. Bill Head knew it and saw it, and was pleased. They were good men, large-handed and proud of their oral word, loving laughter and freedom; they could curse and storm and fight passionately when their authority was questioned, but they could be kind when that had passed. Yet upon this one subject they had an adamant singularity. A man who ran sheep became an enemy, no matter how long he had been a friend; an enemy beyond the bounds of decency or scruples. It was a passionate belief, so imbedded in them as to be like a religious conviction—and their sense of its rightness made them merciless. A man who ran sheep flew in the face of clear warning, and he had no pity and no generosity coming to him. Peyrolles bent in his chair, his desires impetuous and glittering in his eyes. Dutch Kersom was stolid, as always, yet Bill Head knew that this man's mind had locked out Torveen forever. Ab Cameron bowed his pale, benignant face. He spoke in a grieving way. "I am sorry to hear it."

"Sorry?" challenged Bill Head—and flung his willful glance on Cameron.

"We will send an outfit up there and find the sheep," murmured Peyrolles. "We will destroy them."

Sheriff Ranier said anxiously: "What do you think, Martin?"

But Martin Head looked upon them with a fixed, hooded stare; and not the power of all their eyes could detect his sentiments. He said briefly: "It is my son's show."

A ranch hand came to the door and said laconically: "Man here wants to see you, Bill."

Bill Head wheeled out of the room at a long stride. There was a rider near the corner of the porch. He made a formless, topheavy shape on the pony, and the darkness of the night covered his identity. But when he spoke to Bill Head the low, vast roll of his voice betrayed him.

"I didn't tell you to come here," said Bill Head irritably.

"Sheep's started in," said Blackjack Smith. "You wanted to know that, didn't you?"

"Where?"

"On the pass road."

Bill Head turned back into the house. He said: "The sheep are coming in."

Peyrolles was out of his chair in a single motion. The angular frame of the man bent and turned. "We'll stop that, now."

Bill Head said sharply: "Wait a minute," and checked Peyrolles with a shake of his head. "We don't do it that way. Torveen's primed for trouble tonight. He'll be waiting for it. No. Let him bring his sheep in. There's plenty of other nights to come. We'll do this in our own way."

Peyrolles' smile was a bright, sharp thing. "You got an idea, Bill?"

Bill Head said: "When I call on you fellows for help I want to know I'll get it."

"You'll get it," said Dutch Kersom. They all rose and stood a moment; and they seemed to await Martin Head's final word. But he said, "Good night, gentlemen," and nothing more, and then they left the room. Bill Head went to the porch and stood there until they had ridden away. Afterwards he came back into the room. He rolled himself a cigarette and lighted it—and waited.

"Bill," said Old Martin, growling out his anger, "only a fool would take a posse to Torveen's to get a man—and go away without the man."

Bill Head's pink face showed a resenting defensiveness. He was not quite easy in the presence of his father. He

47

said: "I told you Sam had fixed himself up to make a fight of it. Why throw lead in his own yard?"

"You've been taught better," grunted Old Martin. "Never start a play you can't go through with. Either you should have known better than to have gone up there, or else you ought to have taken this Surratt, regardless. So you made two mistakes—going there underestimating Sam Torveen, and going away with your hands empty. You backed down."

Bill Head flushed. He was restless and angry. "Never mind. I'll take that Surratt when I want him."

"Who's this Surratt?"

"A stranger driftin' through the hills."

Martin rolled his shoulders. "It wasn't a stranger that killed Leslie. Somebody did that who knew Les too well. Surratt's clear of that."

"I know it."

"Then," said Old Martin bluntly, "what you want him for?"

"I don't intend to have him strengthen Sam Torveen's hand any."

Old Martin judged his son with a cold, black glance. There was something unsparing in this man that would not relent, not even for his son. "You're a schemin' man," he said at last. "I do not trust your word. I have been harsh in my time and I've done things I regret now. But they were honest mistakes. You're not honest, Bill. I sit here tonight and listen to you speak about sheep, and all the while you are not thinkin' about sheep but about Sam Torveen whom you hate."

"One reason or another," said Bill Head coolly; "I'm after Sam Torveen."

Old Martin's hands gripped the chair arms. He pushed himself forward and let the full blast of his temper thunder out. "If you've got a quarrel with the man, go out and settle it—but don't lie about your reasons! God damn a man who's deceitful!"

His voice rushed along the walls and filled the room massively—and died to a creeping silence. Bill Head stared at the floor with a still strain. He said, very quietly: "Yes sir. You want me to carry you upstairs now?"

Old Martin remained crouched in the chair, inspecting his son in that bitter, friendless way. "It is my opinion that Nick Perrigo shot Les. I knew Perrigo well. A tricky little scoundrel who worked for me long enough to hate all

Heads, and Les in particular. The man never forgot an injury and never forgave one. If I had two sound legs I'd go find Nick and I'd kill him. Since I cannot do it, you will do that for me."

Bill Head pulled up his chin and stared. "I'm to personally do that, sir?"

"Les was no good," stated Old Martin. "But he had our name and we'll see that it is protected. There's our answer to the hills. You go get Nick Perrigo." Then he added with a dismal grimness: "They are not Christian reasons, Bill, but they're honest ones."

"If . . ." began Bill Head; and stopped. A woman's voice come through the door. "Dad's gone home?" And afterwards Judith Cameron walked in. She crossed the room, smiling at Old Martin, and bent down and kissed him on a cheek. Old Martin sat motionless, his hands still gripping the arms of the chair. He was a seldom-smiling man, but when she drew back, laughing a little at his stony manner, his eyes softened and were pleased. He said, more brusque than usual: "Ab's gone. A girl like you, Judith, has got no business rammin' around these hills at night alone. Ride home with her, Bill."

Judith looked at Bill thoughtfully. She said: "Is he supposed to be protection, Martin?"

Old Martin scowled at his son. "If he turns bad on you, Judith, use a gun."

Judith walked out with Bill Head following. Martin Head lifted his voice again and yelled: "Pokey!" A thin, time-whipped little man came instantly in and stood in front of Martin Head, his countenance faithful and sly and sad.

"Who rode up here with news for Bill?"

"Blackjack Smith."

Old Martin's throat growled. "We're havin' fine company on the ranch these days, Pokey. Turn me around—and get out."

Pokey swung the chair toward the fire and left at a silent shuffle; and took up a kind of sentry duty on the porch. Martin Head leaned back against the chair, with his eyes on the lithograph of Jeb Stuart. He spoke to Stuart, across time, as an equal to an equal.

"There ain't as much honor and courage in the world as there used to be, Beauty. And the fun is gone. You died young, which was proper. It's hell to be old."

49

Judith and Bill Head went down the trail in silence until they came to a meadow dimly shining in the night. Bill rode abreast her at this place. He was disgruntled and irritated. "Was that the sort of thing to say to the old man?"

"About your dependability, Bill? Well . . ."

"Judith," he burst out, "treat a man a little kinder!"

"You get kindness," she told him softly, "by being kind."

"You can cut the heart out of a fellow with your words," he said, vehemently. "Good God, what do I have to do if I want a little encouragement from you? Don't hold me off like that!"

Her talk was candid and hurting. "You don't like being held off, do you, Bill? You like things all your own way. If a dog doesn't come when you whistle, you whip him. If a woman doesn't smile, you want to whip her."

He pulled in his horse and reached over to catch her reins. "Listen, Judith. No man's going to stand against me, as far as you're concerned. Maybe I'm not sentimental enough for your fancy. But I can fight for what I want."

"You can use the whip," she retorted.

He spurred his pony over and caught her before she could lift an arm. His gloved hand scraped across her face and pulled it around; and he kissed her with a sudden brutality and let her go. Her other arm came up then and she slashed him across the head with her crop. His hat fell off and his pony fiddled away. He started to swing toward her again, his breathing heavy and fast in the quietness of the hillside. Her voice stopped him definitely. "Quit it, Bill, or I'll follow your Dad's advice."

Rage raked his voice: "What are you prowling around here at night for?"

"I like to ride at night."

He said, wickedly: "The habit will get you in trouble, Judith. Where were you the other night when Les was shot?"

She flung her horse at him and her crop smashed him violently on the face again. And then, without speaking, she galloped down the meadow and disappeared in the lower timber. He didn't follow; he remained there in the meadow, holding a hand across his stinging cheeks, turned mad by his injuries.

Chapter Six

AFFAIR AT
MORGANTOWN

Hughie Grant, who was a Crow Track rider, came up the road from Morgantown and saw Nick Perrigo loitering there at the Torveen gateway. Hughie Grant made a sweeping turn on his horse and came to a stop; he had a big, weathered body and an impressive coal-black mustache—and he rolled freely in the saddle. He said, genially: "There's a fellow that used to work for the Heads. Nick, I never liked you and you never liked me. For a fact, nobody likes you. I'd guess you don't even like yourself."

"Keep goin', Hughie," Perrigo said.

"You own this road?" suggested Hughie Grant, and reached into his hip pocket. He hauled out a flat pint whisky bottle, holding it up to the afternoon sun to measure its contents. He uncorked it with his teeth and transferred the cork to his hand while he downed a drink. He shuddered faintly and corked the bottle. But a touch of magnanimity appeared to get possession of him then. He urged his horse toward Perrigo and inclined the bottle.

"Have a little taste of the hair of this dog."

Perrigo said instantly: "No." Yet his eyes clung to the bottle, and his hands moved and stopped.

"Hell with you, Perrigo. Proud, or something? Well, you never could handle liquor anyhow."

Perrigo suddenly grunted, "Give me that," and seized the bottle. He flung his head back, drinking with a sudden gusty thirst. Hughie Grant's eyes narrowed and contained a shrewdness that didn't belong to a drunken man. He said feebly: "Leave some of that."

Perrigo lowered the bottle. He held it flattened against his hand, darkly glowering over it. He stood this way, thin and waiting and morose.

"You sure was dry," grumbled Hughie Grant.

51

"Ain't drank for six months, Hughie."

"Prohibition," said Hughie in disgust. "Well, give me my bottle."

Perrigo tipped the bottle again quickly and drained it and handed it back. A little flush of blood brightened the man's honed cheeks. He scanned Hughie Grant angrily. "Why in God's name did you come draggin' that bottle past me for?"

"It's my regret," stated Hughie Grant, "not yours. Empty—damnation!" He flung the bottle over into the trees and sat with his shoulders drooping and his eyes studying his palms as they lay folded on the saddle horn. He waited a little while; then looked at Perrigo and came to a decision.

"Well, I'm blasted if I ride home on an empty stomach. Next time, Nick, don't ask me any drink out of my bottle. I'm goin' back to town for another one." He wheeled his horse down the road. Ten yards away he turned. "You comin'?"

"For a drink?"

"What else was I talkin' about?"

"Wait a minute," said Perrigo. He went back into the trees and got on his horse and came out beside Hughie Grant. They trotted toward Morgantown, Perrigo dismally scowling.

"That shows you," pointed out Hughie Grant. "Six months without a drink ain't good for anybody. Why stunt your frame like that?"

"Booze," said Nick Perrigo in sultry disgust, "is my poison." Instantly he hauled up to a stop. "You know that, Hughie. What're we going to town for?"

Hughie Grant didn't look back and he didn't stop. He said: "Don't bother me. On mature thought, maybe you hadn't ought to come. Old Martin's there and so's Bill Head and the bunch."

"Wait," said Nick Perrigo, and came on at a rush.

"We just got through buryin' Les Head," reflected Hughie Grant. "I don't like that kind of work."

"You may be buryin' another," said Nick Perrigo, and all his little features were violent and inflamed. "I've got no use for a Head, nor for any Head rider."

"I'm one," pointed out Hughie Grant equably.

"What of it?" gritted Perrigo.

Hughie Grant's reply was summer-mild. "Nothin'. We was talkin' about a drink wasn't we?"

So they trotted down the hill and rounded into Morgantown's main street. Perrigo stiffened in his saddle and his free arm began to swing forward and back, brushing his gunbelt at each passing. Sunlight was a low flash in the west, and bright purple currents of twilight flowed along Morgantown's south walk and touched the men scattered there. Ranier loitered at the jail office beside Old Martin Head's wheel chair. Nick Perrigo passed him without a side glance; and he didn't turn his eyes at the hotel where Bill Head stood in idleness. Crow Track riders cruised this street and a group of them were at the doors of the Elkhorn saloon. Perrigo wheeled in here and dismounted, a scarlet flush crawling down his narrow neck. He left his horse at the rack and went around the rack and stalked through the Crow Track riders sightlessly, into the saloon. Hughie Grant followed him to the bar. A man immediately lifted his bottle and slid it along the bar, moving away from Perrigo. The humming thickness of talk in here dropped definitely, and other men's faces wheeled in the shadows of the place and watched Perrigo with an indrawing interest.

Perrigo said to the bartender: "It'll be rye," and stared at himself in the backbar's shining mirror; something in that whipped and peaked reflection seemed to lift the hackles on his neck. His eyes turned narrow and red. When the bartender slid bottle and glasses down to him he helped himself to a drink and hooked both arms on the bar's edge and lowered his face—and stood that way.

Hughie Grant abruptly clapped his hands to his chest. He said: "Now where's my money?" and turned to leave. Perrigo's hand instantly shot out and seized Hughie Grant by the arm.

"Where you going?" demanded Perrigo.

"I'll be back," said Hughie Grant very softly.

Perrigo stared at him unrelentingly; and the room's silence grew. Afterwards Perrigo released his grip. "You damn right you will, Hughie. Or I'll come and find you. I don't drink alone."

"Sure," said Hughie Grant, and left the saloon rapidly. He passed the Head riders and winked at them, and cut across to where Bill Head was. He took off his hat and a fresh, full sweat curled down his forehead. He wasn't drunk and never had been. He let out a tremendous sigh, then spoke to Bill Head. "There's your man, Bill. But, listen. I never do that again."

53

Back in the saloon Neal Irish, who ran the poker game, suddenly laid down his cards. He said to the players, very quietly: "Cash in your chips, gentlemen. Play is over for a while."

Buck Surratt was in the Torveen yard with his back propped up against a corral, enjoying the sunset, when Annette Carvel came out of the trees at a rapid canter. She crossed the yard to him and jumped from the saddle and took a pose of interest there. He pushed himself to his feet then, saying casually: "Hello."

Her hands rose in an expressive way to touch her hair and sweep it back from the graphic outline of her face. Her lips changed to a faint smiling; her shoulders straightened and the light of her eyes became direct and personal, as he had noticed it to be in Morgantown two days ago. He didn't quite understand the frankness of that silence, nor could he perceive the change that occurred in her. But the change was there, for this was a girl sensitive and pliable to the ways of men; and her eyes saw that Surratt was young and tall and that he smiled back.

She said: "Is Sam here?"

"Everybody's gone but me."

She speculated on him, her interest very strong. Against the whiteness of her skin her lips made a full, soft, crimson contrast. "My name," she said finally, "is Annette Carvel. My mother and I run the dressmaking shop in town. You're Buck Surratt, the new man."

He said, "Yes," and let it go like that, but her personality came warmly across the space to disturb him. Her voice, when she spoke again, dropped to a faintly husky note, approving and gently inviting.

"You're very brave to stand against Bill Head."

He didn't answer, and he saw immediately how responsive that pretty face was to the least change in her mind. Her lips moved, they showed disappointment. Her shoulders lifted. "Well," she said, "then you'll have to do, I guess. Nick Perrigo's in the Elkhorn saloon, drunk as a fool, and all the Head crowd is there. They hate him, you know."

He said, "Thanks," gravely. She waited a little longer, her expression hopeful and pleasing in the sudden fall of twilight. Her breasts stirred to the lift and fall of her breath. She wheeled away with a quick impatience and swung up to her saddle, saying: "Sam would want to know about that. But if you're alone . . ." Then she had a long, straight smile for him. "There's always a dance in town on Saturday nights, Buck." Unaccountably she laughed at him and galloped down the meadow, into the trees.

Surratt tried another match on his pipe. The light ran along the gravity of his cheeks and died, and he stood in the forming twilight and thought of Annette Carvel's hands because they were, to him, important. But it was a thought that faded swiftly into the back of his head where so many other things were stored. He turned to the bunkroom for his saddle and came out and caught up his horse. When he was ready to ride he sat in the saddle a moment, considering Nick Perrigo brought to bay in the Elkhorn saloon. It was a picture very clear. Out of his memory he could produce other pictures like this, the details blurred by dissimilarity, but the central scenes all the same, all making this dark pattern of a man backed up against a wall and other men starkly waiting for him. Nothing changed. He went down the meadow and through the trees and got to the road. Turning toward Morgantown he had but one question in his mind: How had so wary a hand as Nick Perrigo gotten into the trap?

When he reached Morgantown twilight had faded into another black night, with a low young moon on the horizon shedding no glow. The house lamps of the town were flushing through window and door, laying yellow hurdles across the dusty street; men strolled indolently through these alternate patches of light and dark and made stray outlines in the deeper shadows, their talk coming to him in murmuring eddies of vague sound. This was supper hour, the hour of peace; but because the undertones of life were always strong to him, he could feel the creep of suspense on this street. He trotted on and curled into the hitch rack, the undertow of his arrival leaving a lively wake behind. A few riders stood outside of the Elkhorn's doorway and he knew, by the way they turned, that he was identified. He walked by them, put his shoulders to the doors and passed inside.

Before the doors had swung behind him he heard a man out there say: "Go get Bill Head." The tone of it was eager, it was wicked; and Surratt's lips thinned and were remotely touched by a smile. He stopped here, undiscovered for a moment, to absorb the scene before him.

He had not been wrong. Under the strong full light of

the saloon's bracket lamps was a scene that had nothing new in it. Men stood loosely together in this room, faced toward the back end of the place. There were thirty or more of them, all waiting out the silence. Looking past them, over their shoulders, he saw Nick Perrigo backed against the wall. Perrigo's insubstantial body swayed from side to side, and the weight of his drawn and lifted gun seemed to tip him forward. He stared at the crowd, but it was the blurred, unrecognizing stare of a man blind drunk. His voice came across the room, thick and past caring.

"Gentlemen, why don't you come at me?"

The Elkhorn's bartender, standing with his hands flattened against the bar, caught Surratt in the corner of his eyes and turned to look fully; and opened and closed his mouth without sound. Surratt spoke in a tone strong enough to carry across the shoulders of this crowd to Nick Perrigo.

"You want to go back to the ranch, Nick?"

A ripple ran through that mass; and all those dark and eager and partisan faces veered on him. Perrigo said:

"Who's talkin'?"

The crowd swayed. A little lane opened and a motion of defense carried these men back toward the walls. He faced Perrigo down the lane and saw Perrigo's bitter red eyes stare and find nothing. Perrigo said again, plaintively:

"Who's talkin'?"

"Surratt. You want to go home?"

"Surratt," breathed Perrigo. "Get me out of here." And then he swayed from the wall, all his will exhausted, and fell face down on the floor.

The glow of the lamps sharpened everything and Surratt saw his surroundings with a fatal clarity. The room was long and narrow, the bar on one side and a row of poker tables on the other. For a moment the Crow Track men remained as they had been, recoiled from that little lane down which Surratt had his view of Nick Perrigo. And then an unspoken thought stirred them, and the lane closed up and Nick Perrigo was imprisoned behind the solid wall they made.

He heard men coming rapidly along the walk outside. He heard their voices rising, suppressed and excited. But in here the silence grew insufferably thin. He shook his shoulders a little. His hand touched the butt of his gun and he said gently: "I'm taking Nick home, boys," and he

56

lifted his gun and moved forward, his lips still pressed into that remote, constant smile.

It was the weight of their numbers that held them uncertain during this moment. Men in a mass always waited for the voice of a leader to start them, for a sudden motion or a swift word to start them. This was something the years had taught him and it guided him coolly across the room to the solid edges of the crowd. The moments were ticking on, and the stillness here was ready to ignite and explode. He came against a man, not stopping and not speaking. But the muzzle of his gun was against the man and so was the full weight of his eyes. It was a trick, this piling up of threat against one individual in a mob. Singled out thus, the man wheeled and made a little break in the solid wall. Surratt walked into it slowly; he pushed on and set all his will against the next man. He had made a hole. But a moment later the shifting pressure veered around him and the hole closed up and he was locked solid within the Crow Track crew.

Somebody said angrily from the background: "What are you fools doin' over there? Get at him!"

The weight of that purpose crushed against him at once. A man in front threw his chest into Surratt and reached up with his hands. Surratt smashed him over the head with the gun, knocked him back, and shouldered on. Fury began to boil through the room, talk rose gutturally. The fellow in the background yelled again. "Get at him—get at him!" A hand reached out from Surratt's left side and tore at his neck; he broke away from it and threw his knee into a Head rider, who cried and struck him in the face. Hands groped for him once more and this mob surged at him, and men struggled against other men and were blocked by their own closeness. Surratt lowered his head; he plunged on. He slashed his gun barrel across a countenance so white and hating as to be ghostly—he saw that face tip and drop. He got all his strength together and braced his feet and whirled a complete circle, beating them away. He felt the hot blast of their breathing and the slanting blows they landed on his back. His shirt was caught and torn, and he was caught around the neck again, from behind. But he didn't stop; he squatted and bucked his way ahead, carrying the man with him. He shook that encircling arm free—and slugged a Crow Track rider on the temples and slammed him aside. The back wall of the saloon was before him. He jumped at it and put his shoulders to it—and so faced them. Nick Per-rigo was at his feet.

His gun held them off a moment, his lips holding that same thin laughter; he reached deep into his lungs for the wind he had to have. They were growling at him like wild dogs. The man by the bar still kept up his insistent yelling, but those directly facing him looked at the point of his gun and stood uneasy and sullen and watchful. He dropped to his knees and got one hand around Nick Per-rigo's waist. He pulled the man half upright and threw him over a shoulder—and stood erect with a hard wrench of his muscles.

He remained like this, considering the saloon door thirty feet yonder—with that crowd waiting stubbornly, savagely for him to start back. Somebody suddenly jumped to the top of the bar and reached out with his hand and killed the lights there; somebody else ran along the opposite side of the room to repeat that gesture and to at once turn the room dim and smoky. There was but one lamp left burning, this directly behind Surratt. He laughed at them then—openly—and swung about and lifted the lamp from its holder. He yelled: "Fire!" and flung the lamp straight into the heart of the crowd.

Glass smashed over the floor, the spilled kerosene ex-ploded into a pale flame that rushed up a man's oil-soaked coat. The man let out a high-pitched yell and wheeled and slashed his way through the crowd. A quick fire flashed and smoked in the sawdust scattered along the boards, filling the room with its acrid odors. This Crow Track crew was touched by a sudden terrible fear and stampeded for the lone doorway. One rider alone pushed through the crowd and tried to extinguish the fire spreading out from the bro-ken lamp. The uneasy, shuttering blackness of this room was all at once filled with a savage, senseless grunting as this Crow Track crew slugged its way toward the door. Sur-ratt ran straight for the thin glow of that doorway, ram-ming into the stormy swirl of all those beating bodies. Ta-bles fell and were smashed. Somebody broke a window and jumped through; the swinging doors were clawed down. The weight of that unreason squeezed against Surratt. He bucked his way ahead, beaten by blind blows; he stepped on a man who reached up and grabbed his legs. He had to kick his way free. The pressure around the doorway was like the pressure of a vice, and Perrigo's body put a dead weight on his shoulders; and then the fierce drive of men at his rear shot him through the doorway. He ran around the hitch rack and reached the street—and stopped there.

The lights of the hotel and the adjoining stores laid a bright spot in the dust. He was caught here, exposed and surrounded. The up-running Crow Track crew saw him and wheeled to make a ring that closed him in—and on the hotel porch Bill Head stood and looked at him with a stubborn triumph.

"Put Perrigo down," Bill Head ordered. "You've had all your fun."

It was a scene again, like other scenes on the back trail. Darkness all about, and here one bright flood of light. Men were watching him, the aroused instinct to kill stained somberly and hungrily on their cheeks. There was a cripple in a wheel chair next to Bill Head, an old man with a black beard and a black glance cutting into him. That one bent from his chair and gripped his hands on its arms, as though he wanted to throw his power into the street against Surratt.

"Drop him," repeated Bill Head.

Blood dripped along Surratt's lips. The wild fury of the moment ripped through him and recklessness had its way with his cheeks, strengthening the smile so thin and permanent on his lips.

"I think," he said, "I'll finish this job."

Bill Head cried: "You want to die, you damned fool?"

There was a weight in Surratt's fist. His gun still hung there. He threw Perrigo more securely over his shoulder.

"It's an even break," he said. "You want to try?"

"Grandstand stuff!" breathed Bill Head. He made a stiff and enormous shadow in this yellow light. He didn't move; the bully cast of his features never changed. "Move up behind him, boys—and get the gun."

"Is it the lamplight that makes you look so yellow?" murmured Buck Surratt. The rage in him was enormous, without reason. But he stood here and was trapped. He knew it. The crippled man suddenly slapped both of his hands on the wheel chair and lay back and seemed to grow furious behind his beard. Bill Head looked down at the cripple, with a deepening of ruddy color. Surratt heard him speak hotly to the cripple. "I play this hand my own way, sir."

But there was interruption here. The circle broke and the blocky shape of the marshal drove through. Bolderbuck came up to Surratt. His face was without imagination, without the hint of friendliness or anger. He ranged himself beside Surratt. He said, clear enough for the street to hear: "Put him on his horse and pack him home, son."

"Wait a minute," challenged Bill Head. "I'm running this."

Bolderbuck turned in a manner that was like the settling of a great weight. His voice remained wholly unmoved, it continued its stubborn and polite run. "I handle the law in this particular town, Mr. Head. Take your man and go, Surratt."

But a man cried out instantly from the ranks of the surrounding Crow Track outfit: "No you don't, Mary Ann!"

Bolderbuck wheeled his square body again and faced the sound. He said placidly: "I'll kill the one that draws a gun."

Surratt looked at Bolderbuck. He shook his head. "I'll apologize for misjudgin' you," and carried Nick Perrigo across the street to the horses. The crowd there gave sullenly; but it gave. He threw Perrigo across his saddle and got up and readjusted the little man on his knees crosswise like a bag of flour. He caught the reins of Perrigo's horse and turned up the street, bearing one burden and leading another. But he halted a moment, the thin laughter growing stronger along his lips. He saw Bolderbuck implacably holding that crowd still; he saw Bill Head standing on the walk with a bilked rage flushing his big, handsome face; and he saw the obscure glance of the cripple shooting out at him from beneath those shaggy brows. It was the cripple he remembered as he trotted up the street and left Morgantown behind.

Bolderbuck held his position—and thus held the crowd in place—until the echo of Surratt's pony vanished from the night. He turned after that and walked through the circle, ignoring it, and went on to the jail office. He sat down in a chair and got out his pipe; and was smoking it in ruminative silence, with his thick hands laced across his belly, when Sheriff Ranier came quickly in and shut the door.

Ranier stared at Bolderbuck. "Why did you do that, Tom?"

Bolderbuck spoke around his pipestem. "I admire courage."

"The man's a fighter."

"Yes," murmured Bolderbuck.

Ranier was jerked by a nervous excitement. He fell into

60

a restless tramping, going around the room. His face broke and settled and broke again, and his lips kept moving. He came to a stand. His question burst plaintively out of him. "What are we going to do, Tom?"

"Stick fast."

"No, you don't see it," exclaimed the sheriff. "The old ones will fight for their cattle. They've held this country solid. But there's a lot of young ones and poor ones who'll harken to Sam Torveen's example. They've been still. They won't stay still when they see this man Surratt laugh in Bill Head's face. They'll take courage and swing with Torveen. My God, Tom, you know what a neighborhood war does to you and me? Which way do we swing? Where do we stand?"

"We stand fast," murmured Tom Bolderbuck, and kept on smoking. Long afterwards he mused, half to himself: "It was pretty, the way he stood out there with Perrigo on his back. It was pretty."

On the street Bill Head threw a surly order to his crew. "Get your horses and get out of here!" He swung about and showed Old Martin the burning resentment that was in him. His tone was stiff. "It's my understanding you don't approve the way I handled this. Surratt's a gunman. It sticks out all over him. I won't be baited into a fight he wanted me to start. There's other ways of handling this. I wish you'd hold your judgment till this affair is over."

"I'm staying at the hotel tonight," said Old Martin.

Bill Head started to wheel his father into the hotel. But the old man's hand lifted in sharp dissent. He said gruffly: "Get on home. Pokey—Pokey come here."

Pokey came up. He got behind the chair and pushed it into the hotel lobby and down the hall to Old Martin's room. He closed the door and stood waiting. Old Martin looked oddly at this little, unimportant man.

"What you think of him, Pokey?"

"Surratt?" said Pokey. He let his eyes fall to the floor; he was diffident and vaguely embarrassed. "Seems kinda like a tough one, Martin."

"Tough!" roared Old Martin. "God blast you, Pokey, he stood out there and he didn't care about the whole of Bill's pack around him! He was laughin' at 'em in a way that made 'em cringe back and think twice!" Storm rushed through Old Martin, and his temper was a huge thing that crowded and heated the room. "And it's our luck to have

61

him against us when I'd give the world to have a son like that."

"Bill was just bein' careful," said Pokey.

"No man has a right to be careful when another man calls him yellow," growled Old Martin. "There's no way out of this for Bill now. He'll have to face this Surratt across a gun. He's no son of mine if he doesn't. Pokey, I'm sendin' you on a trip. You go across the desert to where this Surratt came from. I want to know all about him."

"Yeah," said Pokey.

"Start tonight," said Old Martin, and sent Pokey out of the room with a wave of his hand. After the little man was gone Martin Head sat very still, thinking of what he had seen. It impressed him enough to murmur: "One man—and he made it stick. It is strange to understand."

Surratt came across the Torveen yard and lugged Nick Perrigo into the bunkhouse. The kid was there with Ed; they both got up and stared. Surratt dumped Nick into a bunk, turning back without explanation. Torveen had heard him arrive and was in the office doorway.

"I brought Nick home from Morgantown, dead drunk," explained Surratt.

But there was a little light from the office shining on Surratt's battered face and on his torn shirt. Torveen saw this and pulled Surratt into the office. He rapped out his question.

"What was it?"

"The Carvel girl came up here and said he was in town in the saloon, with Crow Track on his neck. So I went down there. I had to pack him out."

"With Crow Track there?" said Torveen.

"Yes."

Torveen stared. His eyes began to flicker. "It's all you've got to say—and you're smilin'?"

Surratt shrugged his shoulders. "Bolderbuck surprised me. He stepped in to help me out."

Torveen said: "Somebody must have got to Nick with a drink, before he went—or he wouldn't have gone to Morgantown. He knows better. Liquor's poison to him. I——"

His mouth was open like that, framing the word, when the sudden boil of shot echoes came out of the north in subdued eddies. He put out a hand to push Surratt aside, but Surratt had already turned through the doorway and was running for his horse. The kid and Ed came from the bunkhouse on the dead gallop. They were all up in the saddles and turning into the meadow within half a minute of that first sound. Torveen yelled back at Surratt: "The sheep! I left Chunk Osbrook with the herders!" He raced into the trees on the north side of the house, down a narrow trail leading toward the upper meadows where the sheep lay. It wasn't more than half a mile ahead, and the sound of shooting there turned general and strong, many guns beating up the darkness. Torveen had quit talking, but the kid came just behind Surratt with a savage, jumpy cursing. Up there, two rifles sent flat explosions through the blunter noise of revolvers. Surratt heard them speak steadily for a matter of two or three minutes, and afterwards heard them no more. The revolvers bore down insistently for a little while, and a man yelled. That seemed to be a signal, for the firing died out with a last cracking shot.

They came into the meadow. Sheep milled whitely in front of them, and Torveen had to turn aside and sweep around. There was a crash of horsemen over on the left, flailing through the trees toward the ridge. Torveen yelled: "Hey, Chunk!" He went on toward the herder's cabin recklessly, calling again. Surratt said, "Be a little careful, Sam," and brought up his horse and got down. The kid went by him, still cursing; but Ed also stopped short and jumped to the ground. He came abreast of Surratt as they walked on toward the house. A sheep lay on the meadow, shot but still moving. Surratt swept the edges of the far trees—and listened and heard nothing. He came up to the house then and found Torveen crouched down by the door. A match burst in Torveen's cupped palms.

Its light glowed down on Chunk Osbrook's face. There was a little glitter of blood on Osbrook's chest. One hand lay up over the hole, as if to check the blood; but he was quite dead.

Surratt reached over and killed the match in Torveen's fist. He raised his voice, calling through this thick dark: "Hey, you herders—come up here."

"No," said Torveen, matter-of-fact with his words. "They'll be running. It was Chunk who stayed to take the beatin'. Well, that's one of us. They've got five more to go, Buck."

Surratt said: "Send one of the boys for my blankets. I'll camp with the sheep."

63

Chapter Seven

THE WAY OF
A WOMAN

They got Chunk Osbrook's body across Torveen's saddle. Ferd Bowie was swearing around the darkness; the others stood grouped together, tensed to the night's mystery. A disturbed bleating came over from the sheep, and the wind ran its steady way through the trees. Powder smell faded from the meadow; the last echo of the raiding party died up in the ridge.

"Crow Track," murmured Surratt. "They left Morgantown just a little while ago."

"Maybe," said Torveen.

"Who else?"

"Met Hank Peyrolles yet?"

"In the jail office, other day."

"You'll know him better," stated Torveen. "Well, there's no use waiting here. Those herders have bunched this job. I don't blame 'em much."

They crossed the meadow and traveled back along the trail, Torveen leading and Ed and Bowie holding Chunk Osbrook's body in the saddle. Surratt followed with the extra horses. A coyote in the deep timber broke the liquid run of these dark shadows with a shrill half-barking call to the remote stars, invoking a far-off answer. When they came to the ranch Torveen helped Ed carry Chunk Osbrook to a storeroom beyond the kitchen. He came out of there and closed the door quietly; and remained on the porch a moment to roll a smoke. When he scratched a match across the boards the light trembled in his fingers. Surratt stared at that sight with a puzzled attention and then was relieved to know that anger did this to Torveen, not fear. For Torveen's voice was packed with hot emotion.

"Dog eat dog," he said. "Well, we'll have our turn at it. You sure you want to watch them sheep alone?"

"I'm a little harder to shoot at," Surratt remarked dryly, and went into the bunkroom. Nick Perrigo lay where he had been dumped, huddled and snoring. The kid sat at the table with his sallow chin cupped in a palm. He stared at Surratt with the vigilant watchfulness of a wild animal; and the smell of this night's blood had put a cast in his eyes that warned Surratt. The thing haunted Surratt as he rolled his blankets. He threw the roll over a shoulder; he turned to the kid.

"How old are you?"

"Twenty," said the kid reluctantly.

"Where's your people?"

Bowie shrugged his shoulders indifferently. "I dunno. Dead maybe. Was in Oklahoma Territory when I run away."

Surratt found nothing on that face which pleased him. Ferd Bowie was a white savage, and all the decency in him had been starved out long ago. Yet something prompted him to speak a civil word of advice. "Get out of this business. Ride over the pass and put this country behind. If you stay you'll kill somebody, or you'll be killed."

The kid said evenly: "That's all right with me."

Surratt left the bunkroom and put the blanket roll behind his saddle. He went across to the office, seeing Torveen inside. "In the morning . . ." he started to say. But he stopped and swung his head to the far end of the office—and discovered Judith Cameron posted quietly by the far wall. Surratt removed his hat. "I didn't know I was butting in."

"That's all right," exclaimed Torveen. He showed a faint embarrassment. "Judith rode down to pass a word with me. She's a regular Indian for prowlin' at night."

"I'm going to the sheep camp," said Surratt. "Be back for breakfast."

Judith Cameron came from the end of the room. She murmured: "Wait a minute—I'll ride that far with you." She smiled a little at Torveen. "Time to go home. Dad's a little touchy lately about the way I drift."

"I don't blame him," said Torveen. "You worry me, too."

"Closing the gate on me, mister?" said Judith, swifter with her smile.

Torveen flushed. "I'm thinkin' about you, Judith, not about me."

Judith turned beside Surratt, near the doorway. For a

65

moment Torveen's cheeks were plain and unexpressive. But Surratt observed something then that gave him the whole story of Sam Torveen's heart. Behind the labored neutrality of expression irritation stirred—a flash of jealousy showed. Torveen tried to hold it out of his voice and wasn't quite successful. "You're a handsome-lookin' pair, but that shirt's kind of irregular, Buck."

"Remember what I told you," Judith said.

"Sure," grunted Torveen. "Better get goin'."

Surratt stood aside to let the girl pass out, and afterwards he went to his horse. She walked around the house and presently came riding back. Torveen remained in the doorway, closely watching. When they started off he sent a call after the girl almost humbly: "Good night, Judith."

She raised her hand to Torveen and said, "So long," in a way that ran like a slow measure of music through Surratt's brain. At the trees he dropped back to let her take the lead, seeing her slim shape vaguely away ahead of him. They reached the sheep meadow a little afterwards, and he came abreast of her again, but there was nothing said and the silence was suddenly thick with this girl's presence, rich and satisfying with it. He saw the meadow cabin's dim outline reach forward—and felt a deep regret then for the shortness of this ride. He got down and pulled off his blanket roll.

"Good night," he said.

"I want to talk with you."

She followed him into the cabin. He tried a match against the gloom and found a lantern sitting on a board table in the middle of the place. When he reached down to lift the globe he felt it still to be warm. A smoky yellow light flowed slowly through the place and reached over to touch the girl. She leaned back against a wall, her shoulders small and square and resolute against it. Her hair was a fresh tawny gold in this obscure room; and the shadows etched out the strong, clear candor of all her features. There was a blend of things in her that troubled Surratt by their fullness—a pride and an honesty and a deep, mysterious grace of heart and body—that woke in him the flame of hungers he could not understand. The knowledge of Sam Torveen's latent jealousy oppressed him then, for he realized why Torveen should feel that way about this girl.

Her voice ran the room gently; her eyes explored his face with a soft, slow attention. "You were hurt tonight,

66

in Morgantown. They bruised you and wanted to kill you."

"We got out of it all right."

Her question came as a low whisper. "Will you get out of it next time?"

"Next time? It's better that a man be blind as to the future. Life's trouble enough without borrowing from tomorrow."

She shook her head, enormously sober. "There's a sadness in you I do not understand."

"I want something I can't have."

"What?"

"I think," he said, carefully choosing his words, "it is peace. I'll leave ambition to other men. To men like Sam, who's staking his hide on it."

"You're staking your hide with him, Buck."

"That's friendship—not ambition. When this is all finished I'll be riding on."

"You know why Sam's ambitious, don't you?"

"He's a young man and he's a poor man. It isn't money that matters with him. It's standing equal with any other cattleman in the district that matters. Something whips him on to that and he'll never rest until he gets it. I can see the pride in him that won't let him ask a woman to step away from a big house to a little one. So he's going to get a big house first, before he asks. I do not blame him—for you are the woman."

She murmured: "Yes, that's why he's doing it."

He watched her with a driving curiosity and could not penetrate the hazel mystery of her eyes. Sam Torveen loved her, but he could not break down her reserve to find how her heart went. It was a thing strangely and powerfully important to him, though he did not know why. He felt restless and depressed for lack of an answer.

She said: "You know what this means, don't you? This band of sheep in the meadow has made outcasts of you all. There were six of you. Now there's five, and it will never end till you're all dead or driven out. Why should you go on with it, Buck?"

He asked her abruptly: "What's your wish?"

"To see it stopped before somebody else dies!"

"No," he said. "Things like this are written in the book. Nobody can say Sam Torveen willfully started a war. It goes deeper. These sheep are like time. They move on and nothing can stop them. It's always been that way and always will be. If it wasn't Sam who started this, it would be somebody else."

Her arms rose and crossed her breasts and she said in a small, quick voice: "I am afraid."

They stood thus faced, deeply engrossed in each other, with something strong and vivid and unsettling running between them. He came around the table and looked down, and her eyes came up and were very bright. He locked his big fists behind him solidly, thinking that she was the full image of man's desire. The strength of her presence rocked and tore at him; it was a hammer beating at his strength; it was a wildness and a beauty lifting him higher than he had ever been lifted. He said, blunt and rough: "I think you'd better ride along."

"I do not think you know fear," she murmured, long watching him. "But you're very lonely, Buck."

"Good night," he said.

Something quick and surprised widened her eyes. She looked steadily at him a moment, reading his face; and she turned immediately and went out. He didn't follow. Motionless by the table, he listened to her pony trot around the house and go up the hill trail. A little afterwards the echoes of the pony died in the timber.

He thought angrily: "What did she see in my head then?" and lifted his chin to catch the fresh rumor of a pony running steadily up the meadow. He lowered the lantern's wick and stepped back a pace, waiting out that arrival. But a moment later he heard Torveen's voice call him. "That's all right, Buck." Surratt reached over and turned up the wick again and found Torveen framed in the doorway.

The mood of this man was written plainly on his face, distrusting and aroused and angered; and Surratt understood instantly that Torveen had been across the meadow watching the cabin during Judith Cameron's visit. Faint anger stirred Surratt—and went away; and he felt sorry for Torveen.

Torveen spoke unevenly: "I thought I'd drop over and see if you was sure you wanted to stick it out here."

"It's all right. Don't be so damned spooky, either about these sheep or anything else."

Torveen jerked up his chin. Irritation got the best of him. "By God, Surratt, you're too clever at reading a man's thoughts!"

"Steady up, kid."

Torveen came into the cabin, his nerves and his fears jerking at him. He made a complete circle of the room; he swung on Surratt, the ragged emotion in him pouring out.

"Listen, Buck. That girl's my life. It's been that way since we were kids. There was a time when I stood well with the old-time cattlemen in this country. I was welcome anywhere. But when I got older and saw what a piddlin' spread I run it cut me pretty deep. To hell with the money or the fame. But I've got to have my part of this range— for Judith. I'm too honest to rustle, so it's sheep. Now I'm an outcast and I've played right into the hands of Bill Head, who's been wanting my scalp ever since I took Judith home from the first dance. He's always laid for me and the sheep give him the excuse he wants. Well, it's open season on Sam Torveen—and I've made it that way because I won't be in the position of poor white trash askin' a rich man's daughter to marry me. I'm playin' my stack on this and God knows where the end is. That's all right, Buck. It's all right—just as long as there's daylight for me. She's the daylight. She's always been."

"Told her this?" asked Surratt quietly. "You've got an agreement on it?"

"What kind of a fool would I be to lay this war on her conscience? Why do you figure she came tonight? To try to keep me out of trouble. Well, we'll play it like this—all the way through."

"Sure," said Surratt. He was smiling across the interval, a little sadly, a little humorously. "We'll play it all the way through."

Torveen scraped a hand across his cheeks and let out a long breath. He stared at the floor with his shoulders wearily dropped. He shook his head and came around the table. A grin streaked wryly across this man's roan, fighting face. He put his hand on Surratt's shoulder.

"Sometimes I'm batty as hell. How long have I known you? Three days. Well, I'd trust you to the end of creation—and that's the way I've felt from the beginning. You're shoulders above the pack, which includes me, and I'm proud of my luck in runnin' into you. Forget it."

"Forget it," agreed Surratt quietly.

Torveen turned immediately out of the cabin, and a little later galloped across the meadow. Surratt picked up his blankets and killed the lantern. He walked from the cabin to lead his horse around to the margin of the near-by timber, to put it on a picket there. He drew his rifle from the saddle boot, strolled twenty yards from the horse and spread his blankets just inside the trees and rolled up for the night, the rifle above his head. The stars were all dimly agleam in the black sky, scattered like crushed diamond dust; the wind poured down these deep hills, strong with the smell of pine and rich upland grasses. All his bones were tired and his desire was for a dreamless sleep; yet he lay there and knew that his life had trapped him again in the strong jaws of friendship. He could not stand in the way of this fiery, lovable Torveen who trusted him; he could not take away, even if it were possible, the man's hope. Silence was his part, as it had been before. He remembered then the strong, supple shape of Judith Cameron against the cabin wall, and the curve of her lips—and loneliness bore him outward on an ebb tide.

Chapter Eight

SECRET MEETINGS

Surratt came down to the ranch house for breakfast; and afterwards went over to a corner of the meadow where the crew had dug a grave for Chunk Osbrook beside the graves of other Torveen people buried there. Day's thick and drowsy warmth already filled these hills, but the long shadow of the pines covered this little cemetery with a cool, still pleasantness. They brought Osbrook from the house and laid him in the grave and were dismally silent awhile. Considering these odd companions, Surratt understood something about them then. Tough as they were, they had an ingrained respect for death. They were embarrassed from knowing they owed Chunk Osbrook a more decent ceremony than they could render. It was the sense of a lacking propriety that held them thus paused here, waiting for Torveen to say what should be said.

Torveen's gravity thickened on him. He looked around the group and out upon the yellow meadow, and turned a little toward a small headstone beside him, engraved: "Thomas J. Torveen, 1820-1881." He considered the stone a moment.

"My father," he mused, "once told me the prime duty of a man was to live in such a manner that dyin' would come easy to him. These old-timers lived strong, but they all seemed to get fun out of their days. They had a faith nobody could shake. I saw it in old Tom many times, a stout belief that his ticket read all the way through. He laid himself down without doubt and he died with a smile, like he wanted to show me it wasn't much of a chore. It's something that seems to be gone out of the world. I haven't got it and I know few people who do have it. I don't know what death is—I don't even know what life is. Maybe we'll find out and maybe we won't. Chunk wasn't a bad boy. His riding is done, and whatever else may come to him at least he's got a rest, which is more than we can say for ourselves."

They waited a little longer, until they were sure he had finished. Ed and the kid put their shovels into the fresh dirt and began to fill up the grave. They worked at first reluctantly; then faster, eager to be done with it. The others presently stepped in and spelled them off on the labor. When they were through they all walked back to the yard. Nick Perrigo sat down on the edge of the porch, the aftermath of his drunk leaving him shaken and white and physically ill. The thinness of the man was more pronounced; his eyes burned. Ferd Bowie stood sullenly in his tracks. Ed remained in the background, leaning on a shovel. Sam Torveen scanned them with a practical glance.

"You want to remember," he warned them, "that this is the beginning of something, not the end. There's five of us left, but it won't stay like that. We're running sheep, which makes us about as low in the scale of things, according to the view of a cattle rancher, as it's possible to get. I'm not cryin' about it—I'm just tellin' you the way the country looks at us. We don't get any more mercy and we don't get any more warnings. Was I a big cattle owner I'd probably feel the same way. If any of you fellows want to drift over the pass tonight it's all right with me."

"I've been considering the sheep meadow," reflected Surratt. "I don't like it."

"Why?" asked Torveen.

"Too exposed—too easy to raid. Up on the ridge yesterday I noticed another clearing along the edge of the river. That yours?"

"Yes, but it's five miles away."

"Still, it gives us one less side to watch. We better move the sheep up there tonight."

Torveen thought about it. Nick Perrigo lifted his head and spoke sourly: "I don't take to the suggestion."

But Torveen finally nodded. "All right. We'll do that tonight."

Perrigo reared up, crossed the yard to his horse and rode off. Bowie went into the bunkroom, Ed walked around the house. Torveen was remotely grinning. "You got this crew eatin' out of your hand. They're not happy about it, but they're mindin' you after a fashion." He came forward to squat in the sunlit yard and to draw stray patterns across the dust with his forefinger. "Friend of mine rode by last night who was in Morgantown when

72

you put on your party. The way he told it I wish I'd seen it. Seems like you kind of printed yourself on this country's memory." He looked up, bright and severe. "You damn fool, don't cut your string so thin next time! It came near breakin' on you."

"It didn't."

"Supposin' it had?"

Surratt murmured: "Sometimes a man can't afford to think of what might happen."

"And you smiled at that bunch," marveled Torveen. "You called Bill Head yellow and he took it. I want to correct you on that little point, for it's important you get the man straight. There's no yellow in him. What you see is a cold brute patience that never gives up and never gets tired. Any other man, even a yellow one, would've been stampeded into a play last night. But Bill will let the whole damn country consider him yellow and keep drivin' at his purpose. You can set him back on his heels, but you can't stop him and you can't swing him off his trail."

Surratt listened with an absorbing attention. He put this picture of Bill Head back in his mind, to consider and to remember.

"It ain't the sheep, with him so much," went on Torveen. "It's me he wants—and my land. The Heads haven't got any open range like this. My meadows shut them into the hills. Bill's been lookin' my way for years. So, there's the story."

Surratt said: "I'll mosey back to the sheep."

Torveen had something else on his mind. He got up, choosing his words with a great deal of care. "Like I said, you've printed yourself on this country's memory. People think you know a good deal about Les Head's shooting."

Surratt had turned away; but he swung about now and studied Torveen thoughtfully. "Maybe I do," he suggested.

There was a definite worry on Torveen's homely cheeks. "Anybody might have done that killin'. Les Head had few friends. He was an insolent man and was hated for it. He was a man to chase after women—and there's men who hated him for that too." Torveen's eyes contained a studied, enforced inscrutability. "For that matter I might have shot him myself. I had reasons enough. I wouldn't go borrowing trouble, Buck, if I were you."

"Maybe I don't follow you," said Surratt.

"Maybe you do," retorted Torveen. But he added: "It's bein' said you've got some clue to the killin'. I wouldn't go turning over old boards. Something might fly up and sting you."

"Were you on the ranch the night of the shot?"

"No," said Torveen, readily enough.

"Was Perrigo?"

This time Torveen's answer came reluctantly. "No."

"Seems like everybody was ridin' through the hills that evening," said Surratt.

Torveen's question went out of him like a shot. "Who else?"

But Surratt only grinned at his partner. He went over to his horse. Torveen called after him swiftly and imperiously: "Don't carry your curiosity any farther, kid." Surratt made a stray gesture with his hand and cantered away, his grin dying. He let his arm fall briefly across his shirt pocket; then got out his pipe and stopped in the trees to fill it. Down the trail he saw the disappearing rump of another horse cutting crosswise through the brush; he lighted his pipe and caught it tightly between his teeth, riding on with a quick lift of his nerves. Coming out of the trees into the sheep meadow he found Annette Carvel waiting there for him.

She said frankly: "I thought you'd be back along this way."

He tipped his stetson, and was at once afraid of this moment. She wore a buckskin split skirt, heavily beaded, and a silk shirt fastened at the collar with a dark string tie. Hatless under the strong sun, her black hair glistened; and there was a shining, eager recklessness all about her. He looked at her attentively and saw that his glance was expected and awaited. Her lips, very red, broke into a quick smiling, and then she was a woman fully, lush with life.

She fell beside him, pleased and softly laughing; and rode across the meadow to the little cabin. He waited a moment in the saddle, but she said: "Are you camping up here now?" and got down and went toward the cabin. He dismounted and stood by his horse. His silence turned her head and her back-thrown glance was made to please him, yet in a moment she shrugged her shoulders and came back, to watch him with a growing soberness. Her eyes then were very wistful; as though his silence struck her a blow she didn't deserve. She was, he suddenly thought, a child loving warmth and afraid of darkness.

She spoke in a way that was humble, that was disappointed: "Men are funny. They keep thinking women are either bad or good. And when a woman comes first to a man, the man always thinks the woman is bad. Why is that? Don't you ever get tired of the same old things said in the same old way?"

He said, gently: "Why ask me a question like that?"

"I thought," she murmured, "you were different. But then I always think that. I guess there are no different men."

He said: "Let me see your hand."

She looked carefully at him, her head held a little to one side. She put her right hand forward, and her cheeks filled with color and her breath quickened. He took the hand, looked at it and turned it over, and let it go.

"Why?" she breathed.

He reached up to his shirt pocket. But some impulse stopped the gesture. He said: "Do you wear doeskin riding gloves?"

Her mouth opened. She drew in a quick, gasped breath. Alarm sprang through her eyes and a pure whiteness covered her face, turning her lips scarlet against such pallor. Her expression then was haunted and miserable.

"Give it to me!" she whispered.

"Does it belong to you?"

"Give it to me—please! It came from my store."

He said, in a regretting, apologetic way: "I'm sorry I mentioned it. I have no desire to pry into anybody's life."

She had seen his hand touch his shirt pocket. She threw herself against him vehemently and her fingers ripped at the pocket and reached into it. He stepped backward and pushed her hands down. He had to brace himself against the violence of her body for a moment—until her burst of strength went away and left her trembling there in front of him. She cried at him:

"I knew you had it—and I'm not the only one that knows you have it! You won't give it to me?"

He said gently: "No."

She whirled back to her horse and got into the saddle. "You can be killed for that!" she exclaimed and went across the meadow at a full gallop, disappearing behind the trees.

Surratt remained in his tracks, somebody displeased at his own conduct. He had no desire, he told himself strictly, to tinker with people's secrets or crack the whip of fear over anybody's head. Yet this was what possession of that doeskin glove in his shirt pocket was coming to mean. In the beginning a pure impulse had caused him to take that glove from the floor of that cabin in which Leslie Head lay dead—a sudden and instinctive desire to protect the unknown woman who owned it. But his mind, always seeking answers, kept reaching into the mystery surrounding the glove, and though he had thought this his secret, Annette Carvel's warning seemed to indicate it was no secret to the hills. So the glove became a major problem, a liability burning a hole in his pocket. He had a duty here to its unnamed owner; and that duty forbade him giving the glove to anyone else.

A threshing of brush behind the cabin wheeled him around. He saw Nick Perrigo ride forward, anger making the little man's eccentric face very old. Perrigo remained in the saddle.

"Surratt," he said, "you leave that girl alone!"

Surratt eyed the man carefully. "What's that, Nick?"

"Never mind," snapped Perrigo. "Don't encourage her to come to you again! She's a kid any man can fool. She'll believe you if you lie to her and she'll come to you if you smile. . . ."

"Perrigo," ordered Surratt, "say no more on this subject."

"By God, I will! What've you got she wants?"

Surratt studied the little man. "My friend," he said quietly, "if you ride through muddy places late at night and don't want men to know where you have been, it's always a good idea to brush off your pony's legs before morning comes. Have I said enough?"

"You know too much!" said Perrigo in a lunging tone. "Your eyes see too much!"

"Better let well-enough alone."

Nick Perrigo fell silent, struggling with the wicked flux of his temper. He seemed to conquer it, for he said in a milder way: "I have made many mistakes, Surratt, and my life has been no good for anybody." Then the mildness, like a flurry of air, passed and left him dismally antagonistic. "You've got my thanks for pulling me out of Morgantown. That's all you've got. I do not trust you and I do not like you."

"I doubt if you like anybody," observed Surratt.

"All men are dogs," grated Perrigo. "Leave that girl alone." He quit on that warning and wheeled and charged back into the trees.

Surratt stood quietly in the sunlight a little while, narrowly considering the mad strangeness of this Nick Perrigo. Going back into his memory he found no precedent; the man's distorted, untrusting behavior was new to him, long ago warped by some major catastrophe. The day had turned steadily hotter, the wind was gone and far above him the Gray Bull peaks threw their angular iron shapes against a flawless azure sky. The sheep lay scattered along the meadow, browsing. On impulse Surratt stepped into the saddle and swung north into the higher trees. There was no need of guarding this flock by daylight; it was by night that men brought trouble to men.

He cruised steadily along the shadowed aisles of these heavy, red-haired pines and was touched by a pure ease. Now and then a shaft of sunlight cut diagonally through some break in the treetops and laid a yellow, sharp-edged pattern in the twilight and burned brilliantly on the humus flooring and turned the surrounding air a smoky blue. Dreaming stillness held the hills; the smell of this forest was spiced and resinous and wild. Somewhere to his left he began to pick up a long, low murmuring.

It was middle-morning when the rising trail brought him out upon another meadow making a tawny splash in the emerald solidity of the hills. Traveling across it he brought up before the unfenced rim of a canyon. Almost vertically below him, a matter of six hundred feet, lay the sunless surface of a river.

Across the way ran a spur of the foothills, considerably higher than the ground upon which Surratt stood. The river swung out of the high hills through a narrow channel that threshed up its water and made white rollers glisten even in the dull light, and passed below him smoothly for a quarter-mile and swung again and went charging through a sheer break in the yonder ridge. Looking far down there, Surratt saw three or four buildings of a little settlement beside the edge of the river where it turned, lost in the depths of this dark hole.

He wheeled to consider the meadow, which he had sighted from a higher peak the day before and had considered as a good place to hold the sheep. Then, the riding impulse strong in him, he tipped into a yard-wide ledge cut against the face of the canyon and began an angling descent to the river. At occasional muddy spots in the trail he saw the round neat-cut print of deer side by side with the heavy plantigrade tracks of bear. Twenty minutes afterwards he stood at the margin of the river where it shallowed across a gravel bar. He forded here, his horse splashing up to its shoulders. On the far side he struck a wagon road and followed it to the settlement.

It was a saloon and a store and one gray ancient house of shakes and hand-hewn timber sleeping on the toes of the ridge rearing high to the sky. The dusty road ran on along the edge of the river, through the narrow chasm, toward the suggestion of a gentler valley beyond. Surratt came to the saloon and drew in there; three men sat on the porch, dark and obscure men, enigmatically interested in him. When he saw them he knew their kind; and looking beyond them to the saloon doorway he found the gross and loose-tissued body of Blackjack Smith filling it.

Surratt got down and climbed the porch, remotely smiling. Blackjack's liquid glance was wary and waiting; the pendulous mouth shifted by degrees, neither friendly nor otherwise. Surratt was quietly laughing then.

He said: "Hello, Blackjack."

Blackjack turned his head to the three men on the porch. "This is Surratt," he grumbled, as though he added the information to previous talk. All three looked at him alertly. Smith said: "Come in, Buck," and retreated to the deeper shadows of the saloon. He walked to the rear of the bar. "Still drinkin' corn whisky?"

"Sure. Your place, Blackjack?"

"Yeah," said Blackjack. "Mine." He seized a bottle and two glasses and kept going down the bar to the back end. There was a rear room there; he went into it and set the bottle on the table. When Surratt came in, Blackjack called all the way through the saloon to the porch: "Take Surratt's horse behind the shed." He closed the door. "It's all right," he said to Surratt; and sat down by the table and fell ponderously silent.

Surratt grinned. "Glad to see me, Blackjack?"

"No," said Blackjack frankly, "I can't say that."

"This joint got a name?"

"This is Carson Ford."

"What's on down the river?"

"Cameron Valley," said Blackjack. "The Head outfit's above me, back yonder is the hills."

"You always did like to get in the middle of a lot of beef," observed Surratt. "But this looks like an inconvenient spot for your business."

"Better than it looks."

78

"Still like other people's beef?"

"Why not?" grunted the big man. Then he burst out: "You sure have messed up the works for me. I'm gettin' along fine and now here you are. I don't know why you come, but you sure make things different."

"I'm not after you, Blackjack. We had our little battle once, but that was a long time ago, across the desert."

"No matter," said Blackjack. "You make it tough on a man. You know me. I always play the strong side of politics against the weak side. Maybe I rustle a little beef, but I got a way of finding friends to take care of me in case of grief."

"That's Bill Head."

"Sure. But you come ridin' through and damned if you don't hook up with this Torveen and Bill Head's bound to have your hide nailed to the side of his shanty, and I'm playin' with Bill in this business."

"Fair enough," suggested Surratt imperturbably. He lifted his glass and drank the pale corn liquor. Blackjack reared back in his chair and pushed his arms in front of him. He said devoutly: "No sir, kid. I don't want any more of your kind of battle. I won't fight you. Not anywhere, any time. I want you to know that. What'd you come to this country for?"

"A rest," murmured Surratt. "A rest I won't get. It's the same old thing. Man that carries the gun dies by the gun."

Blackjack's tone was smooth and marveling. "Well, you take me back just two years to another night. My God, you walk into Morgantown and brace Head's outfit and carry Perrigo out. And you get away with it! You always do. But I doubt your luck this time, kid. You're buckin' too much. Sam Torveen can't stand against these cattlemen. They're bound to wipe him out. It's all arranged. I wish you'd get clear of it."

"Torveen," said Surratt quietly, "is a friend of mine."

"Sure," said Blackjack in a deep, regretting way. "That's always your style. It's a funny thing. I'm no saint and you sure chased me to hell and gone over a lot of acres. But I'm gettin' older and there's things I admire against my will. You got what I admire, kid—and I never thought the day would come when I'd tell you that." He lifted his hands helplessly. "What'm I goin' to do?"

"Play out your hand, of course."

"I'll never lift an arm against you, kid. Well, it's tough. You'll make this country lift its hat to you before the music's done. But in the end they'll get you. I know Bill Head."

Boots scraped across the saloon floor and a voice said definitely: "Blackjack."

It was a voice Surratt knew. He looked up at Blackjack, who had risen. Blackjack nodded. He said quietly: "That's why I had your horse put out of sight. I knew he was comin', and didn't think you wanted to meet him. There's the back door."

The big man opened the door into the saloon and slid through and closed it. He said warily: "What's on your mind, Sam?"

It was Sam Torveen.

As quietly as possible Surratt left the saloon by the back door, found his horse and left the settlement, recrossing the river and climbing up to the meadow.

Chapter Nine

IN DEEP NIGHT

The road through Cameron Valley passed within a stone's throw of Ab Cameron's house, paralleling the river. It was a well-worn road, the main artery into the hills. This way the Heads always traveled, riding up from the desert to their high ranch; the Peyrolles used it when coming out of their lower valley to Morgantown, via the bridge here and the trail over the ridge; and this way drifted many shadowy shapes bound for Carson Ford and the Gray Bull pass and the lonely safety of the deep canyons yonder. Tonight the traffic on the road troubled Judith; many men were adrift, more frequently passing by, more hurried in their pace. She had lived her life here and knew the moods of the land better than her own moods. Intangible rumors flowed thickly in this night, and the wind was telegraphing its messages from canyon and peak.

She looked at her mother, who sat so placidly by the table, engrossed in an endless knitting; and at her father seated at the other side of the table. Lamplight touched up the benign qualities of his face. His lips moved as he read the book in his lap.

Her mother said unexpectedly: "You fiddle around so much, Judith. Can't you rest your body?"

Steve Koerner, who was the Cameron foreman, came over the porch and put his head through the doorway. He nodded at Judith. "The Carvel girl's here."

Judith was half across the room before Ab Cameron's order came quietly after her. "Wait." It turned her around. A little color showed along the strong modeling of her features. She noticed he showed his worry. "The Carvel girl," he said. "That trinket. There's a word in the good book which describes her. What's she doing here?"

"To talk to me," Judith said. Then she added more quietly: "Sometimes I think I'm the only friend she has."

81

"You're not choosy enough," commented Ab Cameron. "You'll pick up anything, sick cats and stray dogs—and a common girl like this Annette."

"Ab," said Mrs. Cameron. For Judith's color had deepened. It turned her lovely and resisting. Cameron spoke in an anxious way: "Don't ride tonight, Daughter."

Judith went on out to the porch and across the yard. Annette Carvel was a small, swaying shape on her horse. Faint moonlight blurred the outline of her face. "Judith," she said, "I've found——"

"Wait."

The men of the Cameron crew stirred near by. They were grouped by the door of the blacksmith shop beside the road. They loitered in the semiopaque shadows of the cottonwoods. It was strange, this unrest that caused them to be here. Over the river's murmurings came the swift echoes of a traveler pounding up from the lower reaches of the valley. Judith moved away from the yard, Annette following.

"Now," murmured Judith.

Annette's voice was low and uneven. "The new man—Surratt—has the glove!"

"I thought so."

"Oh, Judith!"

"Do you think he knows who it belongs to?"

"He looked at my hands!"

"He looked at mine too, Annette."

"I had to tell him they came from my shop."

The arriving rider came up at a steady canter and called out to the men at the blacksmith shop. "Hello, boys." He hurried on. It was, Judith knew, the voice of a Peyrolles man.

The breeze was pleasant on her cheeks; and a current of wildness came out of the black hill mass and woke a responding unrest in her slim, smooth body. She was remembering Surratt's shoulders against the sun and the sadness of his voice and the sleeping danger behind the smoke-gray surfaces of his eyes. The discovery of it had sent a small shock through her; the remembrance of it freshened all her senses now. But she said calmly: "We are safe with him, Annette."

"No man is safe," said Annette sullenly.

"He is."

"Don't trust him."

"I do, Annette."

82

Annette Carvel leaned down from the saddle and her white face showed a dreamlike wonder. "No—never be like me, Judith. That would break my heart. I went up to see him and he smiled at me and I thought he liked me."

"All men smile at you, Annette. That is your fate."

"He asked me if I wore doeskin riding gloves! And apologized for asking! Why did he do that? I tried to get the glove but he wouldn't give it. Supposing somebody else gets it from him?"

"No," said Judith softly, "I think nobody will."

"People know he has it now. And somebody'll try."

Judith Cameron was a little angry then. "Annette, why do you always throw yourself at men?"

"I guess," said Annette Carvel in a small, childlike tone, "I want somebody to love me. Oh, God, Judith—I get so hungry for that!"

"Annette!" breathed Judith, and reached up and touched the girl's arm.

Annette pulled her horse about. "Mom will be worried about me, and scold some more. But it makes me so desperate. I can't sleep for thinking about that glove—and you, and me. Bill Head's so damn cruel. He's going to kill Sam Torveen, I know that. And he'll kill Buck Surratt. You see!" With that she stormed down the road and raced across the bridge, the old structure rolling back a long booming.

Steve Koerner drifted from the shadows, very tall, very quiet-spoken. "She shouldn't be ridin' alone. Neither should you."

"Steve," Judith said, "what's happening?"

But he crawled into a reticence that could not be shaken. He turned away. "I don't know, Miss Cameron."

She went on into the house and stopped and stared at her father, bringing up his bland attention. She was angry then. "Isn't there room enough in these hills for everybody?"

Worry was more clearly disturbing the clerklike gentility of his face. "It isn't for me to say, and not for you to ask."

"Isn't it?" countered Judith. "Whatever happens, you must share the responsibility. Sam Torveen has the right to run his own range his own way. Chunk Osbrook has been killed. Isn't that murder, Dad? Do you approve?"

Mrs. Cameron tried to catch Judith's glance; she showed distress. Ab Cameron marked the page of his book and closed it. To Judith her father had always been a fair and just and kind man. His manner, as long as she could remember it, had been mild; it had been serene, as though untouched by any trouble. But it occurred to her now, with a definite astonishment, that worry was real in him.

"I wish you'd been a boy," he reflected. "I'm getting along, and some things I can't fight against."

"What?"

He looked toward his wife, quietly shrugged his shoulders. "I suppose it is high time Judith knew. Well, Judy, our years here have not always been pleasant. I am not the kind to wish for fighting, and fighting is the breath of life to the Heads. I made my peace with Old Martin long ago. Martin's the sort that has to be king. It was twenty years back that he came here with six men. Those hills up there belonged to me. But he had his mind made up to possess them, so I sold them to him. I knew if I didn't I should have a hard enemy. We have been good neighbors because I have let him have his will. Peace meant more to me than war. And still does—but Bill Head now repeats the whole thing, and Bill is a less scrupulous man than his father."

"A brutal man," said Judith. "He whips his horses—he whips anything that stands against him."

"Yes," agreed Ab Cameron quietly.

Judith flamed up at once. "I'd never, never let him use a single man of our crew to put against Sam Torveen! Never!"

"No?" murmured Ab. He kept shaking his head; and to Judith he seemed older than he was. "It is easy to say, Daughter. But you know nothing of the will of the Heads. I have lived my life under that will. It is a hard thing. This is why I wish you were a boy. I have remained humble, because this someday will be your ranch and I do not want you to inherit the Head anger. You could not fight against Bill."

He left his chair and walked into another room. Judith said: "Mother, how long has it been like this?"

"Your father," said Mrs. Cameron, "has tried to be a Christian. In this country it has been hard to practise. I have often seen him come home bitterly humiliated." She looked up at her daughter and she smiled sadly. "He has had his troubles, Judith, for he was never meant to live in a wild land."

84

"I didn't know," protested Judith.

Mrs. Cameron shrugged her shoulders, a gesture of resignation Judith had often noticed before. "Life can't always be as we dream it to be, in youth. Don't you get in too much of a hurry to find that out." She quit talking, and her smile became dim and impersonal.

Bill Head stood at the doorway, stiffly polite. He removed his hat and said, "Good evening," and came in.

Mrs. Cameron nodded. Rising, she went back into the kitchen and swung the door behind her. Bill Head bowed a little, his stiff yellow hair accenting the ruddy, bold health along his solid face. He said to Judith, "I regret my temper. You can sting a man hard sometimes," and stood waiting. But Judith kept her silence, suddenly proud and cool in this uncertain moment. Bill Head's hazel eyes were thoughtful. They were turning angry again.

He said: "I have heard talk of a glove this Surratt's carrying in his pocket. I intend to get it."

The devil of malice was in her. "So far, Bill, you haven't had much luck with the man."

His light skin swiftly took on a deeper stain of color. A dumb, wicked anger boiled against his setup barriers and showed through. "I intend to get it," he repeated stubbornly. "Do you want me to bring it to you?"

"Why?"

"A woman's glove in Leslie's possession leaves scandal against any woman who ever went with him. You know that. And you went with him now and then."

"Yes," she murmured, "I went with him. For there were times, Bill, when he was gay and charming. He treated a woman always as she wished to be treated, neither more nor less. And he wasn't brutal. He never was that."

"He was a devil!" ground out Bill. "I understand him and I know it would be just his way, in dyin', to leave that glove on the cabin floor to tell me he won something from a woman I couldn't get."

"I'm the woman you mean."

He burst out: "How can I help believing it sometimes!"

"Believe it if you want," she told him. "Your opinion doesn't matter to me. It never will."

His lips rolled and came together and he held himself in a way that told her his desire was to beat compliance into her with his big, savage fists. Yet even then he caught his rage and held it in the full grip of his will. This, she thought then, was the most dreaded quality in him—a stubborn streak that wouldn't surrender. His voice was at once full of heavy authority. "You have had your fun torturing me, Judith. I know that. But wait. I have a turn coming."

He went out with his shoulders slunk forward, the darkness of the night momentarily blinding him. He collided with a Cameron rider. He put his hands forward and seized the man and tightened his fingers into that man's flesh until the other cursed at him. He threw the man aside and plowed on to his horse, galloping up the road under the dim shining of the moon.

Some distance beyond the bridge he swung into the trees and pulled to a walk. Darkness here was a dripping, curdled substance; and out of that darkness emerged a cautious voice.

"Bill Head?"

Head threw his horse around, swinging to face the sound. He drew his gun and trained it on the blackness. He said, "Yes," listening with his head cocked.

"This is a tip," said the voice. "Torveen's shifting his sheep tonight. Going on up the hill to the meadow across from Carson Ford."

"Who are you?"

"What do you care? Take it or leave it. Go there and you'll see. Now ride on and don't be curious."

After Bill Head had circled around and gone up the trail—quite a long while afterwards—the man came out of the brush and rode down the hill. Near the Cameron place he walked his pony and bent low in the saddle; at the bridge he dug in his spurs and crossed on the gallop; and kept this fugitive flight all the way up the ridge. This was the kid, Ferd Bowie, racing home.

They had the sheep already moving away from the meadow into the uphill trail. They were waiting for Bowie, grumbling and restless from the suspense. Torveen said irritably, "Here he comes," and they all turned to watch the shadow of horse and rider break forward from the darkness. Bowie was breathing fast when he stopped in front of them.

"Where the hell you been?" demanded Torveen.

"I got cut off by a couple fellows. Had to duck all over the country. It was Hughie Grant, I think, and that black rascal I don't like—Steve Koerner."

"Get up there in front of the sheep," grunted Torveen.

Bowie vanished. Perrigo and Ed were already out of

sight. The sheep milled palely at the trees, feeding into a trail narrow enough to hold them without flank-guards. The shuffle of their hooves and the quavering, defenseless echo of their bleating softened. Surratt followed, at once enveloped by a churned-up forest dust. Torveen, behind him, swore in a jerky, discomfortable fashion. "How long does it take a man to get used to woollies?"

A slow wind ruffled its waterfall echoes through the treetops again. A chill came off the Gray Bull peaks. Out of the hills—out of the far sweep of canyon and ridge and pine-deep—prowled the ghostly, abysmal feel of loneliness, of mystery primitive and unsolvable. This was night, with night's riddle walking on his nerves. It was, Surratt thought, the cold touch of a nameless and timeless question, reaching out of a black sky into a man's heart. His thinking went down a long spiral, wistful and hopeless. There were no answers for him. A little sunlight and laughter, the memory of a man's farewell grin by camp-fire, the brief flash of a woman's shining eyes—these were all he had or ever would have to answer the riddle. Time ran on. His life was a series of stray pictures fading out behind him; he rode now with a band of sheep, and presently from some other hill in some other year, this too would be a fading picture. There was a melody in the world, for he had heard it, and there was some meaning for men in the world, for he had seen other men's faces light up on discovering it. Neither was for him; vaguely, as a traveler on a lonely trail, he had seen the lamp-glow of hope far away—and then had passed on.

"You can be damned silent when you please."

This was Torveen's voice in the rear; fretted and pitched to uncertainty. Torveen was a man with ambition, and ambition made men feel the risk and the disappointment of living too much. For one without hope nothing much mattered. A day was a day. He pulled himself out of this remote thinking with a real effort.

"I was wondering," he said. "The big ranches all seem over to the north, yonder of the river. What's the other way—south?"

"Just hills and timber—and some small fellows running a few cows in their vest pockets. What's that?"

Listening, Surratt heard nothing, and said so. Torveen swore indistinctly. "I'm not a man to ride easy, like you. Some things I will never understand. How could you smile at the Heads, with Perrigo on your back and the wolves snappin' at your heels?"

"When you're a wolf, kid, you get to know wolves."

They drifted this way for an hour or more, the dust and the sheep smell rolling back. Faint glittering patches of sky broke now and then over them. It was colder; the wind had steadied to a straight, westerly run. Through the trees Surratt saw a cigarette tip jiggling. A horse sneezed. The sheep walked faster and the shape of a rider floated down the trail. "This," grumbled Perrigo, "is the place."

Surratt rode into the clearing. Ed and the kid came back and all of them halted here on the edge of the trees. "You sure you want to stick at this alone?" said Torveen.

"That's all right." Surratt walked his horse across the meadow and stopped at its northern edge. The river murmured sibilantly along its sightless bottom. Far below, the lights of Carson Ford were winking through a thin fog mist. Torveen had followed. He remained beside Surratt, indecisiveness plainly controlling him. He scratched a match and lifted it to his cigarette; his cheeks were strained, with none of his old laughter visible. When the match died the darkness was a deeper thing. He watched the lights of Carson Ford.

"They make a pretty show," he murmured.

"It's a land that gets under your skin," said Surratt.

"Yeah," murmured Torveen. He turned away, "I'll bring some grub up to you first thing in the morning."

Perrigo's voice came across the meadow, curt and quick. "What you doin' over that way, Sam?"

Torveen stopped. He said: "What?"

Perrigo's tone ran up the scale: "Surratt—that you?"

Surratt spun on his heels. Torveen grunted: "Surratt's here with me." The sheep were shifting in the meadow, as they had been before; but they were recoiling from the far trees, spreading gently and uneasily this way. It was a sign. Surratt's eyes swept that darkness with a risen vigilance. Perrigo's challenge slammed across the darkness.

"Then who's walkin' in that yonder corner!"

Torveen became a hunched, moving shape. His voice was low; it snapped back to Surratt. "Get out of here, Buck." He went charging toward Perrigo.

Surratt stood fast, identifying a shape over on the southern edge of the meadow; it moved away from the trees, and blended with that darkness—and became distinct again. There was a pressure yonder, pushing the

88

sheep steadily. He lifted his gun. He called: "Sing out, you over there," and stretched the barrel on that shifting figure. There was no answer. But Ferd Bowie's voice rose unexpectedly on his right, where Torveen was.

"That you, Surratt?"

"Shut up, kid." Surratt let a long moment run by; and fired.

The shadow wheeled away; it faded and he saw no more of it. But the long echoes of his gun struck all the surrounding trees and woke a disaster latent and crouched on that southern side. A voice, as calm and as sure as fate, said: "Push 'em over," and riders slashed from the brush in one broadside rank and rushed deliberately against the sheep. Dropped to a knee and coolly sighting his target in this confusion, he saw the wool-white tide break toward him, body jammed to body, a senseless bleating lifting up. He fired then and discovered no break in that wall of advancing riders. Torveen and Perrigo and Bowie and Ed let go a solid blast. It rocked that line of riders; it broke that rank's solidarity. Horsemen streamed tangentially against Torveen's position and the night pulsed with the abrupt, opening explosions of a general answer. One shot withered past Surratt. But then another bullet sliced the ground in front of him and its sound was on his right hand where he had no reason to expect hostility to be. He swung that way, trying to penetrate the black. Dropping alertly back on his haunches he saw the pale bloom of muzzle-light flash up in the trees, not far from where Torveen should be standing.

A sheep struck him and rolled him over on his elbows. He swung himself to his feet, at once involved in this pale stream rushing at him. He made three long jumps, was caught in the tide and carried with it; and dug in his feet and lunged again. There was a sapling pine at hand. He got behind this and put his arms around it and braced himself there. Looking behind him, he saw the end of Sam Torveen's woollies; they were at the lip of the canyon and the leaders were falling over and the mass struggled forward, confused and blind and witless, pressure throwing them out into that space. He saw the white, solid glow they made at the edge of the canyon, like water at the edge of a falls. The sound of their bellowing and dumb whinnying was oppressive in his ears. The thing turned him mad. He braced himself by the tree and spotted roving shapes in the meadow. He fired and struck; a horse went over in a sailing circle. Torveen and Torveen's men were drilling away with their guns, and the attacking crew now was scattered and withdrawing. An even, controlled voice rallied that crew, in the trees.

"Back here—back here."

The voice bothered him, until his memory supplied a name. It was Bill Head over there, faithful to his own stubborn intentions. A few stray sheep ran the meadows in circles, and dropped and struggled as they were shot down by the Crow Track men. A bullet struck the tree behind which Surratt stood, shivering it. Powder smell began to roll with the wind; Torveen's furious calling sought out Bill Head and damned him and blasted him. But the sheep in the meadow were nearly all dead and the rest were at the bottom of the canyon, sending back no complaint. Head's men remained screened by the far trees, taking desultory shots in the darkness. They were moving around the brush and Surratt thought they were swinging aside to have a try at Torveen's position. Then Bill Head's voice came casually into the clearing. "There's your sheep, Sam. It should be a hint to you. If it isn't, I'll make it a little stronger in the near future."

A round blast rushed from Torveen's position by way of reply. A Crow Track rider at once swore in a stricken way and somebody began violently to argue with Bill Head. The crew, Surratt guessed, wanted to come on and finish the job. It was Head's indomitable will that held them from that, for Crow Track's firing suddenly ceased and the party retreated through the timber. Listening closely, Surratt heard the bunch reach some near-by trail and go along it without haste. In a little while silence came fully to the meadow.

Torveen called out anxiously: "Surratt?"

Surratt left his tree, mind narrowing around the meaning of those two shots thrown at him from the right flank, where no Head rider had been. He walked across the meadow slowly and reached his partners and identified the three dissimilar shapes of Torveen and Ed and Perrigo vaguely grouped there. He couldn't see Ferd Bowie at all. A long, prowling anger was in him then, but he held his voice to softness as he called. "Kid."

Ferd Bowie answered, ten yards away. Bowie's feet were moving along the brush, unevenly. "Yeah?" he said, and continued to shift position.

"What was your idea of callin' to me just before the ball started?"

Torveen murmured: "What's this?" Surratt saw him turn and step nearer; Perrigo and Ed were swinging up, the sound of his voice seemed to attract them. Ferd Bowie's feet were still fiddling; his body remained out of sight. His answer was flat, it was sullen.

"I didn't want to go throwin' any lead till I knew where you was, Surratt."

"So," murmured Surratt. The others were listening carefully. They were waiting for him to speak again. But he didn't speak and the silence began to carry a strain. Perrigo softly retreated.

Torveen rolled a cigarette in this stillness and struck a match, which was pure carelessness; for the light made a plain target out of him. Surratt saw the man's face to be loose and discouraged then. In the following darkness Torveen spoke as though all his energy were gone. "Well, we lost the sheep."

Surratt's tone ran out easy and gentle. "I told you this was a wolf's game, Sam."

"What's left now?" said Torveen.

"Turn wolf."

Chapter Ten

ODD ENDS

"What?" said Torveen.

In this darkness was a puzzle. Surratt's voice was changing; it was amused now, seeming to catch the tune of a laughter he felt. The group came nearer him, closely listening. "I told you," he murmured, "that this was a game no man learned except in sorrow and when he learned it he wasn't the same man any more. I'm telling you, because I know. Which road would Bill Head be taking home?"

Torveen said: "He went down the hill, so he'll cross the ridge and go around by Cameron's bridge."

"There's a closer way," Surratt remarked. He was smiling, though they could not see that. "We'll ride a little."

Torveen broke in doubtfully: "Wait. . . ."

"No," said Surratt, "you've got nothing to lose. This is my fun."

He went into the trees for his horse and came to the meadow and crossed it, waiting at the edge of the canyon for them to follow. He said: "Perrigo, you and the kid ride in front of me." They hung back a moment and he heard Perrigo's wind whistling in his throat. His voice sharpened. "Go ahead." It pushed them forward, into the slanting trail. They went down that uneasy ledge single file, into the rustling blackness of the canyon. A single sheep, somehow surviving the slaughter, stood halfway down the trail. They drove it ahead and came to the margin of the sibilant river. There was an eddy just above the ford and as they took to the water, following the shallow gravel bar across, the bodies of dead sheep drifted from the eddy and bumped them and turned the horses nervous. They gained the far shore.

Perrigo was leading. But he stopped, not knowing what to do.

"Take us the quick way to Head's ranch," ordered Surratt.

"There's Carson Ford," pointed out Perrigo. "It's Blackjack Smith's town. We got no business passin' through it."

"Play a poor stack as strong as a big stack, Nick. Go ahead."

They went along the road, swinging toward the settlement at a steady canter. There was a light shining across the street like a yellow fence; and a man came out of the saloon, warned by their approach, and turned his face toward them. But they went through Carson Ford without stopping, and on along the bend of the gorge. A little later Perrigo spoke back to them: "We turn." His shadow shot across this road, into another one slanting up the side of the gorge's right-hand shoulder. The pace dropped to a walk. Five hundred feet above the road, Surratt saw the river vaguely shining below and the wink of the saloon lamps; afterwards they passed into the trees.

Surratt said: "How far?"

"A mile."

"Push faster."

The wind scoured down this stiff-pitched slope and the touch of the night was cold. After a while the slope leveled and they were running freely through a black arch, along a corduroy trail. They swung out of this presently and came upon another road climbing from the lowlands. Directly above them the lights of the Head ranch made bright beacons against an obscure sky.

"Watch out," said Torveen. "We're going to run into something here."

Surratt pushed ahead of Perrigo and, thus leading them, came into the Crow Track yard. The doorway of the ranch was open, a yellow beam flushing out of it; and Surratt saw a man sitting there on the porch. It was, he realized, the cripple he had seen in Morgantown—Old Martin Head. But at the moment he was keening the yard for deceit, his senses reaching swiftly out. On the right stood a bunkhouse, vaguely showing its lampshine through the windows. One solitary man walked forward from that direction.

"Keep him under your wing, Ed," murmured Surratt.

Martin Head's body swung forward in the chair. His challenge rapped them taciturnly. "Who's there?"

93

Ed had gone over to the advancing puncher. Ed's voice was a murmur, soft and easy. Surratt's straying impressions came back to him, with no discovered trouble. The place was unguarded. "Go to the bunkhouse and drag out everything you can move. Put it all in a pile. You'll probably find a kerosene can there. Dump it on the pile."

Martin Head called: "Who's there?" He did not need to speak again, for they crossed over the beam of light from the house, plainly in his view. Surratt dropped from his horse and walked up the steps.

"Your son," he said, "just paid us a visit and we're poorer for it by a band of sheep gone over the cliff. Your ways are severe."

"You've got the nerve of a better man," growled Old Martin. His hands lay above the blanket covering his legs. The big, square torso lifted and thickened. Even in a chair he was impressive, with a quality of savage authority flowing from him; it was easy to understand why other men feared him. One voice rose from the bunkhouse area in bitter protest. The sound of things being smashed came distinctly to the porch. Old Martin said:

"I'd judge you better, Surratt, if it wasn't for the dog you keep in your company."

Surratt had not known until then that Perrigo stood behind him. The little man had crept that quietly up the steps. Turning, Surratt saw a queer and mortal hatred pouring from Perrigo's eyes across the interval to Old Martin. It was a strange thing to see—the heights to which a man's passion could go. The temper of this little man threw its toxin through him; it shook his throat when he spoke.

"I don't forget you kicked me off this ranch once."

"Perrigo," stated Old Martin brutally, "I have ordered you to be shot. Sooner or later my son will do that."

The quick swing of Perrigo's shoulders was something Surratt expected and waited for. He threw his body against Perrigo and reached out and caught Perrigo's lifting hand. He drove his knee into the man's stomach, and got the risen gun with a wrench of his arm. Perrigo fell off the porch; he landed on his knees and crouched that way, sucking back the breath Surratt had knocked out of him.

"No," Surratt said evenly.

Ed came around the corner. "You want that pile lighted now?"

"Go in this house and find Bill Head's room and drag out his personal belongings."

He was watching Old Martin Head, and there was an admiration in him for the bulldog qualities he saw on that rocky face. Old Martin's stare had a force that was like a physical blow.

"I thought you had nerve. What's a bonfire of personal belongings? If I was in your shoes it would be man for man."

But Surratt was smiling and he was reckless and laughter came out of him softly. "This is your ranch, I take it. Well, it is your son and the men he led that I'm payin' my compliments to. Not you. There's no point in this little visit—except a warning to them."

Old Martin lifted his hand and pointed a heavy finger at Surratt. "This was not your quarrel in the beginning. Why is it now?"

Surratt looked at him, slow and soft with his answer. "Torveen did me a favor."

"So," grunted Old Martin. The sharpness of his glance was an interesting thing. "I saw you smile in Morgantown. I see you smile now. Is there that much fun left in life? It is no idle question. I have long wondered."

Ed came from the house carrying a load of Bill Head's clothes. They had lighted the bonfire, its glow brightly rising through the dark. "The fun," said Surratt, no longer smiling, "lasts a little while. It is something to look back on when a man rides down the trail alone."

"You have a reason for coming here," growled Old Martin. "I still do not understand what it is."

Torveen came away from the fire with the others. He said: "They're comin' up the trail, Buck." He wheeled to the foot of the porch and put his eyes on Old Martin. "You tell Bill——"

"You tell Bill," broke in Surratt evenly, "that no trail in the world runs straight. Sooner or later it comes to another trail, where other men ride. I have found it so. He will find it so."

The plunder from the bunkhouse made a high broad blaze in the night as Surratt ran to his horse. There was even then a murmuring down the road and all the men here were anxious to go. Torveen led them past the fire, into the darkness of the hills again. Surratt crowded up against Perrigo, returning the man's gun without comment.

He was laughing softly to himself as they ran down the

stiff slope. Carson Ford was directly below, but they came out of the timber well away from the settlement, reached the gorge road and cantered north with it as far as the Cameron bridge. They crossed here, racing up another ridge. An hour afterwards they were home.

Torveen said: "Nick, you'll take the first watch."

Surratt sat at the foot of the porch, under the late afternoon's hard sunlight, with his pipe bitten between his teeth, with the smoke rolling up from its bowl. Idle thus, his mind kept returning to Ferd Bowie, and his glance lifted to the far skyline and remained enigmatically there. The kid was twenty, but all the evil ways of the world were known to him. There was an excuse for this—for a wild life that knew no gentleness—but nothing could excuse treachery. It was Surratt's slow decision. He had a job to do here and hated it.

Torveen came from the office and squatted in the yard. He said: "I still don't get the reason why you went to Head's last night."

"Bother you?"

"You're not a man to make idle moves," pointed out Torveen. "You had some reason in your coco for doin' that. It's the reason I can't get."

He held his peace. A horse in the corral began to lash out at another horse and for a little while the whole bunch in there whirled around the compound, beating up heavy dust.

"An experiment," mused Surratt.

"Did it work?"

"We'll know more about that later."

Torveen grinned. "You're a hell of a mysterious guy."

"A good many things puzzle me, Sam," observed Surratt. "And it's men that make the puzzles. I like to find out why."

Torveen's grin disappeared, leaving him uncertain and irritated. "Well, Bill Head knocked the props from under us and it looks like our move next, but I don't know what it is."

"Wait."

"Wait for what? They done what they wanted to do, didn't they? They got rid of the sheep—and I'm busted. That's the end of the story."

"You sure?" asked Surratt. But he shook his head and

explained himself. "We can do one of two things. We can strike back or we can wait out Bill Head's next play."

"How'd we strike back?" demanded Torveen.

Surratt smiled in a tight, narrow way. "Turn Indian. In three days, if we were industrious about it, we could tie up the roads in these hills so tight nobody'd care to use 'em. Drop a shot in front of a man ridin' along the trail and you make that man pretty nervous."

"So, why not?" suggested Torveen, who always liked quick results.

"Better to wait," opined Surratt shrewdly. "Have no fear. Head will not let it stand like this. He's played his hand well. But it is my observation that when a man wins one jack pot he never has sense enough to quit tryin' for another."

"You don't know Bill Head."

"Maybe—maybe not. But if he's as cool a fellow as you suggest he'll lose no time catchin' on to the meanin' of his junk burned in his own yard. I meant that as a little reminder of what four stray men can do. It was a way of tellin' him that he didn't win any battle by driving a band of sheep over the cliff. As long as we stay in the hills neither he nor any man in his crew is safe. It's an experiment, like I said. The experiment is to see how long it takes him to find that out for himself."

"Then," said Torveen vigorously, "we've got no business hangin' around here where he can hit us."

Surratt smiled a little. "When you set a trap, Sam, you got to have bait. We're the bait."

Wang walked from the ranch kitchen, slamming the door behind him. Surratt didn't pay much attention to this tall Manchurian until he saw Torveen square around. Wang had a bundle wrapped by burlap under his arm; he wore his good clothes. He stopped by Torveen.

"I go and not come back. You pay me now."

Torveen got up. "Leavin'?" He looked at Wang carefully. "You're too young a man to be goin' back to China yet, Wang."

"You pay me," said Wang distinctly.

Torveen said: "You been here twenty years, and now you pull out on five minutes' notice. Why?"

Wang divided a black, fathomless glance between the two men. Afterwards he looked to the ground. He gripped the bundle more securely under his arm. His free hand rose and his finger began to mark off each word he spoke, lifting and dropping. "Head boy die. Osbrook die. By'm by more boys die. Too bad. You pay me."

Torveen stared at Surratt. "He seems to have it figured for himself." He went over the yard to the office. Wang turned his glance on Surratt.

"You," he intoned, "you watch."

Torveen came back with a small stack of silver dollars. He put them into Wang's reaching hand. He said, "All right, Wang," briefly and crouched in the dust again. Wang watched him a moment, purely expressionless. Then he said, "G'bye," and walked across the yard, toward the Morgantown road.

"First China boy I ever knew that wasn't loyal to his outfit," muttered Torveen.

"He's playin' his hunch," said Surratt. "No Chinaman likes to fight a white man."

"How does he know there's goin' to be a scrap?"

"Any Chinamen in Morgantown?"

"Sure. Lots of 'em. Every ranch around here's got one."

"That's how he knows," said Surratt. He had his eyes on Wang, watching that stolid shape trudge into the trees; and he saw a rider come forward from the trees at a gentle trot and immediately afterwards draw up to a discreet walk. Surratt stood up. His pipe stiffened between the set of his teeth. Torveen had his back to the newcomer, but the sound of the man's travel reacted instantly on his high-strung nerves and made him instantly rise as the newcomer crossed the bridge and entered the yard. He was, Surratt thought, a cheerful young man with a very matter-of-fact face. His eyes went around the yard observingly. After a moment's pause he said, "How, boy," and remained in the saddle, his manners keeping him there until an invitation came to get down. Surratt studied Torveen to discover what the situation meant. He saw Torveen relax a little and show friendliness. "Mornin', George. What you doin' over here?"

George gave Surratt a square, frank look. "You're this Buck Surratt?"

Torveen said: "This fellow's name is George Bernay, Buck."

"I keep a few cows over south of Morgantown," Bernay explained to Buck, as though he wanted himself fully explained. "That is, when I can find 'em. This fellow"—indicating Torveen—"and me used to do our scrappin' together at the Saturday dances."

"You can get down now," said Torveen amiably. "What's in your craw?"

Bernay got out his cigarette materials and built himself a smoke, squinting at his fingertips. "I'll stay in the saddle. Your yard's full of fleas anyhow."

"Hell with you, George."

"Sure. Understand you lost a couple sheep." He was, just then, licking his cigarette together, but his glance darted to Torveen to catch the redhead's reaction.

"Yeah."

"What next?"

"Look in your crystal globe," grumbled Torveen, "and see if you can tell us."

George Bernay lighted his cigarette and took a deep drag, and seemed satisfied with his handiwork. He punched back the brim of his hat; there was a white scar irregularly marked across the sun-bronze of his forehead. "Something always comes next. That's the kind of a country this is. Funny thing. Billy Temple and me and Jud Horsfall was a-talkin' about you last night. Poor topic of conversation, but we was. We sorta decided sheep wasn't much of a crime."

"Your moral support helps a lot," said Torveen ironically.

"It ill beseems a sport like you to be a-talkin' of morals," chided George Bernay. "Well, just thought I'd mention it."

"So, what was it you come here to borrow?" demanded Torveen.

"Listen to him," remarked George Bernay. "Fact is I just wandered in to have a look at Surratt. Kind of captured my fancy, that Morgantown business. Any man," he concluded idly, "who can run his hand into a nest of bees and not get stung must have a pretty shookum brand of personal medicine." He threw his cigarette into the dust. He rubbed the scar with a slow finger. "See that, Surratt? I got it one time when I almost licked Bill Head. Some years ago when I thought I was fast enough to dodge anything. Well, that's the size of my politics. If you see me again at any time you'll anyhow know who I am. I'll report to the boys that you look like you could fight. So long." He turned and went off at a rocking canter and vanished behind the yonder trees.

"The scoundrel always did talk in parables," complained

Torveen. "It'll take me a couple hours to get at what he was tryin' to say."

Surratt was gently smiling. "He reminds me of a man I used to know—a fellow you'd regret to leave."

"It's odd," observed Torveen, "that something always seems to remind you of something you knew before."

Surratt gave Torveen a quiet, shadowed glance. "The morning half of a trail is always fresh and full of new things, kid. But the afternoon half is a tedious journey, for there's nothing on it you haven't seen before. It's a fact I'm telling you. I hope you never have to find it out for yourself. Where's the boys?"

"Went below Morgantown to have a look."

"Let's have a little scout toward the high meadow."

"Company again," said Torveen and stopped his walking. A rider came from the northern trees, out of the ridge that held this meadow away from Cameron Valley. He kept a steady gait all across the meadow, but his arm lifted as he approached. Torveen's manner turned at once unfavorable. "I don't get this," he muttered.

The rider came up, a dark-jawed man with the accent of nervousness about him. He stared briefly at Torveen and then threw his attention toward Surratt. He reached into his shirt pocket, producing a folded note. He bent down and gave it to Surratt.

Surratt opened the note, his head bowed seriously over it a moment. Afterwards he stared up at the rider. "Yes," he said without expression and closed his fingers around the paper.

Chapter Eleven

<hr>

ACTION

Showing an open relief, the rider pulled his horse about and went away from the place rapidly. Surratt was frowning at that disappearing shape, but he could see the sudden red and violent flush creep across Torveen's roan cheeks. He said to Torveen: "Who's that rider?"

"A Cameron hand." Torveen wheeled definitely toward Surratt. "Didn't you know it?" he said, challenge riding his tone.

"I wanted to make sure," answered Surratt. He folded the note along its original creases, and refolded it, his eyes half shut. Torveen's silence grew enormous, with an unspoken demand for an explanation in it. The late, low sun threw its bombing brilliance higher against the trees and shadows were beginning to spread in blue, irregular pools at the lower edge of the meadow. Surratt put the note in his pocket. "I'm going on a little ride, Sam."

"Be back soon?" The indifference of Torveen's question was strained and false; he stared down at the ground, his mouth pressed together.

"I'll be late," Surratt said and went to his horse. He rode away to the north, without looking back.

Torveen didn't immediately stir from his position in the yard. He rolled himself a smoke and as long as Surratt remained in sight his glance covertly followed. He dragged heavy gusts of smoke into his lungs and expelled them vehemently. The flushed anger remained on his face; he was like a boy then, sulky and hurt and suspicious.

"So I guess," he grumbled, "I'm supposed to hang around till somebody gives me different orders."

He dropped the cigarette and stamped it with his boot. He wheeled over to his horse. In the saddle, he remained quiet a moment and seemed to argue with his own impulses. But there was a rankling emotion in him he could

101

not help and could not kill. For a little while he debated following Surratt's exact trail. Then he rejected the idea, galloped over the meadow to the northern ridge and entered the trees. There was a good spot on top of this ridge, he knew, where he might stand and watch the Cameron Valley. If Surratt was traveling that way he'd sooner or later know about it.

He was a little ashamed of himself. Yet Sam Torveen, so rash and ready with his impulses, was possessed by a jealousy stronger than his shame. There had been in him since boyhood a single-minded devotion to Judith Cameron; and there was in him as well these last few days a devout admiration for Buck Surratt. He owned a loyalty to both these people that had mixed in it a possessiveness and a queer feeling of inferiority. He could not explain these things to himself, yet it was true enough that in Buck Surratt's slow talk and rare smile was a quality that made him feel humble and somehow inexperienced; and always he had seen in Judith a womanliness that everlastingly made him doubt his ability to win her.

He was a very human man. And when he had seen Surratt and Judith standing so serene and so fully wise, side by side—these two whom he regarded as better people than he could ever be—he had a deep and foreboding fear that he would lose them both. Strangle the breath of that jealous thing as he might, it came to life again and blew against his nerves. His own loyalty was an absolute emotion; and he could not bear to think of their loyalty to him being any less absolute. These two owned a strength he had to share. To be left out of their thoughts was like sunlight going from the sky.

Vague to his understanding, these queer and human reactions pushed Sam Torveen up the side of the ridge, past the woodcutter's camp, across the corduroy road and to the summit. Jogging more leisurely toward a cleared spot on the ridge, from which he might command a view of the Cameron buildings, a far sound of ponies pounding through yonder brush arrested him. His nerves had been cocked for trouble these many days; and now he slipped off the trail and swung about and stared into the thickening twilight.

They burst around the bend, these riders; three of them in single file, with the leading man strained forward in his saddle and the one at the rear lagging a little and keeping his glance behind. It was that rear man, Perrigo, Torveen identified first. He pushed his horse out of the brush then and into the path.

Ferd Bowie led the file. The sudden shadow of Torveen across the trail wrenched Bowie back in the saddle and his arm dropped and for a swirling moment some blind impulse trembled in him. Torveen called again, more sharply. Ferd Bowie swore: "By God, Torveen!" He hauled his horse to a plunging halt. Ed and Perrigo overshot the trail and came abreast; all three of them stared at Torveen. They were deeply breathing, they were charged with an electric excitement.

Perrigo said: "We got to get out of here."

"What?"

"It's Peyrolles and his bunch comin' behind," growled Bowie.

"Where you been?" demanded Torveen. "What you doin' over here anyhow?"

The answer lagged. Perrigo kept stirring in his saddle. He said at last: "That's all right, Sam."

"Come on—come on," muttered Bowie. He moved his hand at Torveen, he shoved his horse at Torveen. "This is no place to stay."

Peyrolles was down the trail, riding fast with his outfit. The sound of that pursuit was filling the stillness of this hill.

"How many?" Torveen snapped.

"Eight-nine, I guess."

Torveen said: "Get into the brush. We don't run. Why should we run? Whose trail is this? To hell with Hank Peyrolles! Get in the brush!"

"Here, here," grunted Perrigo. "You ain't . . ."

But Torveen stared at the little man savagely. "Run, if you're afraid, Nick." Stung raw by his thinking, he went rash and wild. There was no consideration in him. The injustice of the recent hours was all that his head could hold; it could hold no thought of safety now. Five minutes of reflection would have changed his mind, but the moments rushed him to his decision and so he acted on his strongest impulses. Ferd Bowie put his horse into the brush, Ed soon following. Perrigo circled and got into the timber. They were all out of sight save Torveen, who faced the up-drumming echoes of the coming Peyrolles.

Perrigo said insistently: "Get in here, Sam!"

"I don't shoot my turkey without fair warnin'," retorted Torveen bitterly. He stood up in the saddle, he sat down.

He drew his gun and rested it across the horn. Stiff and still in the shadows, he watched the column of Peyrolles' men turn and bend and rush forward.

"You're on my range!" yelled Torveen. "Turn around and get the hell out of here!"

The sound of his warning flattened against that group; it broke Peyrolles' outfit into fragments. Horses wheeled and bucked against the dimming light; and riders boiled into the shelter of the trees. Peyrolles was a defiant shape still on the trail. He yelled: "You fresh young punk!" And then took a snap shot at Torveen and threw his horse aside.

Unmoved by the shot and too stubborn to give ground, Torveen began a steady firing.

Peyrolles' horse dropped without a sound and Peyrolles yelled again. A rider behind Peyrolles slowly reeled out of the saddle; then the trail was empty and the firing began to slash and strike and cry through the thicket. There was no clear object on which Torveen could pin a bullet then. He pulled against his reins, reluctantly backing into shelter. He poised his gun, waiting for a quick aim. Of a sudden a bullet whipping through these woods slugged his shoulder with a definite blow. His horse kept backing away; Torveen tried to lift his gun and could not. He tried to seize the horn to keep from tipping, but his arm refused to obey. He fell slowly out of the saddle and lay in the dust, none of his muscles helping him. Somebody rushed at him through the brush. He heard Nick Perrigo's voice taut and singing, calling his name; the smashing echoes of this wicked fusillade grew deeper. Blackness rushed across the world. He said in a windless whisper, "Perrigo," and knew nothing more.

Leaving the ranch, Surratt went up to the near-by sheep meadow and crossed it and entered that trail along which the sheep had been driven the night before. He had read the note hurriedly. Now, to make sure of what he had read, he pulled it from his pocket and smoothed it. The writing was a woman's writing, the paper was the sort a woman would use—and a Cameron man had delivered it. So it seemed genuine. It read:

Unless something very urgent keeps you away, please be at Carson Ford this evening at 7 o'clock. I've learned something you should know. Remember what I told you the last time I saw you. Judith.

He lighted a match and touched the edge of the paper. He stopped long enough to watch it char and drop to the ground; and he got down and stamped it beneath his boot. The sun was gone. The world swiftly turned blue and pale violet and a wind began drifting down the slope. There was someone riding behind him rapidly. He got into the saddle and pulled about—and discovered Annette Carvel coming behind him.

She smiled at him frankly. "You going my way or am I going yours?"

He lifted his hat to her, whereupon her eyes began to light up. He said: "Which way is that, Annette?"

"Oh, any way. It doesn't much matter. I like the way you speak my name."

She fell beside him as a matter of course. Her eyes strayed to his face and studied it, the smile still softening her lips; and then she settled back in her saddle and rode silently with him.

She had a free, careless way that rose either from boldness or from childlike faith. Curious always as to the motives of people, he quietly considered this girl and remained puzzled. One thing was strong in her, stronger than any other quality: a love of life that made her eager and pleasing. The lifting of a man's hat could make her gay, the quiet calling of her name could make her eyes glow. In her vivid personality goodness and badness seemed close together, so close that no man knew where one left off and the other began, or if either mattered much. There were hungers, he told himself, that sometimes made nice distinctions in morals unimportant.

A mile onward she spoke to him very quietly: "Do I bother you?"

It startled him. He said promptly: "No."

"That helps," she said candidly. "I don't want to be a nuisance. But it was a nice feeling to talk to you the other day. So I thought I'd like to do it again." Her eyes sought his face for expression. "Don't you ever get lonely?"

"For what, Annette?"

Her shoulders stirred. She spread her arms toward the closing twilight, as if to grasp something that could not be seen, could not be captured. "Oh, there is so much in this world. It must be so, or else why should people feel the loss of things they never have had? That's—that's what I mean. Things just beyond you that you'd go to find, if you knew where to find them."

"Yes," he said.

She clapped her hands together, enormously pleased. "I knew you'd be a help. Buck, where are they to be found?"

He hated to answer. But honesty compelled him. "You are going to be older—and much sadder—before you get the truth of that."

She had a way of pondering his words. She rode now in thoughtful quietness, a faint scowl penciled across her forehead. He could see that vaguely in the thickening shadows. They came out of the trail into the upper meadow, where the sheep had been destroyed. She followed him to the edge of the canyon. There was a remote break in the hill solitude, a ruffling of faint sound waves somewhere to the west. He listened carefully to them. The lights of Carson Ford glittered far below. He got off his horse and sat down at the edge of the descending trail.

"You're going there?" she asked him. "It's a bad place for you to be."

"When it gets darker."

She dismounted and came over to sit beside him, near enough for him to feel the occasional stirring of her shoulder. He thought then that she had a high sensitiveness to the world; that it kept troubling and lifting and turning her. Gray and steel-black shadows were filling the canyon in a way that made it seem without bottom. The murmuring of the river grew fainter below. Her shoulder rested frankly against him. She was speaking with an intensity that was strange.

"That's what I'm afraid of, Buck. That gloomy blackness down there. It's so cruel. Like the end of the world. I hate the thought of getting old. I lie awake at nights thinking about it—that I shall get old and never be pretty again. And I pray that before I get ugly I shall have found something. I don't know what. But when people are young it is not just for sleeping and eating. If there's a feeling like craziness in me I know it was put there for a reason. Maybe for love, maybe for heartbreak. But I know it wasn't meant to be bottled up. It would be cruel of God to put so much feeling in anybody just to be wasted. I pray that I may have whatever is meant for me before I grow old, so that I can laugh and cry—and then be content. If it isn't to be that way, I'd rather die now."

The fire and color of her words struck into his imagination. She was a vessel full to spilling; her voice sang with the richness of her desire. He sat bowed and taciturn and moved to a pity that was infinitely tender. He could not tell her he had seen the shapes of such dreams over his own campfire—and had watched them fade; and that, save for the blind operation of chance in a blind world, they would fade for her. Surratt heard her voice lift to him, soft and whispered and urgent.

"Please."

He swung toward her, puzzled again. Her face was round and graphic in the smooth darkness. Her shoulders were turned to him and she was waiting wordlessly.

He said: "It wouldn't mean anything."

That murmured, begging word came again to him. "Please!"

"Don't make a mistake about this, Annette," he told her. He reached out and brought her forward with his long arms. Her face was there for him; and then the wild, primitive fire of this girl came through her lips and shook him more than he believed he could be shaken. There was shock in that troubled and passionate and desiring kiss. It woke something near to savagery in him. He pulled her solidly against him and felt the deep willingness of her response. He drew away and got to his feet, thoroughly disturbed.

He said gruffly: "I'm sorry."

She was up beside him; her cheeks were pale in the faint moonlight, her breathing very rapid. But he saw how she smiled, so wisely, so sadly—yet so shiningly tender. "Sorry! Oh, I'm not! It was like a world opening up for me! Don't be sorry!"

"A man's kiss?" he said, more and more disturbed.

She murmured: "No—not just any man's kiss, Buck." She came to him again and lifted on her toes, and her lips brushed his cheek briefly and coolly. She was laughing in the darkness; she was happy. "That's my thanks to you."

He said: "It would be safer for you, Annette, if you knew more about men."

She walked away from him to her horse. "I know more about men than you dream. But you are not like other men—and that's why you've made me happy. This is one of the things I can remember a long time from now, like I told you. You shouldn't be sorry—and good night, my dear."

She was away in the darkness before he could answer. He got aboard his horse and took to the narrow ledge leading into the bottom of the canyon. He was remembering all this with a growing wonder; it rode with him across the gravelly ford. But, going down the dark river road toward the settlement, the tricky qualities of this night aroused his attention and pushed the recent scene to the back of his mind.

A hundred yards this side of the saloon he stopped to examine the settlement carefully. Two horses stood in front of the saloon and a broad beam of light ran across the road. One man loitered on Blackjack's porch. Elsewhere he could see no life. Not particularly satisfied, he advanced on the saloon, left his horse and went inside.

Blackjack Smith was behind the bar, idly polishing a glass. He looked at Surratt. His head turned and ducked toward the back room. "Go in there."

"Blackjack——"

The gross-bodied man shook his ponderous chin. "It's all right, Buck. I'm tellin' you."

Surratt walked to the rear room's door and opened it and stepped inside. He closed the door quickly. Judith Cameron was poised in a far corner, against a wall; and he saw the worry in her eyes.

There was one moment then in which he was ashamed of himself for his part in the scene at the top of the canyon—in which he felt dismally angry for remembering the shape and force of Annette Carvel's lips. For there was a fidelity in Buck Surratt that governed him and kept him on a straight track; seeing Judith across the room, fair and proud, he knew then where his faith belonged and had belonged since the first meeting. He couldn't help it. There was grace in her shoulders, a straight and shining beauty in her eyes. It was the irony and strangeness of this world that his idle drifting had brought him to these hills to find her—and to know even then he had found her too late.

He said: "When I got your note I started riding."

Her voice lifted curiously. "Note?"

"Your note."

She said: "No, Buck. I wrote none. But—is this yours?"

He went across the room at a swift pace, suddenly aware of trouble. He looked down at the paper she held. A few words said: "Can you be at Carson Ford about 7 tonight." It was signed with his name.

"This," he said, "is a trick. I——"

The door opened then and Bill Head walked in, his big shoulders rolling. Blackjack followed through and closed the door and moved over to a side of the room, his obscure eyes turned beady with a growing interest. Bill Head's ruddy cheeks swung to the girl, to Surratt. He said in a way that was too calm to be real:

"I made a good guess. I guessed that you two people were thick enough to answer any call the other might make. You remind me of Annette Carvel, Judith."

She was speaking. But Surratt's attention was engrossed by essential things; he was looking at Blackjack Smith now with a smoldering, aroused interest. He stepped back against the wall. His hand fell slightly against the cold butt of his gun.

Blackjack said: "Don't do it, Buck."

"That's the way you feel?" challenged Surratt.

Blackjack only shook his head; his pear-shaped cheeks were solemn and wholly enigmatic.

Bill Head slowly said: "I told you, Judith, I meant to get that glove from Surratt. You seemed to doubt I would. This is my way of showin' you. You got the glove, Surratt?"

Surratt was idly murmuring: "You're a smarter man than I thought. It is a mistake I made—to underestimate you."

"The glove," said Bill Head.

"No," replied Surratt, "I guess not."

This was all unforgettably clear. Judith stood beside him, pale and still against the wall, her hands risen to her breasts, her breathing soft and fast. Bill Head remained doggedly in the center of the room, huge under the light, his purpose too plain and too violent for anybody to mistake. Over in the corner Blackjack Smith had established himself like an umpire, no feeling and no partiality escaping him. Out in the saloon was the scraping of feet—Blackjack's companions listening.

Considering all this, Surratt knew how inevitably he was trapped. This was a pattern again and he felt himself answering it in his old way. There were times when a man had to remember the sweetness of life and use caution and quiet speech. There were times when it was best to forget all that. He felt cool reason creep away from him. He held his place, a bitter dissent thumping along his arteries. He was then as he always had been in time of trouble—and always would be—with a flame and a savage pleasure having its way thoroughly with him. He was smiling, though he did not know it. But Blackjack Smith, who knew the man well, waited for the smile, and when he saw it he settled back on his heels.

"Don't try it, Buck," he grunted. "There's other boys outside the door, if you got that far."

"The glove," repeated Bill Head stubbornly.

Blackjack said: "Miss Cameron, you step outside a moment."

Judith's face swung around to Surratt, very pale. Yet it was calm and it was held by faith. Surratt nodded, his admiration for her deeper and deeper. He watched her walk across the room, unhurried and slowly graceful, and leave it.

Bill Head spoke. "Put your gun on him, Blackjack. I'll get the glove."

"Wait," ordered Blackjack. "Both you boys unbuckle your belts and drop 'em right where you stand."

Bill Head stared at the big outlaw, taciturnly surprised. "When did you get that idea? I've already told you what to do."

"You'll do it my way," responded Blackjack evenly. "Drop the belts."

Surratt's smile was long and thin and bitter-bright. He obeyed the order; the belt, with the gun in it, dropped. He kicked it aside. Bill Head still stared at Blackjack, a violent and mistrusting consideration in his hazel eyes. "If I thought you were fooling me, Blackjack . . ." But his massive shoulder rolled back, and he unbuckled his belt and laid it on the center table. "Maybe," he said narrowly, "this is a better way. You been making some comments about my character. It will give me some satisfaction to change your mind, Surratt."

The man had the strength of a rock-crusher. There was that immense impression of power in Head's ropy shoulder muscles, in the girth of his neck, in those thick wrists and fists which gave to his arms the appearance of heavy-knobbed clubs. He had a solidity and a massiveness, a body too vast to feel the hurt of blows; his temper burned sullen and steady.

Surratt murmured: "It is my hope you enjoyed the bonfire."

That malice-pointed phrase visibly jabbed the man. He lowered his shoulders and his knees bent from the pressure put on them and he threw himself across the room. One remote cell in Surratt's mind told him then he had made another mistake. Head wasn't slow, he wasn't clumsy. Surratt started out from the wall, but never got away from it. Bill Head slammed terrifically into him and threw him back against it. Surratt's skull struck the boards, his brain roared. Head's fists were like axes chopping into his temples. They drove daylight and memory out of him. Strength left his legs entirely, and thus blinded and stunned and momentarily helpless he reached for Bill Head's waist and caught at it to weather through the storm.

Head rapidly retreated, avoiding that grip. "Oh, no," he grunted, and seemed to bear a respect for Surratt's tricks. He poised this way, breathing fast. It was a moment's respite; the mist cleared away from the room and Surratt saw the man teetering for another rush. He dropped to his knees as Head flung himself on. He caught Head like that, rolling his body into Head's legs and completely upsetting the big one. Head went crashing into the wall. The whole building shook.

Surratt rose and found himself steady again. He wheeled and waited. Blackjack Smith came forward swiftly and lifted the lamp from the table and carried it back to this corner. Once more posted there, he held it high over his head to illumine this scene.

Bill Head threw himself up from the floor, shaking his yellow poll. He was turning slowly, he was for one slim interval not quite on his guard. Waiting for that chance, Surratt plunged in. He beat aside a huge arm and smashed the man full in the mouth. His knuckles ripped across the other's lips as though they were scraping back wet paper; and the bones of his hand seemed to snap Head's teeth. He had his moment here and made use of it, driving solid, savage blows at Head's chin, at his temple, at his eyes, at his chin again—the dull and fleshy sound flatly horrid in the room. Blood came rolling through Head's lips; his eyes were aflood with a tawny rage. He cried out and steadied himself against the wall and threw himself at Surratt again. Surratt deflected one blow; but the next one, slashing through his defensive elbow, hurled him back against the table. He carried the table with him and went over with it, and under it.

Pulling around, he saw Head's feet walking forward. He threw the table aside. A foot lashed out at him. He seized it, and rolled, and brought Head down, that fall jarring all the building. Head crawled at him and drove his fist across Surratt's neck in the way he might have used a hammer. They were lunging and wrestling wickedly around this floor, striking and missing, and gutturally heaving up their hatred in bitter gusts, and striking again. Surratt tore free from the man and rolled and rose. He found Head slowly getting up. Crouched low then, he ran on and met Head in the center of the room. He felt Head's fist crack through his ribs and bury itself in his lungs, the pain of that a pure agony. But he had forced Head backward and the man's face tipped higher and Surratt ripped one stiff blow to the shelving point of the exposed chin. Strangeness came all across Bill Head's features, turning them wide and alarmed and astonished. The will that held him up so hugely snapped like a tight-draw wire. He went down on the floor and tried to crawl, his breath large and groaning and incomplete. He did not get up. Blood flowed along his cheeks freely; his body shook with some involuntary spasm. Then he was wholly still.

There was that troubled silence, with the panting of the two men springing through it. Surratt could find no room in his lungs for the air he needed. A thousand needles stung his fists, and all his face seemed broken and pulpy. Enormous weariness flowed its cold way through his muscles. He hadn't the spirit to move; and so he stood and stared down at Bill Head who was unconscious on the dirty boards.

The silence was a signal to those beyond the room. The door opened at a jerk and Judith Cameron came through. Turning toward her, Surratt saw the dread in her eyes for a moment before it changed to an inexpressible hurt. She cried: "My dear—my dear!" And ran over to him, and caught his arms and looked up at him. The reserve disappeared from her eyes, like the lifting of a curtain. It was for a moment only; when it came back he was stirred and shaken by what he had seen—and then ceased to be sure that he had seen it.

His lips were difficult to shape when he spoke. His words weren't clear. "I must look like the wrath of God. It's the way I feel."

Blackjack Smith moved from his corner and tried to lift the table. But its legs were broken and its top was splintered; and he stared down thoughtfully a moment, still holding the lamp in his hand. At the doorway Blackjack's men made a solid rank, all their cheeks dark with interest. Judith Cameron slipped an arm through Surratt's elbow and held her place beside him; her chin lifted and there was something flowing out of her that called his attention.

Color had returned to her cheeks. She was proud then—and quietly defying the threat in the room.

Surratt stared at Blackjack. "You were in on this. There's your boss on the floor. You were the man that wasn't going to lift a hand against me."

"And I didn't," said Blackjack. "Sure I was in on it. But I had a little idea of my own, like you heard Bill Head remark. You saw it didn't please him."

"What?"

Blackjack was shaking his vast, pear-shaped countenance in a bemused way. "I have known you a long while. Your way of fightin' is familiar to me. The tougher things are, the better you are. I have never known the man you couldn't whip. It was my desire for you to whip this one here. It is a thing he needed, it was a fight I wanted to see. Well, I'll remember it. You're a fellow that no man ever forgets."

"Blackjack," challenged Surratt, "where do you stand?"

"And now that's a funny thing," sighed Blackjack. "It has been the policy of my life to string along with the winnin' side. I never yet broke that rule. I have played with Head in this matter and made a comfortable thing of it. Nobody can say Blackjack's been a fool. Yet here I am, partin' company with the man and throwin' my meal ticket away. You're licked now and Sam Torveen's licked, but I said I never would lift my hand against you again and I never will. I guess I better start ridin' before Head sends his boys after me. I do not understand it."

"Blackjack," murmured the girl. "You are not so bad."

"And not so good either," reflected Blackjack skeptically. "So I guess that makes me out just another sucker, which I never thought I'd come to be." But he stopped talking and looked at the girl. He put his lamp on the floor, going to the door. He turned there, his black eyes sharpening. He said to Surratt: "Understand this, friend Buck. Bill Head will come after you with a gun." He said only that, and closed the door.

Surratt turned across the room and bent over to pick up his belt. The top of his skull pounded, and the drying sweat pulled at his skin and its saltiness stung the mashed edges of his lip. He had begun to stiffen up. Bill Head lay without motion, seemingly without breath, plunged deeply into a slugged slumber. Surratt considered him without anger; and turned toward Judith.

She had retreated to a wall. She stood against it, hands behind her. He saw a shadow of fear darkening the love-

113

liness and the candor of her eyes. It had not been there before. Her voice whispered at him.

"I have to tell you this, Buck. The glove belongs to me."

He looked down at his belt. He buckled it on, his fingers very awkward. Afterwards he reached for his pipe and packed and lighted it. The smoke made a bland, pure relief in his lungs. He clenched the pipe between his teeth and felt the steady, asking weight of her glance on him. He pulled the glove out of his pocket—a small doeskin riding glove—and crossed the room and handed it to her.

She waited for him to speak. But he didn't. Long afterwards she broke the silence gently. "No questions?"

He shook his head. "There would never be a time when I'd ask you a question about that glove. There won't ever be a time, Judith, when I could bring myself to doubt you."

"Buck!" she called, almost crying.

She had a strength and a pride and a dignity. She had a womanliness that touched his senses like tremendous music; it turned all his past barren, it made him a hungry man now. But he looked down. He said casually: "I'd better ride. Sam's not much comfort to himself these days."

"You like him greatly."

"Yes." He looked at her and could not help asking what had been in his mind since his first entry into the hills. "You do, don't you?"

"Of course." He listened to the tone of her talk; he watched her eyes. But her answer was incomplete, he did not understand it. Elusiveness controlled that even, soft voice. He shrugged his shoulders and opened the door, observing that Blackjack and Blackjack's men had gone out to the porch. He walked with her that far and saw her climb into the saddle. She lifted her hand at him and said, "Good night," and galloped down the road. He went on to the rack, mounting with all his muscles in protest. "So long, Blackjack," he said, and trotted away.

He crossed the ford, climbed the hill and struck down the dark trail. He had an hour's riding here, with time to revive the powerful sensations of all this night's action. But weariness grew greater in him and he was drained dry of feeling. So he rode through the sheep meadow almost stupidly and came into the Torveen yard. There were no lights burning.

He called out, "Hello," and got down. After that he

wheeled with a quicker step across the yard, the strong surrounding shadows closing his throat to further sound. He went into the office and struck a match. By the bright glow of it he saw the room overturned and in confusion. It was for him a clear and dangerous warning, compelling him to instantly kill the match. He stepped back to the porch, crossed it to the bunkroom. He closed the door here and tried another match, cupping it in his palm. He let it burn only long enough for one brief and sufficient survey. Here too was a stripped room.

Going back to the porch, he noticed then that the corral gate was open, the horses gone.

Chapter Twelve

THE SEARCH

Pokey came into the Head yard with a good deal of riding dust on him and went immediately to the house. This was morning, but Old Martin still lay in bed smoking a cigar. Pokey stood beside the bed, looking down at his boss with a plain concern. "You sick?"

"I get tired sittin' in that confounded chair," grumbled Old Martin. "You find out something about Surratt?"

"Yes," said Pokey. But he remained quiet a moment, the information he had gathered still a little strange to him. He didn't know that he could make it clear to Old Martin; it wasn't clear to himself. "I went over the desert to Thunder Butte. They knew him there, but it wasn't his town. So I crossed the hills to prairie country and stopped at a place called Crow. I sat me down in a poker game and kept my mouth shut. Well, that was his town all right."

"Crow," murmured Old Martin. "Ain't been there for fifteen years, which was when I ran down the Patton boys."

Pokey said: "Martin, he ain't no outlaw."

"I knew that before I sent you," retorted Old Martin. "I can still judge a man."

"This Surratt's dad ran a big horse ranch yonder. He was a tough one and he never stood back from anybody. The wild ones over that way were always aimin' for him. As I get it, this old man Surratt had his fun fightin' 'em, never asked no favors, and never asked no help. So, a couple years ago they finally drygulched him. It left this Buck Surratt under the gun. The way the story goes he went out and found the fellow that did the killin'—and left him right where he found him. But there was always one more fellow to take up the trouble and come after Surratt." Pokey's eyes narrowed at the wall, visualizing what had

116

happened. His voice was soft. "He had to meet and kill four men, Martin. Which settled that particular wild bunch for good. Like I said, I kept my mouth shut and played poker—but the man left his mark on that town, for they're still talkin' about those fights."

"But he didn't get any peace out of it," remarked Old Martin.

"How'd you know that?" inquired Pokey, puzzled.

"Go on," growled Old Martin.

"No, he didn't get any peace. Seems like his reputation for bein' fast on the draw spread with the wind. It was honey for the bees. Pretty soon a lot of tough ones came driftin' in to have a look at him. He had one more fight on the streets of Crow. Then he sold his horse ranch—and drifted out. That's how he got here." Pokey quit talking for a moment. He shook his head. Then he said: "He's not the kind to run, Martin. What'd he do that for?"

"You don't understand, Pokey?"

"No," said Pokey, "I don't."

Old Martin's eyes were black and bright behind the cigar smoke. "Never think the boy was runnin' from trouble. Never think it. He was runnin' from himself."

"What?"

Old Martin said quietly: "Surratt's smart. He saw the end of the trail. So he pulled out. Listen, Pokey. When a man starts the killin' trade it does something to his brain and it does something to his sleep. He becomes a maverick wolf, he's kicked out of the pack. He runs alone, with other maverick wolves huntin' him. He quits bein' civilized, there's no trust for him and no love—none of the things a man ought to live for. And someday he dies up in the hills in the way a maverick wolf always dies, miserable and tormented. Surratt knew that. He was runnin' from it."

Pokey said, faintly regretful: "Well, he found no peace here."

"No," growled Old Martin, "he didn't. It's the boy's fate. He could run to the end of the earth now and it would catch up with him. He knows it, too. I heard the sound of it in his talk the other night. Pokey, there's the kind of a boy I'd like to've had for a son."

These two men let the somber silence drift on. Pokey held his place by the bed, obediently waiting for Old Martin to speak, as he had been doing for fifteen years. There wasn't much in this little man except that implicit unquestioning loyalty to Martin Head. Old Martin burst out bitterly: "It's a hell of a thing to contemplate. Bill and Surratt are bound to meet. It can't be escaped, and neither will avoid it. One of 'em will die."

"Unless Surratt runs again," suggested Pokey hopefully.

Old Martin stared at his henchman. He shook his head. He was impatient. "You know he won't."

Pokey cleared his throat and showed diffidence. "There's another way, Martin. Stop this fight with Torveen altogether. I don't love sheep, not at all. But I saw sheep in the yonder country. I guess sheep will come here, too. Not regardin' what we do."

"Pokey," said Old Martin, "I have got to tell you something you apparently ain't noticed yet. I own this ranch, but the runnin' of it has passed out of my hands. The crew takes orders only from my son. And my son will not take my orders."

"The pup," growled Pokey, displaying his first resentment.

Old Martin sat up in bed. "I have but one desire. Nothing else matters, but on that one thing I will have my way. I can't get Bill to act quick enough. Therefore, you must do it for me. You take your horse, Pokey, and start roamin' these hills. Don't come back until you've found Perrigo and settled him. You understand what I mean?"

Pokey took the full, iron weight of Old Martin's glance without flinching. He shrugged his little shoulders. He said, mild and matter-of-fact: "All right, Martin."

"He is a dog to be put out of the way," said Old Martin emotionlessly. "It's my full belief he killed Leslie and for that I'll have my own kind of justice, without recourse."

He closed his mouth and leaned back on the pillow. Bill Head walked across the living room and appeared at the door. Seeing him, Pokey's eyes went shrewd with interest, for the scars of the Carson Ford fight were livid and purple on that ruddy face. He had taken a smashing. Pokey said: "What happened to you?"

"Another fine scheme that didn't work," commented Old Martin ironically.

Bill Head stared dismally at Pokey. "Where you been?"

"That's his business and mine," interjected Old Martin.

Pokey turned out of the room. Bill Head wheeled and started to follow and was halted by Old Martin's order. "Stay here, Bill. I want to talk to you."

Bill said, "Wait a minute," and tracked Pokey to the porch. He put out his big arm and shoved Pokey against the house wall. "You runt, I asked you a question. Answer me."

Pokey's voice remained soft. "Your dad answered you, Bill."

Bill Head's crushed lips curved and showed a savage impulse. "You won't always have Old Martin to hide behind, Pokey. When that time comes you'll answer to me."

"When Old Martin dies," replied Pokey, "I'll be going from this ranch."

Bill Head swayed nearer the little man and his broad fist closed and lifted; the desire to strike Pokey was clear in his eyes. But Pokey looked back at Bill Head, strictly still, a gleam creeping into his glance. Unaccountably, Bill Head wheeled into the house again. Pokey went over to his horse and climbed to the saddle, for a moment remaining thoughtfully there. Afterwards he passed into the trees. He had been given an order, and it was the habit of his life to obey Old Martin.

Bill went into the bedroom and took his sulky, angry stand. His father had taught him as a boy to be silent and to be respectful in front of older people, and though the time of his obedience had long passed he still found the habit of attention hard to break. Old Martin's eyes were biting into him, without affection, without kindness.

"Bill," he said, "you were always a brute stubborn lad, no doubt a quality you got from me. It was never that I blamed you for. You have felt I cared little for you since you started into manhood, and it is true and I think the time's come when you should know why—for I doubt if you and I will have much more to say to each other."

"Have we got to talk about that?" Bill asked.

"Stubbornness," stated Old Martin, "is a thing I do not condemn, bein' a kind of courage in its way. But I never have ceased to hate deceit—and you started lyin' to me young. Maybe there were reasons I never understood. Maybe I wasn't the sort of a father you could trust the truth to. At any rate, here's my apologies for bein' the sort of a father that couldn't draw better things out of you. It must be my fault, for Les was no better that way. Yet there is one thing you got neither from me nor from your mother—a streak of meanness that makes you do brutal things deliberately. This is what I have wanted to say to you, so that you'll know why I have no love for you as a son and no respect for you as a man. I'd be sorry to see Judith Cameron make the mistake of marryin' you."

"You're all through talkin'?" breathed Bill Head.

"No, you whelp!" thundered Old Martin. "I'm tellin' you this! You have made a miserable mess with Torveen and now you've got only one thing you can do, which is meet this Surratt who has condemned you to the whole country. If you do not meet him and settle that challenge I'll use a gun on you myself! No man is going to carry my name around and let people spit on it! You hear?"

"All your life," burst out Bill, "you've been obsessed with somebody hurting the name of Head!"

"For fifteen years of my life," replied Old Martin grimly, "my own sons have used that name shamefully. Go on away, Bill." He stopped talking and passed a big hand over his eyes. His next words were slow and gray. "Only God can pass judgment on you and Les and me. If the blame's on me I'll bend my knees willingly to a deserved punishment."

Bill Head went out of the room, out of the house. In the yard he stopped to build a cigarette and light it. The smoke stung his injured eyes; it built up the morose wrath all day accumulating in him. He stood this way and watched one of his riders, Hughie Grant, come up the hill.

Hughie Grant shook his head. "No trace of Torveen or any of the crowd around their ranch. They skipped out."

"I sent Benny and Stuke Jackson to cover the upper trail. See them?"

"No, I just been watchin' Torveen's house."

"I'll find him," grunted Bill Head. "Send somebody to cover the pass road. Send somebody to scout the river. Then you go to Kersom's and tell him I want him to be in Morgantown at suppertime. Go on, Hughie."

He went to his own horse and trotted out of the yard. He was in front of Ab Cameron's house twenty minutes later. He saw Ab Cameron standing by a corral and called him over.

"I've got men all through the hills," said Bill. "He won't get away."

"Peyrolles was just by," explained Ab. "He thought his shot caught Torveen. There was blood in the brush this mornin'."

"We'll find out."

Ab murmured: "Henry Tanner died a little while ago. It was Torveen's bullet that got him fair. Peyrolles saw Torveen aim and he saw Tanner fall."

"I want to see you in Morgantown at suppertime."

"All right," agreed Cameron, without enthusiasm.

Bill Head sourly studied Ab Cameron. "You been hearin' about a woman's glove Surratt was supposed to have found by Les Head?"

"Yes," said Cameron and closed his lips.

"It was Judith's glove," said Bill Head. "She took it from Surratt last night."

Cameron said in a humble way, "God's pity," and walked off. Bill Head watched him go straight for the house. It made him grin to observe how Ab Cameron's face sunk, to notice how the old man's pride fell. He galloped down the river toward Peyrolles' place.

At first daylight Surratt shook himself from his blankets and came out of the trees to Torveen's house close by; and looked again through the place to verify his quick inspection of the night before. There was nothing new to be seen. Torveen had apparently taken his things and had run, the evidence of haste clearly here. In the yard, Surratt had a careful look at the ground. Pony tracks came out of the meadow from the ridge to the house; and pony tracks swung away from the house, turning toward the trees and the upper sheep meadow. Surratt followed these prints into the trees, picked up his horse, and rode to the edge of the meadow.

But caution came to him as he studied the green undergrowth surrounding the meadow. A full day came up and sunlight was a bright promise over the Gray Bull peaks; and the sense of trouble was real enough to swing him completely around the meadow, via the brush, and so arrive at the meadow's higher side, where the trail struck into the timber again. There had been some confusion here, marked by a scatter of men's shoe indentations in the ground and a long, dragged pattern where something had been laid. He got down to have a look at that, and found the dull, round scum of blood drops in the dust. They had carried a man this far, had put him down to rest. They had remounted and carried the man on.

He continued this way. Sunlight rushed fully across the sky, its strong color breaking through the close web of pine tops and lifting the twilight in here one full octave of brightness. Dust particles glistened in the windless air; heat began to come on. It was those dust particles that, half an hour later, reminded him to be on his guard. Bending with the trail, he saw their increased, shimmering thickness in the soft forest atmosphere. The tracks on the ground were too confused for him to read anything more than a story of forward travel; but the suspended dust—and its faint sudden smell—indicated a more recent traveler. And then, from some yonder course of the trail, he heard an approaching echo. He put himself instantly into the brush.

Two or three minutes later he saw a pair of riders drop down the slope, traveling fast. He kept still until the sound was gone. Out on the trail again, he pushed along faster and presently reached the meadow hard by the river canyon. There was a man out there on the edge of the canyon, about ready to tip down the trail to the ford; this was a hundred yards away. Surratt gently retreated without being seen. A little later, again looking, he found the man had disappeared into the canyon. But it was increasingly clear to Surratt that these hills were being dragged by Head's men and that no trail was safe. So he again took to the timber and wove his way laboriously around the meadow and got to its upper side.

It was his guess that Torveen had traveled a straight course, always deeper into the hills; confused and churned as now were the prints of travel on the trail, he believed this way the right one. But it was quite apparent that Crow Track was on this trail too.

Obeying his judgment, he veered into the timber and began a tedious march around brush clumps and deadfalls and rocky hummocks, paralleling the trail. Half an hour later he cut into the trail without intending to; and found that it swung from north to south at this point, keeping beside the river as the river also turned. The tracks still were heavy in the soft dirt. Pulling away, he took the new direction, hearing ahead of him the murmuring roar of water deeply in the canyon. It grew greater in his ears and then its sound diminished as he got by it. The morning went on, with an overhead sun throwing its thin golden lances through the interstices of the trees. He cut back to the trail again.

He had, he discovered, overshot the fugitives. The heavy print of their retreat wasn't here. One rider only had passed this way recently. Somewhere back down the trail Torveen had turned off.

Time ran fast and he wanted to waste no more of it. Knowing he did a reckless thing, he followed the trail back and ten minutes afterwards came upon Torveen's turnoff. The redhead had swung into the timber on the river's side; and Surratt was paused like this, reading the story in the dirt, when a faint rattle of brush jerked him upright in the saddle. A rider suddenly appeared on the trail fifty yards below him and swung to continue upward with it.

He saw Surratt there, a tall and stiff shape in the shadows, and recognition jerked at him. He reached for his gun and wheeled his horse smartly into the brush; and whipped two shots rearward as he retreated, those echoes tearing the hill's dreaming quiet completely asunder. The shots were wide of the mark and Surratt, sliding away, heard the man crash downhill. He would, Surratt understood, be back soon enough with other men to help him. It caused him to travel faster through the brush and so reach the river's edge.

Torveen's tracks tipped down a twenty-foot bank and were lost in the gravel; but it was plain that the crossing had been made here. Looking over the shallow water, Surratt saw the solid green forest wall on the yonder side broken by a small aperture which represented another trail. The rush of the falls was deeper in his ears and he had only to look a quarter-mile downstream to see mist curling heavily up from the sunlight where the fast-running water dropped into sudden depths. But he had little time to view it, for the thought of pursuit was strong in him now and the ford was a risk he had to take and put behind him without delay. Accordingly he slid down the bluff and pushed through the water, the muscles along his back involuntarily tightening. He came out of the water and rushed his pony up the bluff, into the timber again—and stopped. Perrigo stood directly in the trail.

Perrigo shook his head solemnly. "That was a damfool thing to do, Surratt."

"Where's Torveen?"

"We're camped a long ways off. I came back to cover the trail. Knew we'd left tracks plain enough for anybody to follow. Been four different men come out to that bank and have a look at the river. You're the only one that's been brash enough to come out of cover."

"Who was shot?"

"Sam."

"Bad?"

"Not good," grunted Perrigo. "Come on."

He went into the brush for his horse and afterwards took the lead, running freely into the rising timber. He had some method here, for afterwards he swung into the trackless pine deeps and traveled at the same rapid pace until he reached some other dim-traced way. This he followed for a little distance, and abandoned it for the pines again, and again struck some trail. Thus erratically was Surratt towed southward. They came finally to a broad road and paused to reconnoiter it before crossing. Up its length Surratt caught a glimpse of the Gray Bull peaks. Then they were once more closed around by the somber pine blanket, running constantly south. Surratt guessed they had traveled a good eight miles when Perrigo swung downhill and reached the river. They forded it without much prior inspection—Perrigo seeming to feel himself on safer ground—and went a good two miles along a narrow and rocky way. It was around noon when Perrigo stopped and called down the trail casually:

"All right, Ferd."

Ferd Bowie put his head out of the brush. They went past him and were at the river's bank, turning through what once had been another channel but was now dry and half overgrown by brush. A sheer rock wall confronted them and showed them a broad hole smashed out by some ancient current. They rode into this tunnel for a dozen yards and got down and walked on through the semi-darkness. A piece of a fire burned on the gravel. Ed sat cross-legged before Torveen, who lay in his blankets with his face turned up. He seemed to be sleeping but the crunch of Surratt's feet opened his lids. The pallor of the man was distinct. He grinned remotely. His voice was only a whisper.

"Hello, kid."

"What were you doin'?" demanded Surratt.

Ed said: "We was bein' chased back by Peyrolles. Sam came up and we made a stand of it, on the ridge near Cameron's." Ed looked anxiously at Surratt. "The bullet hole looks to be near his lungs. You know anything about those things?"

"Let it alone," murmured Torveen. "I can lick this."

"Sure," agreed Surratt quietly. "Sure you can." But he was watching Torveen's lips settle and didn't like what he saw.

"Glad you got here," muttered Torveen—and closed his eyes.

Ed stared at Surratt, secretively shaking his head. Looking around the cavern, Surratt observed they had saved

124

their blankets and not much else. The place, even with the fire burning, was damp and draughty. He stood a moment, watching the labored lift and fall of Torveen's chest; and turned out to the mouth of the hole, signaling Perrigo to follow. He stopped in the sunlight. He filled his pipe.

"Got anything to eat?"

"No," said Perrigo.

"That boy needs a doctor."

"And how would you work that?" countered Perrigo. "Doc Brann's the only one—in Morgantown. You got any ideas?"

"Sure. I'll fetch him."

Perrigo surveyed Surratt morosely. "You'd be nervy enough to try. But it won't do. For one thing, these hills are full of Bill Head's men. He's huntin' us. By the middle of afternoon every stray rider in the country will be beatin' up the brush. No doubt you can get through to town. How you goin' to find Brann when you get there? The place is poison to you—you can't stick your head out on Main Street without gettin' it shot at. If you get Brann, how can you bring him back without bein' followed? No, Sam's got to tough this out alone."

Surratt said: "What's this Brann like?"

"A fat fellow with white hair. He's all right. This quarrel don't mean anything to him, one way or another. His office is over the bank. He lives up there, too. But you can't do it, Surratt. You pushed your luck twice in Morgantown. It won't hold up three times. Don't consider it."

"It will be late tonight before I get back," decided Surratt. He smoked his pipe idly, and in equal idleness considered this hideout. The timber reached down to the ancient river bed. A high bank of gravel, studded with brush and seedling pines, locked it in from the water. The river ran quietly past the far side of the gravel bank and this gravel bank screened the tunnel from anybody who might be across the river.

"Where are we?" he wanted to know.

"This is George Bernay's country. We're south of the pass road. It is about twelve miles northward downgrade to Morgantown."

"We'll try it," decided Surratt. "I don't like Torveen's look." He knocked the ashes out of his pipe; he swung into his saddle.

"Wait," said Perrigo. "You maybe might not find it easy to get back. But Doc Brann knows this country. Tell him it's the place where Modoc Niles' bones were found the year after Martin Head had fence trouble with George Bernay's dad." Perrigo looked carefully at Surratt. His voice softened and quickened. "What was it you said about Ferd Bowie's callin' to you the other night?"

Surratt's answer was dry. "It is my affair, Nick. I'll take care of it."

Perrigo spoke in a grudging, reluctant way. "I'm forced to admire a man that keeps his mouth shut." Then he said, more and more taciturn: "If a bullet came at you from the wrong direction, Surratt, it wasn't mine."

Surratt climbed back through the brush to the top of the bluff. Perrigo watched him go, but a moment later he followed quickly. Ferd Bowie was in the trail when Surratt went by, and Perrigo came up to Bowie and stood beside the kid until Surratt had vanished somewhere down the timber. Perrigo's eyes kept watching Bowie. Bowie made an impatient swing with his shoulders. He said: "What you want, Nick?"

"Nothin'," said Perrigo. Yet he kept staring at Ferd Bowie, a dead darkness making his glance wholly obscure.

Surratt took his way through the hills carefully and without haste, knowing he could do nothing in Morgantown until darkness covered him. So his trail was one that circled and zigzagged, avoiding all clear country. In the early afternoon he had sight of a small ranch sitting well down in a bowl-like meadow, with men working in nearby corrals. Later he struck a road and was careful to erase his prints when he crossed it. At five o'clock, thus vigilantly riding, he came out on the timbered ridge back of Morgantown and saw the settlement sitting all yellow and hot under the harsh flare of a late sun. He sat down here and waited the arrival of twilight, meanwhile observing riders come in and increase the traffic of this town. At half-past seven, with the shadows safe for him, he left his horse tied to a tree and crawled to Morgantown's back end and made his way along a between-building alley. He took his station at the corner of the saloon; in the semi-darkness of his position he watched men stroll by him, near enough at times to touch.

Pokey, who took Old Martin's orders always literally, went directly from Crow Track to Torveen's and had a look at the place. He picked up the churned marks of the departing crew and followed them into the hills; a little after noon he stood at the same spot on the river where Surratt had stood before crossing. But Pokey avoided the ford and instead made an enormous detour to the pass-road bridge and crossed there. It took him two hours to get back to the place where Surratt and Perrigo had met. Here he studied the tracks and softly pursued them. When they began to break away into the timber he got down and led his horse and patiently unraveled the puzzle.

There was no hurry in him and no uncertainty; for Pokey was a methodical man who once had been an Indian scout and knew the ways and the signs of fugitives very well. It was growing dusk when he reached the pass road and saw the prints cross and continue southward. Here, with the light too dim to read sign by, he rolled up in the brush and fell asleep. There was no other man in these hills who could have followed all the confused turnings of that fugitive trail; to Pokey it was as clear as ink on paper and he knew that if Torveen still camped in the hills he would find him before noon of the following day. From time to time during the night he was wakened by men riding by and he understood they were looking for the hidden Torveen. Yet he never betrayed his position and he took no interest in their searching. He was, in fact, mildly amused at their noisy beatings through the hills.

Chapter Thirteen

THE REWARD
NOTICE

Standing at the corner of the saloon, obscured by the building's shadow and one step away from the indolent current of riders ranging along the board walk, Surratt saw both Bolderbuck and Sheriff Ranier on the porch of the White House Hotel across the way; and with them was the lank-shaped, sharp-nosed Peyrolles. He watched them with a moment's interest, observing Peyrolles' arms lift expressively as he talked. Then he stood quite still, hearing steps in the alley behind him. He didn't turn. A man circled him in this darkness and veered a curious face at him and went on into the street. Surratt bowed his head a little, bringing the hatbrim down in front of his face. But he saw the man look back before swinging around the corner.

The bank building was across the alley. Scanning its second story, where Perrigo had said Doc Brann's office and living quarters were, Surratt saw a light shining behind a drawn curtain; and then, searching the alley for a side stairway into the building and finding none, Surratt knew that his position had become ticklish. To reach Brann he had to leave the alley, pass the bank corner and enter the stairway from the main street.

He crossed the alley to the bank side—a matter of four long strides. He meant to pause here and wait a moment before stepping into the stream of ambling townsmen; but all this while he had kept an eye on the White House porch and he saw Ranier's head swing toward him and remain that way a moment. It was his nearness to the bank door, Surratt guessed, that drew Ranier's attention; and he couldn't afford to let that casual inspection grow. Pulling down his chin, he turned the bank corner and walked along the front side of the building. Light from the hotel flamed over the dusty street and made a diffused patch on the bank wall. He tipped his head away from the hotel and stepped into the light—and passed beyond it and got to the building's stairway.

He went up the stairs rapidly and stopped to inspect a single hall with four or five doors. Brann's name was on the nearest. The others were unlabeled; but at the end of the hall lamplight and a woman's voice came through an open transom. He went forward and knocked on Brann's door.

The odor of fried onions lay across the remnant of other musty smells in this close, dark corridor. The woman's voice kept on with an inexhaustible energy; the words were plain enough for his listening, but his mind was narrowly on other things and he heard only the out-pour of tone. He had come from a cool night, yet he had begun to sweat. He knocked again; and heard someone swing off the street and start up the stairs.

He turned the door's knob and went into Brann's office, black and faintly rank with the presence of formaldehyde; he closed the door and put a slight weight on it, listening to these steps arrive and pass by. A far door opened, the woman's vigorous talk rising. The door slammed. Surratt came out of the office then and considered this situation with a swifter, more aroused attention. Sweat had gotten below his hatband; the palms of his hands were soft. Save for the woman's room there seemed no other occupant up here; he had little choice in this matter. He went down the hall and knocked.

The woman opened the door, a buxom and ruddy and good-looking woman. "Doctor Brann?" asked Surratt.

"If he isn't in his office or his room," she said, "you'll no doubt find him at the White House eating. Or he'll be playin' poker at the saloon. One of the two."

"Thanks," said Surratt. The woman's eyes were interested in him. She remained against the roomlight; a man at the back of that room slowly turned to have his look at Surratt. Surratt moved away. The woman came forward a step, calling after him. "Well, it will be the saloon. You'll have to go get him if you want him—he's liable to play cards all night. Be just as well if he moved his office down there for that's where anybody finds him most of the time."

"Thanks," repeated Surratt and kept on walking. At the head of the stairs he stopped a long moment, considering. For him the saloon was as far away as China; going into it was wholly out of the question. He went down the stairs and stood in the smooth darkness of the bottom landing. Three punchers went by, their spurs dragging the boards. Looking across to the White House porch he discovered the meeting over there had grown. The short, chunky Dutch Kersom had joined it. And one other man had joined it and now stood head and shoulders above them. Staring at him—at this Bill Head who bulked so vastly against the others—Surratt felt a quick, tense excitement seize him. This game was getting dangerous.

He stepped back and plunged his hands in his pockets, and drew them out. A whole column of cowhands whirled down the street and came to a dusty halt by the saloon. One solitary rider came more casually in the wake of the group. Abreast the lights of the White House, this rider turned in the saddle and Surratt saw the even, supple shape of Judith Cameron silhouetted there before she passed on.

He advanced to the walk and headed for the alley. He kept his face angled toward the bank window; and because he did so he saw the white sign gummed to the glass. It stopped him completely; it threw him for a moment off guard.

REWARD!

Five Hundred Dollars paid in hand for information leading to the capture of Sam Torveen, wanted for murder of Henry Tanner, killed in fight on Cameron Ridge.

Five Hundred Dollars Reward for information regarding one Buck Surratt, for killing of Leslie Head.

One Hundred Dollars each for information for capture of Nick Perrigo, Ferd Bowie, and a man known as Ed, all riding with the aforesaid Sam Torveen.

Cattleman's Protective Association
BILL HEAD
AB CAMERON
T. J. KERSOM
HANK PEYROLLES.

He wheeled from that notice, passing around the bank corner into the safety of the alley. He crossed the alley and stopped by the saloon wall again. Judith Cameron left

130

her horse farther down the street and walked into the dressmaking shop with a quick, striding step. He saw George Bernay for the first time, idly smoking a cigarette over under the shadows of the board awnings. His mind was running hard and fast and reckless now, for the town was full of men and the weight of some deliberate purpose was clearly here. The risk grew greater. He saw Ranier's exploring glance reach out once more toward him. Ranier suddenly detached himself from the cattlemen's group and started over the dust in Surratt's direction.

George Bernay was on his ranch when news of Torveen's flight reached him in the middle of the afternoon. He knocked off work and rode around the country south of Morgantown until he found Billy Temple and Jud Horsfall. They were two-bit ranchers, as he was; they had all worked for one or another of the four big outfits in the hills before setting up their own places. And they were all sound friends of Sam Torveen. It was this that turned them toward Morgantown—three men still young enough to feel like fighting and still poor enough not to be worried over losing very much. On the way into town they discovered the reward notice tacked to a tree. They read it and rode thoughtfully on.

"Bill Head," reflected George Bernay, "always did enjoy squashing bugs under his thumb."

"It's funny," considered Jud Horsfall, "how a man can get to admire sheep when somebody tells him he mustn't."

"Don't let your admiration get the best of you," warned Billy Temple. "We're pretty small onions in this vegetable patch. Look what happened to Sam."

At the edge of town—it was six o'clock then—they found the street already filling up with riders from the big outfits. It was a pretty clear indication of trouble. George Bernay said as much. "Something up Bill Head's sleeve. We better not be together. Suppose we float around and hear what we hear."

They separated. George Bernay left his horse in front of the White House and went in for his supper. When he came out he met Sheriff Ranier face to face in the doorway. Ranier started to go by. But he stopped on impulse and considered Bernay with a worried attention. "Go up to the office a minute, George. I want to talk to you."

Bernay loitered on the porch, building himself a smoke. Afterwards he ambled to the jail office and sat down in a chair. It was five minutes or so before Ranier appeared. Ranier closed the door, which was a thing that lifted Bernay's quiet interest.

"George, what's going to happen?"

"What?"

Ranier walked around the room. He needed a shave and he needed sleep. His eyes kept returning to Bernay, curious and troubled. "These sheep and cattle wars are hell. I'm not fooled. Bill Head's driven Torveen to timber, but that is not the end of it. What're those boys cookin' up? This Surratt is a fox."

"He rides high, for a fact," assented George Bernay casually. His glance measured the sheriff.

Ranier came to a stand. "I've been in other cattle-sheep wars. It always goes the same. The big outfits are strong and they have their way for a while. But sheep's a little man's easy crop. There's a lot of little men down your way, George. Little men never do love big outfits. What'll they do now?"

"Don't know," said George Bernay laconically. He got up. "That all, Sheriff?"

"Nothing more bitter than a neighborhood fight. I'm trying to play things safe."

"When a man straddles the fence," suggested George Bernay, "he can't keep from gettin' a sore crotch." He threw a sharp question at the sheriff. "What happened to Torveen—you know for sure?"

"We think Peyrolles shot him."

"Peyrolles?" murmured George Bernay. His eyes laid a faint glitter on the otherwise blandness of his face.

Tom Bolderbuck opened the office door and walked in. He said: "Hello, George."

"Hello, you baldheaded horsethief. Look, Tom. You a friend of mine?"

"Think so," replied Bolderbuck imperturbably.

"Remember it durin' the next few days," said Bernay as he walked out.

"What's that?" called the sheriff, plainly disturbed.

George Bernay strolled the street with a tight streak of a smile on his lips. He was talking to himself. "The meek shall inherit the earth, except that part of the earth which is cow country." Peyrolles stood in front of the White House, waiting for somebody. George Bernay only looked at him quietly and passed by. One time he had been a Peyrolles rider and he knew the man well enough.

Peyrolles saw him and said: "George."

Bernay turned. The tone Peyrolles used was the old tone of command. It bit into George Bernay but he didn't show it. "George," said Peyrolles, "we may need you to help out in this business."

George Bernay murmured: "To hell with you, Hank," and walked on. Under the board awning of the hardware store he stopped to arrange himself against a post. He built a new cigarette and dragged in its smoke energetically. Dutch Kersom was entering town with his crew; they all wheeled by the saloon, ripping up the dust. Kersom walked over to join Peyrolles. The sheriff and Tom Bolderbuck came down from the jail office to join the two big ranchers. The riders pushed into the saloon. This town grew crowded, the sense of trouble was pretty definite. "And the meek," murmured George Bernay, "shall get their pants shot off."

Jud Horsfall came out of the saloon. He spotted George and walked over. "This is maybe news to you. Bill Head met this Surratt by accident up at Carson Ford and they had a fight. Surratt laid Bill out. Why, my God, he must be the old fruit—this Surratt."

"That," said George Bernay, "is the nearest thing to truth you've said since you was seven years old."

"I likewise hear Blackjack Smith had a quarrel with Bill Head and pulled out of the Ford with his bunch of plugs."

"Where'd he go?"

"Don't know," responded Horsfall, ambling away.

Sound rolled and boiled in the yonder saloon; and more riders trotted out of the hills into this crowding street. Men tramped ceaselessly up and down the board walks. All the store lights threw bright beams into the dust, deepening the intervening shadows. Annette Carvel came out of her dressmaking shop and seemed to watch the night carefully. George Bernay dropped his cigarette. He walked over. She saw him come, but she didn't pay much attention to him. Paused before her, he removed his hat carefully. Bronzed as he was by the sun, his face showed an increased flush. He said rather diffidently:

"Hello."

She murmured, "Hello, George," and gave him a more deliberate glance. Her arms were white in the light of the shop; her cheeks were soft and pale, turning her eyes very black. "What are you doing in town?" she added.

"Just lookin' around," he said.

133

Her glance left him and her thoughts left him. He felt that indifference with a quick, deep regret. It had been this way for two or three years—an emotion in him he could not express to her. He was a man that made no show, who had no flamboyant manners which could compete with all the striking riders of the hills. Always realistic, George Bernay knew this girl was attracted by a color he did not possess; he had no qualities to draw her attention, so that she might really see him. Quietly in the background, he understood where her likings lay and to whom her smiles were given. In fact he understood more about Annette Carvel than she dreamed; yet in the evening solitude of his own ranch house he kept thinking of her—of the mistakes she had committed, of the naïve honesty which made her still so desirable to him.

She uttered a small, quick sound of anxiety. Looking around, he saw Bill Head ride into town with the Crow Track crew. Bill Head swung over to the group of cattlemen on the White House porch; the crew made for the saloon, a solid confusion rising from the turning horses. One other rider paced down the middle of the street and didn't stop. It was, George Bernay discovered, Judith Cameron; she wheeled in at the dressmaking shop and jumped to the boards.

"Annette," she said instantly, "what's happened?"

"You haven't heard about Sam Torveen?"

"No!"

"He had a fight with Peyrolles. They think they shot him—Sam. He's gone from his ranch. With the crew."

George Bernay stepped backward so that the two women might stand together; he kept his glance on Judith, stirred by the picture she made in these moving shadows. She said: "Where is he now?"

"They don't know," said Annette. Her tone was defiant then. "I guess Bill Head would like to. That must be why they've all come to town—to think up a way of catching him."

Judith turned. "George—you're his friend. Do you know?"

"No," he murmured.

She was darkly thinking about it; and the stormy dignity of her features impressed Bernay immeasurably. She was a woman who could fight and still be a woman; it was a real distinction, though he could not define it. Her eyes were on him again. "Will you tell me, if you find out?"

"Yes," said Bernay, and watched the two women go into the dressmaking shop. He ambled along the walk, toward the saloon, noting the solid crowd inside. Across the street Bill Head talked aggressively to the other cattle owners, his big hand dropping with each word. It was, Bernay thought, the only way the man knew—to use his strength to get things done. Ranier was turning away from the group; he was coming across the street. Halfway over he stopped dead, for Bill Head's voice jumped arrogantly after him. "Come back here—I want you!"

Ranier turned in full obedience and went back; and then all the group entered the hotel. Ab Cameron came out of the hill road and pulled up at the White House. He got down so slowly that once George Bernay felt sorry for the old man. Cameron was a mild-mannered character who didn't belong with that pack. It was Bill Head who bullied Ab into line; this was the way it had been for years, as all the country knew. At the saloon's corner Bernay turned to cross the street. A voice said softly to him then: "Step back in the alley, George."

He was no fool, this George Bernay. He knew the tricks of the land. And so he remained paused at the corner a moment, serenely indifferent, while a group of Kersom riders passed. Afterwards he dropped slowly into the alley—and discovered Buck Surratt.

He could not help letting a quick warning fall out of him. "My God, man, you don't belong here! Ain't you seen the price posted on your head?"

"Go get Doc Brann and bring him up to his office. I'll be there."

George Bernay grinned in a small, brilliant way. "All right," he murmured, and went instantly to perform the chore.

Surratt crossed the alley and stopped a moment by the bank wall. The street was more crowded than it had been; but the cattlemen had gone inside the hotel—taking Ranier and Bolderbuck with them—and he felt fractionally safer. He tipped his hat down, stepped around the bank wall and strolled to the stairway. He went up, going into Brann's office. He lighted a match and found Brann's lamp. The room, he saw, was typically a doctor's room. He was waiting there in the middle of it when Brann entered and closed the door and propped his round body against it. He had a face that was half jovial and half professional, with shaggy silver eyebrows; his hair was pure white. He had his look at Surratt, seeming to be amused with what he saw and knew.

"Shouldn't think you'd want to come back to Morgantown."

"You're Torveen's friend?" asked Surratt.

Brann shrugged his shoulders. "I'm supposed to be humanity's friend, son. But when I get dragged away from a pat full house I begin to doubt it. So Sam's been shot?"

"Who told you?"

"Why else would you venture into Morgantown?" retorted Brann. He went over to his table and opened a doctor's satchel there. He got a few things out of a cabinet. "A bullet hole—where?"

"Lungs, I think."

"It hadn't better be," remarked Brann grimly. He reached into his cabinet again. "Well, if I had five dollars for every bullet hole I've treated I suppose I'd be in Vienna now studying medicine under the famous ones, instead of practising buckshot surgery out in the middle of the hills. Yet I doubt if I'd have as much fun in Vienna." He snapped his satchel together and put on his hat; he took a revolver out of his hip pocket and laid it on the table.

"Better keep that," suggested Surratt.

"I never carry a gun except when I play poker."

Men were coming up the stairs. Surratt backed quietly to a corner of the room; he stood against the wall, waiting like that. But it was George Bernay who came in presently with two others Surratt didn't know.

Doc Brann, observing Surratt's whiplike reactions, stepped forward to stand in front of Surratt with a dim and kind and skeptic smile printed along his fat lips. "I like you, son. You're a dissenter, you don't conform easy to the ways of the world. It makes your sleep bad but your days interesting. It's my hope I don't have to fold your hands over your chest, though it is a thin hope the way things stand. Now where's Sam?"

Surratt looked at the two strangers, whereupon George Bernay said: "That's all right. This is Jud Horsfall. This is Billy Temple. Doc knows 'em."

Surratt remembered what Perrigo had told him. "Where Modoc Niles' bones were found."

"Way over there?" said Brann in some surprise.

"Be careful," Bernay warned Brann. "Don't let anybody follow you in."

136

"Teachin' your grandmother to suck eggs?" retorted Brann. "Surratt, you wait till I'm gone before you come. I make better time alone." Saying that, he left the office.

"Time for me to crawl out of here," decided Surratt.

But George Bernay was grinning in an obscure, pleased way that Surratt didn't understand; and Bernay spoke to the other two men. "Well, that's the size of him."

"What?" said Surratt.

They were all looking at him, they were studying him with a care that was strange. They were young and he saw a gleam of recklessness appear in their watching. George Bernay said: "You give a man hope, Surratt."

"I'd like to take back some grub."

Billy Temple broke in: "Think you can move Sam over the pass?"

"Not now."

"Hell of a situation. I just found out what Bill Head's up to. This gang in town is going to spread out and beat the timber all the way to the Gray Bull peaks."

There was a man running up the stairs. These four swung and became rigid. But the man went scuffling down the hall and flung open a far door. They heard him say: "Belle, that fellow who came here was Surratt. They've found his horse back of town!"

The door slammed. Surratt was moving across the room in quick strides. "There ought to be some windows in the back of this place."

George Bernay hauled the office door open, stopping long enough to say, "I'll get my horse and bring it around back," and then ran down the stairs. Surratt pursued the hallway to its end, rapidly, with Temple and Horsfall at his heels. He halted at the door across from the lighted room. He put his hands to the knob, but it didn't give. The man and the woman both were talking in the other room and the man seemed to be coming out. Surratt suddenly laid his weight against the panel, breaking the lock with a force that shot bulletlike echoes through the building. He ran across the darkness of this room toward its back window. Horsfall was still with him, but Temple had stopped in the hall, for the door of the occupied room opened and the couple were looking at him suspectingly. Temple lifted his gun. He said: "Hold it a minute."

The woman suddenly put herself in front of the man and slammed the door in Temple's face. A minute later she had run across to her own window and was yelling out of it into the alley. "Hey—hey—hey!" Temple stood there in the black hall and cursed himself.

Meanwhile Surratt reached the empty room's back window, opened and slid through it and lowered himself the length of his arms—and dropped. That long fall stung his ankles, and he rolled in the dirt and remained on his side, hearing Jud Horsfall plump beside him with a heavy grunt. The woman was still caterwauling into the alley just around the building's corner; she was waking the town.

"Now wouldn't you think she'd be a Christian?" growled Horsfall.

George Bernay was across the street by the White House, up in his saddle and moving quietly toward the alley, when the woman's strident yelling sailed unexpectedly along the street. It was as though the fire bell in the courthouse steeple started to ring. The effect of it was like that. Men wheeled on the walks; men poured out of the saloon—all rushing at the alley. The woman bent far down from her window, flinging out her arms, her hair falling wildly around her face.

"That man Surratt—he's back of the building."

George Bernay kicked his horse into the alley, into the forming crowd. He couldn't make headway against that mob; and Hughie Grant, a Crow Track hand always, suddenly bored a hole through the confused and charging cowhands and reached up to seize Bernay's bridle. He said, cool and alert:

"Where you goin', George?"

Bernay swore in a soft, violent way. He lifted his boot from a stirrup and used it to smash Hughie Grant backwards. Hughie Grant reached down for his gun; he wasn't angry, he was a little bit amused. But he put the gun on George Bernay in a manner that wasn't to be mistaken. "Stay there a minute, George, till we see what this is all about."

Bill Head ran from the White House with the other owners; and Bill Head's voice began to throw some sort of order into this confusion. "Dan—go through the stable!" The alley was alive with riders now, and a gun began to blast up that yonder blackness. A little section of Crow Track hands raced past the bank, into the stable. George Bernay folded his hands on the saddle horn and looked down at all this with a pale, wild and useless rage.

Flat on his belly in the darkness behind the bank building, Surratt heard the pack rush into the alley and come toward him. Horsfall crouched near him, breathing fast. Horsfall murmured: "George better be here with that horse pronto."

"Too late now. You get out of here, Jud." Surratt sprang up and ran on down the rear side of these buildings, into a continuing blackness. He stumbled over broken boxes and loose wire, aiming for the faint glow of light ahead of him, which was the back entrance of the stable. He meant to get in here. Horsfall trotted faithfully at his heels, and he threw a quicker warning at the man. "Get out of here!" Next moment he dropped, and Horsfall dropped. Men turned out of the alley into this back area; and at the same time a group shot through the stable's rear opening and blocked that way entirely. There was no chance to run now, except away from the building toward the clutter of sheds and corrals that occupied the narrow space lying at the foot of the ridge. Surratt threw this chance from his mind as being no good. He lay still. Horsfall was murmuring in his ear.

"If they want it, by God they can have it!"

Crow Track had him trapped—and it went about its business with a sure knowledge that it had. These men were spreading around him, trickling up from the alley, moving away from the stable door. They were boxing him. Someone in the alley kept throwing out quick orders and afterwards Bill Head's voice reached forward, very certain.

"Come out of there, Surratt."

Surratt held his tongue a moment, wickedly considering it. Jud Horsfall, desperate and reckless in this trap, was again whispering. "To hell with 'em!"

But in a moment Surratt quietly answered the call. "Where's Bolderbuck?"

The marshal immediately spoke up from the stable door. "Here, Surratt."

"You come up. I'll give you my gun."

Bolderbuck walked on. Surratt laid a warning hand on Horsfall's back, pushing Horsfall definitely against the earth, and got up and went over to meet Bolderbuck. He handed the marshal his gun and turned Bolderbuck around. They went back to the stable door together, through the forming clutter of ranch hands and on out to the street. Light was shining here, with all the crowding faces turned somber and sullen by it. The tide had set out of the alley, men running up to thicken the surrounding ranks. Bill Head plunged his way through and his ruddy face was doggedly pleased. He said to Bolderbuck: "Bring him to the hotel."

Bolderbuck had Surratt's gun still in his fist. He swung it around the circle. "Make a track here," he said quietly. "Surratt's going to the jail."

"Bolderbuck!" shouted Head, "you mind me!"

"Bill," said Tom Bolderbuck, "I still run this town."

He walked straight ahead, with Surratt beside him, the unyielding breadth of his body making a hole in the Crow Track ring. He got through with Surratt; and kept on toward the jail office. Crow Track kept following, restless and on the edge of a break, with Bill Head's voice low and furious in the background. Bolderbuck didn't bother to look back. He went through the jail-office door; and shut the door. He spoke then, with a little restlessness in his voice. "Up the stairs."

They went up the stairs. Bolderbuck opened an iron-barred door and stood aside and watched Surratt go through. He closed the door and locked it. He put his back to the cell.

Crow Track boiled into the jail office below, the stairway began to groan with their oncoming weight. Bolderbuck listened to it for a dragging moment, and then turned and thrust Surratt's gun between the bars. He said: "Slip this under the bunk blankets. You're cool and I admire you. We've had luck so far, but it may not last."

Chapter Fourteen

THE TURNING HOUR

Tom Bolderbuck turned from the cell door to face the length of this second-story jail corridor. Bill Head came up the stairs, with Peyrolles and Kersom and Cameron and half a dozen of the Head riders following. They came on until Bolderbuck's broad shape stopped them; and they spread out and filled the corridor completely. The dull light of the bracket lamps shined incompletely across their brown and stubborn and partisan cheeks. Bolderbuck, as immovable in his attitude as one of the Gray Bull peaks, studied these men and understood the narrow gleaming in their eyes. It was a stung savagery he saw and carefully marked. His attention remained a moment on George Bernay, who had followed this group; afterwards it switched to Ab Cameron's mild, sad cheeks and then turned more fully to Bill Head.

"Open the door, Tom," commanded Head.

Bolderbuck seemed to calculate the exact measure of danger here; and some practical and very shrewd consideration evidently tipped his mind. He said calmly: "No rough stuff, Bill," and unlocked the door, entering the cell first. When Bill Head and the other three owners had followed him Bolderbuck put up an arresting hand at the rest of the crowd. "Stay in the hall—you." Hughie Grant was in this group. He laughed a little, but he didn't step into the cell. George Bernay worked his way forward and got beside Hughie Grant at the doorway. Hughie Grant looked at him, still grinning. "Don't make no plays here, George," he said.

Bolderbuck stood solidly in his boots and watched this scene with a dogged care. Surratt made a high, tough shape in the middle of the cell, throwing back an expression purely smooth. It held nothing that Bolderbuck could see. Bill Head had come to a massive stop in front of Surratt. Peyrolles and Kersom were to one side of him, old Ab Cameron remained sadly and unwillingly in the background. Bill Head's ruddy face was bitter and brutal in its show of triumph. He lifted his big fists and hooked his thumbs into the armholes of his vest.

"You were up at Brann's office," he said, "and Brann's gone. So you came to get him to go see Torveen, who's been shot. Where's Torveen hidin'?"

"You've got a bright mind, Bill. You find out."

Bill Head's ruddy complexion thickened. The remark raked up a resentment that changed the slant of his lips. He said, with a softness that was wicked: "You'll tell me, friend Surratt. You'll tell me."

"Bring a few more of your crew in here," suggested Surratt. "It'll make you feel safer."

The cool rashness of that talk attracted Bolderbuck's considering glance to Surratt. Surratt was faintly smiling; a devil's temper plainly stirred behind the smoky color of his eyes. The silence lay deep and heavy in the cell; beyond the bars Head's men were as still as statues. Bill Head's face was a furious red. His right foot moved a little backward and his right fist jumped from its idle position, without warning of any kind, and smashed Surratt on the chin. Surratt fell backward against the cell wall; he dropped to his knees. His head sagged down and he supported himself with stiff arms a moment, his shoulders swaying.

"Do that again," growled Bolderbuck, "and I'll bend a gun over your skull, Bill."

George Bernay's voice came into the cell, strained and passionate. "Head, I'd like to kill you for that!" Hughie Grant, beside George Bernay, abruptly cocked his eyes on Bernay. "Easy, George. You ain't among friends."

Ab Cameron spoke out his sickened, heartfelt protest. "That's no way for a white man to act, Bill."

Head and Peyrolles and Kersom swung on Cameron almost in unison, angry at the interference; and Head rapped Cameron with an insolent command. "Shut up, Ab." He wheeled to cover Surratt with a sultry, desiring attention. Surratt got to his feet, he supported himself against the cell wall. But to Bolderbuck it was a strange thing how that faint, ironic smile came back to Surratt; how it laid an irrevocable and relentless will across the room, beyond the power of any man to stop. It was strong enough to impress them all, for Peyrolles shifted his position cautiously and Kersom stirred. Bill Head's profile was all solid and somber. The desire was there to lash out and crush Surratt again, but he kept watching Surratt's face and that desire seemed to be swayed by another thought. He threw a narrowing glance at Bolderbuck.

Surratt was speaking. "I've been a long time figuring you out, Head. In the beginning I misjudged you, but I've got you straight now."

"It will do you no good," said Bill Head in a slow, snarling way.

Surratt didn't answer. He stood straight against the wall, and it was at once plain to them that a wild, killing impulse raged in him. Bill Head stepped back a pace. He said, more under control: "I've got fifty men in Morgantown. They're going into the hills tonight. I can tell you now, Surratt, you're at the end of your own rope—and Torveen's at the end of his." He turned and thrust a long finger toward George Bernay in the corridor. "You're in this, George. I'm givin' you just twelve hours to get out of the country."

The motion of his arm sent all his riders down the corridor and down the stairs. He left the cell, and Peyrolles and Kersom went out. Cameron stood a moment longer, lost in some vague, unhappy speculation of his own. At last he walked over to Surratt. "You're an admirable man to know," he murmured, "and I'll remember this many long days. But I have no recourse and neither have you." He went away then, faintly unsure in his walking. George Bernay didn't stir from the cell door.

Bolderbuck moved into the corridor and stopped by a window commanding the street. He lifted the sash and put his head near the opening, catching the talk that came from below. Crow Track waited down there. His eyes were thoughtful as he came back and locked the cell door.

Surratt said: "You want that gun back now?"

Bolderbuck showed a faint dissatisfaction. "The first dumb thing I've heard you say. I didn't mention anything about the gun, did I? You play your cards like they're dealt to you, my boy, without askin' the dealer any questions. This thing ain't over yet. I know what's in Bill Head's mind and I know what he's apt to try to do. Maybe I can stop him. But I'm damned if I leave a man in a cell without ways of protectin' himself at a time like this." He stared at George Bernay. "You can stay up here for a little while. Don't get any funny notions, you understand?" Leaving his warning flat and final behind him, he descended the stairway.

George Bernay grabbed the cell-door bars in his hands and shook them with all his strength. It was the way he felt. "Surratt, you can kick my pants off and I'd be relieved."

"What's below?" Surratt asked.

Sound kept boiling up from the street. George Bernay fixed himself discreetly beside the window, having his look at the crowd below. The outfits were assembling in a round, restless formation. Bill Head stepped into the saddle; Peyrolles and Kersom rode from some obscure angle of the town to join him. The smell of a dry, scorched dust lifted strongly to George Bernay's nostrils. Ab Cameron stood on the edge of the walk; and Bill Head rode toward the older man, using an arrogant tone on him. "Why didn't you bring your men along?"

"You got plenty men," Ab Cameron said agreeably.

"You can't dodge your part of this work," retorted Bill Head.

"It's your work, Bill, not mine," suggested Ab Cameron.

"What?" said Bill Head. He swung his heavy body downward. He was severe and he was threatening. "Don't tell me that, Ab. I'm going to send a rider over to bring your outfit up to me in the hills. All right, everybody."

They milled forward and fell into a column of twos and left Morgantown at a wild gallop, like the outrushing of wind. Motion and confusion and uncertainty went with them and peace flowed along the street, the murmur of voices tentatively creeping through the quietness. Townsmen appeared on the walks. Lights, dimmed during the occupancy of the outfits, sprang up again. George Bernay saw Judith Cameron come from the dressmaking shop and hurry up the street; Ab Cameron saw her too, for he turned down toward her, calling out in a strange, hopeless way: "Daughter—go back." But it wasn't that scene George Bernay was immediately interested in. Five men—five of Head's men—remained by the jail-office door; they made a compact and vigilant group there. George Bernay sucked in a long breath. He reported what he saw to Surratt.

"Sure," murmured Surratt. "Bill Head wants to be certain I'm in the cooler when he comes back." He walked around the cell; he put his hands to the solid walls as he circled and he came back and stood at the door. His eyes were restless; his muscles were restless.

Bernay wheeled from the window and started down the hall. "See you later."

"George," called Surratt, and brought the man to a halt. "Don't," added Surratt, "try anything rough on Bolderbuck. That fellow is white."

"This is no time to think of that," said George Bernay.

Surratt's voice hit him like the flat of an ax. "Bernay." It widened George Bernay's eyes. It shocked him. "There's never any time to forget a white man," said Surratt, cold and exact with his words. "You remember that."

George Bernay walked down the stairs, not nearly as certain as he had been a moment before. He paused in the jail office. Bolderbuck sat before a flat desk, with his back to the wall and his face bent on the open doorway. But the marshal's face was heavy with his thinking, and he seemed only vaguely aware of Bernay, who went on out of the place. Head's five men were watching him carefully and Hughie Grant was grinning at him. He went by them without comment, but Grant's amused advice followed him down the street. "Don't be rash, Georgie, my boy."

Cameron and Judith had gone on to the dressmaking shop. That way George Bernay turned, his mind marching nearer and nearer a fixed conclusion. At the saloon corner he found Jud Horsfall poised in the alley shadows. George said: "Come on—and where's Billy Temple?"

"Down there," said Jud, pointing toward the dressmaking shop. They fell in step and passed the saloon. One townsman came out of the saloon, and through the momentary opening of the doors George saw the place empty save for the bartender and Neal Irish, who sat bowed over a game of solitaire. They turned into the dressmaking shop. The two girls were there with Ab Cameron and Billy Temple; and a woman—Annette Carvel's mother—sat in the background, saying nothing.

Judith spoke to her father: "It will take you an hour to get to the ranch and bring the boys back here. That's enough—to get Surratt out."

Cameron showed his uncertainty and confusion, he showed his age. "No," he said. "No, Daughter. I can't ask the boys to stack up against Billy Head."

"I can!" said Judith. There was a vigor and a resoluteness about the girl George Bernay profoundly respected then. She was a woman, a full and gallant woman.

145

There was a spirit shining in her eyes now that brought his own stray thinking to that final point beyond doubt. But Ab Cameron shook his head sadly.

"They'd be gone by the time I got there. Bill Head sent a man to bring them to him. Anyhow it would do us no good. They're loyal to me, no doubt. But they've got to live in this country and it would be hell to set 'em against the Head crowd and the Peyrolles crowd and Dutch Kersom's crowd." The silence that followed his statement seemed to arouse him a little. "You don't know Bill Head," he told them simply. "If I crossed his desires in this matter I'd have no men on my ranch within a week. Nor would I ever be able to hire anybody. We cannot help Surratt."

Judith considered her father in a quick, comprehending way, as though she saw and felt what his life had been; and she touched his arm, gently smiling. "I am sorry," she murmured.

George Bernay passed a long look to Billy Temple, and Jud Horsfall came toward the center of the room, and then these three men were silently, narrowly speculating. Horsfall softly suggested the thought. "There's five of 'em up there in front of that jail door, kid."

"It's Hughie Grant that's tough," pointed out Billy Temple.

George Bernay said: "Well?"

The other people caught on then. The thing these three young men were thinking became that plain and that strong. Ab Cameron had a half-smoked cigar in his mouth. He lighted a match; his fingers shook. He turned the full worry of his eyes on George Bernay. "I'd advise you not to try. I have seen a good deal of tragedy in this country. We're all seeing some now. Sam Torveen's about run his course and I strongly doubt if Surratt gets out of that jail alive. Even if he does, nothing can change the end of this affair. This is cattle country. Sheep will never come. The big outfits won't permit it—and Bill Head speaks for the big outfits. You will be one more outlaw, to be treated as such. Don't think of it."

But George Bernay said to Temple: "We'll walk up behind the buildings on the north side and come out there, across from the jail."

Annette Carvel's face turned to George Bernay; it was white and round and surprised. Her lips opened. She seemed to be seeing him for the first time. Her eyes took him in carefully, as they would a stranger. Billy Temple said again: "It's this Hughie Grant. . . ."

"I'll have a look at his hole card," murmured George Bernay. "He seems pretty proud of it. The back door, Jud——"

"No, George!" commanded Judith.

He said: "Judith, that fellow Surratt's my friend, and I don't know why. It's a thing that gets you. There's no fear in the man. Why, hell, I'd——"

He bit the sentence between his teeth and he leaped for the doorway. There was a shot's solid smash filling the street, and one replying echo, and the sudden short rush of horse's hoofs, and a man's voice laid a massive unhurried order across Morgantown. George Bernay went through the doorway. He trotted up the street, colliding with other townsmen coming out of the buildings into the lamp-softened shadows. Even as he ran, he saw horsemen close in on the jail door and surround the five Crow Track hands. There was no more gunplay. Forty feet away, with Horsfall and Temple at his heels, he identified the enormous, shapeless bulk of Blackjack Smith. Blackjack had four riders with him; he had dropped out of the darkness without warning. It was his lifted and pointed gun that seemed to hold Head's men thoroughly silent by the jail wall.

One of Blackjack's men turned in his saddle. He called at Bernay: "Hold up!"

George Bernay yelled: "Hey, Blackjack!"

Blackjack didn't look around. But he identified George Bernay's voice and his voice accepted Bernay. "You'll do, George. Get in here and drop these fellow's belts for me. I hear Surratt's upstairs."

Bernay pushed his way through the horses. Four of Head's men were motionless against the jail wall, their hands risen. The fifth man lay on the board walk. He was on his back, rolling from side to side. Looking down briefly into that set, gritting face, Bernay marked Hughie Grant with a cold pleasure.

"He ain't hurt much," said Blackjack indifferently.

"I'll write your ticket!" gasped Hughie Grant.

"My ticket," said Blackjack, "was written before you were born. Stay around here, boys, while I go inside." He dropped to the ground with an agility strange to so ponderous a shape. He stood a moment, watching George Bernay strip away the gun belts from these Head men and throw them far out into the street; and darkly and taciturnly he enjoyed that scene for a moment. Afterwards he entered the jail office. Bernay followed.

Bolderbuck hadn't risen from his chair. He sat there and looked at the two men with a glance that was unreadable, that was shrewd and stubborn and fixed. Blackjack shook his head; there was a small regret and a perceptible courtesy in his words.

"You know me, Tom, and I know you. But I heard Surratt was here and I want him out."

"The man's got friends in strange places," observed Bolderbuck quietly.

"It's his way, Tom."

Bolderbuck bent forward. He put his elbows on the table in front of him and lowered his cheeks. He remained so, engaged with his difficult thoughts. Blackjack stood mountainously calm, letting the marshal have his silence out. When Bolderbuck reared back in the chair there wasn't any change in his manner. The crisp blue of his eyes steadied on Blackjack. "Surratt's in jail on a warrant, which is legal and proper. I've been a peace officer pretty near twenty years and in that time I never let a man go and never lost one. I'm kind of pleased to think of the record."

Bernay started to speak, and changed his mind. For Bolderbuck's hand had shifted up to his vest, to the thin silver crescent that was his badge of authority. "As long as I'm marshal I'd see you in hell before I gave Surratt up. But it works the other way, too. The boy is in a death trap up there. I cannot protect him against what Head plainly intends to do. I do not know of any other answer to this." His fingers touched the badge and unsnapped it. He laid it on the table, beside a ring of keys. "When a man can't see his way in a plain light it's time to quit. So there the star lays and there's the keys."

Bernay reached for the keys and walked up the stairs. Bolderbuck shot a frosty glance at the silent Blackjack. "Head's a pretty powerful enemy for you to be makin', Blackjack. You've had your parsnips well buttered, till now. You're goin' to discover what trouble is."

Surratt came down the stairs with Bernay behind him. He looked at Blackjack and saw how it was. He turned to Bolderbuck. "Tom," he said regretfully, "this is a thing——"

"Your luck still holds," commented Bolderbuck. "I'm

pleased with the way it goes. But you better be on your horse soon."

Surratt went out of the jail office into the shadow-thickened street; and was smiling as he went to a Crow Track horse and stepped up. Blackjack and Bernay had come from the office. It was quiet here, with a little group of townspeople collected by the White House and looking soberly on.

"Blackjack . . ." said Surratt.

"Go on," grumbled the big man. "Go on and ride. I never thought I'd live to see the day I'd do this."

George Bernay felt the pinch of time. "You better dust, before somebody comes pouring down that road."

"Where are you going now?" Surratt wanted to know.

"Not with you," Bernay instantly answered. "Get Sam out of the country—don't delay it. And so long."

Surratt turned from the group. But he halted here a moment, for his name had been called. Judith Cameron came riding fast up the street. She stopped beside him and her voice dropped low and none of that group heard what was said then. In the end she turned with Surratt and they both rode out of Morgantown.

Blackjack was in his saddle. George Bernay had turned to Horsfall and Billy Temple, and presently these two went back down the street on the run. Blackjack stared at George Bernay, not understanding. He said: "What's this now?"

But George Bernay didn't answer till Horsfall and Temple returned with their own horses and his. Then he said: "Company for you, Blackjack."

Blackjack said sourly: "We're no company for you boys."

"Go along," said Bernay; and then that group whirled away, into the hills. Hughie Grant sat propped against the jail office, cursing at them, but none of the other Head riders went over to pick their guns from the dust until Blackjack's group merged with the night.

Inside the jail office, Tom Bolderbuck lighted himself a fresh cigar and stood up. He ran his finger across the badge which lay on the desk. He had no regrets. A literal-minded man to the extreme, he never crossed a bridge until he reached it—and this bridge he had crossed because there was no other way. Yet he was displeased with himself and didn't know why. He left the jail office, passing the Crow Track men without a backward look.

Bill Head's wrath would visit him soon enough he realized; yet he went to the hotel porch and sat in a rocker there and somberly smoked his cigar.

A mile from Morgantown George Bernay said to Blackjack, "Wait," and his order stopped the party.

"You ain't in a hurry to go anywhere particular?" suggested Bernay.

"No."

"Turn here then," directed Bernay; whereupon the group entered a trail and vanished toward the south.

Chapter Fifteen

DEATH COMES
TO A MAN

As soon as they got beyond Morgantown, Surratt left the pass road. Faint moonlight seeped through the trees, showing him the vague arch of another road leading into the south. Judith said: "Where are we going, Buck?"

"To a point on the river where a man named Modoc Niles was killed."

"There?" she murmured. Afterwards she added: "I know the way."

"Take the lead. I'm just going at it blind."

They ran on through the crisp and pungent night for a matter of three miles or so before she turned to the east and fell upon a corduroy trail leading into the higher hills. They passed much later a ranch house in a low meadow, from which a single light was cheerfully shining. "Billy Temple's place," she said, over her shoulder. Then they were in the solid trees and no light got through this green wall to show them the way. The trail turned, but they left it and pursued a narrowing slash upward. At one point they stopped to let the horses blow and Surratt's attentive ears quested the far, deep stillness for the sound of Head's searching scouts. Judith's voice was as soft as a breath of wind.

"I think they've not had time to spread down this way."

They continued, walking where the hill slopes sharply tipped, cantering when the ground ran level. It was a half-hour later that Surratt saw a streak of moonlight coming down through the pines and knew they were at the edge of a north-and-south road of some consequence. His senses lifted at once; for a rumor struck forward definitely. He said, "Wait," and drew in. There was a strengthening echo over on the left; Judith came beside him then, and her hand reached out and fell on his arm, the pressure of her fingers tightening as the moments

151

dragged. Riders—two or three of them—went by on the road, vaguely visible through the brush. They waited until the sound had faded, then crossed the road and kept rising with the slope. Head's men were spreading fast, laying a loose net through all the hills; thinking of this, Surratt's attentive senses reached more keenly into the tricky, felt-thick shadows. But there was a part of his mind free to have its way with him, and that part was filled with the strange and strong impressions of this girl. Her shoulders swayed faintly as she rode and he saw now and then the trim outline of her head turning gracefully. The tone of her voice, when she broke the long riding silence, was a tone that struck soft and clear and vital across all uncertainty.

She had stopped with a warning abruptness and she was bending forward. Brought stiffly up, he saw a meadow's yellow glow directly to the fore—and the blurred, still shape of a horseman in it. This was only a hundred yards away, near enough to betray to that one the steady draw of their horses' breathing. Yet the man, poised as though listening, seemed not to hear it; and presently he slid on across the meadow and vanished with a minute rattle of the surrounding thicket. Judith veered around the meadow, holding her pony to a slow walk. The meadow dropped behind and afterwards the sightless trail fell between tall shoulders of rock. Sparks shot up from the shoes of Judith's animal, creating a pale spray of light, and the sound of that concussion rode the stillness hugely. They were out of the defile. The ruffled run of water came to them softly then—and the faint odor of wood-smoke was abroad. Judith stopped here and Surratt went ahead of her. It was for only a dozen yards. Halted, he sent a small, gentle challenge at the blackness.

"Nick."

The answer seemed almost under his feet; and it came in a rush of expelled breath. "That was close," sighed Perrigo's voice. "Who's with you?"

"Miss Cameron."

"Go ahead."

"Somebody riding around here, Nick. We saw a fellow cross a meadow just below." He went on with Judith, dropped down the short bluff and followed the gravelly bottom of the old-time river bed. A remote glow indicated the mouth of the cavern, with a shape angularly placed

152

against the glow. Ferd Bowie's challenge met them as they got down.

"That's all right, kid," grunted Surratt. He took Judith's arm and led her into the cavern. Around its quick bend firelight jumped freshly at them and the pungent smoke was thick here. Ed and Doc Brann stood close by the fire; Sam Torveen was a shape under the blankets, his head turned their way. Judith dropped down to her knees, and Surratt heard her voice break and be near to crying. "Oh, Sam—what have they done to you?"

All of them were watching Sam Torveen's gray face brighten. The presence of this girl was a warmth that smoothed and softened his pain. The deep dark-drawn lines of his face eased. There was a faint loosening of his lips into the old, skeptic smile. His one good arm reached up and touched Judith's shoulders. "Honey," he murmured, "I'm sure glad you're here, but it's one hell of a place for you to be."

Judith wheeled toward Brann. "Be honest—how bad is this?"

"He's all right," said Brann casually. "It was a lot of blood he lost."

Sam Torveen never let his eyes turn from Judith. Hope was strong in them and pleasure put spots of color on his drawn cheeks. "It's a help to know you thought enough to come," he said humbly.

"Sam," she murmured; and then she was quietly crying. Bending her head she kissed him on his stubbled chin. Surratt jerked around on his heels and walked back to the mouth of the cave.

He stood there, glowering into the liquid blackness, with a still more profound blackness in his brain. He got out his pipe and automatically packed it. The light of the match, when he lifted it to the pipebowl, showed the bony set of his jaws. There was a pattern to a man's life and it never changed; there was a fate that covered him from beginning to end and neither hope nor bitter fighting could temper that. He dragged the smoke heavily into his hale lungs, all wild and savage-tempered and reckless from knowing he never would have this girl. His eyes, against his own wishes, had looked ahead and saw some faint gleam of luck. He knew definitely and bitterly now that he had fooled himself. The morning half of the trail was always bright with the newness of things, and the way was fresh and full of pleasant prospect. The second half was only regret for what had been and what never would be. He was on the afternoon side of his journey now, with no shade for a traveler along this way until the final sundown came.

Perrigo glided softly out of the night. Ferd Bowie came from somewhere and remained vaguely behind Perrigo. Brann and Ed and the girl walked from the tunnel. They made a loose group there.

"Can we move him?" asked Surratt.

"No," said Brann, "you can't. The boy's lost too much blood."

"Where'd you want to move him?" asked Perrigo.

"Over the peaks, out of this country." The bowl of Surratt's pipe cut a round, crimson hole in the shadows. "It's not my habit to give up easy, but Sam's lost this fight. Bill Head's throwing forty or fifty men into the hills. It is only a question of time till we're found. I wouldn't want Sam to get in their hands now, not with one killing to his credit and a bunch ready to settle that score."

"You can't move him," repeated Brann very definitely. "He's unable to ride or walk."

"Then we'll have to play our white chips like we were proud of 'em. Put out that fire, Ed."

"Nobody can see it."

"No, but you can smell it for a mile."

They stood thoroughly still for a little while, having nothing to say. Surratt watched Ferd Bowie's thin shape sway and swing. The kid went away, his boots scuffling up a small noise. Perrigo turned to follow. Brann murmured, "Well, we'll make a night of it," and went back into the cave with Ed. Judith remained. It was long afterwards when her voice came to him, low and rather sad.

"It's like a light going out, Buck—when you give up hope."

He stared at the shapeless bulk of the gravel bank which separated this old stream's course from the river. A tempest stormed up from that wild, lonely place in him which lay beyond his will, out of that very core of his body where were bred his most reckless angers and his gentlest regrets. He bit his jaws against it. "You had better be riding back."

"No—I'm staying here."

He said, "All right," and moved away from her to the gravel bank. He sat down there. She stood a moment, uncertain and silent, and then came forward. She settled beside him, her shoulder against his shoulder.

"You don't mind?" she asked softly.

"No."

He put his hands across his knees and locked his big fists together. Her hand came out to touch his fists; and the coldness and smallness of that hand did strange things to him, past his understanding. He put it between his palms.

At once she turned, and he saw the pale oval of her face come near to him and rest on his chest. Her body tipped in and she was crying in a silent intense way that shook all the courage and pride and serenity out of her. He laid his arms around her, holding her thus against the moment's despair. He had never seen Judith cry, he had never seen a break in her strength before—and it was hard for him to endure, this hurt he could not help.

His thoughts ran on with an instant's immeasurable clarity. He had held Annette Carvel this way and felt the frank, passionate offering of a girl he didn't want. Stirred as he had been, he had felt only a pity. But in his arms now was a sweetness and a richness that filled all the empty places of his body, allowing him for this short fragment of time to know what completeness could be. This was the full treasure of a man's dreaming. The best of his life was here at this moment, soon to pass away. For he knew he would never hold her again and he knew that the rest of his days would be deeper in want, from the memory of this. The fragrance of her hair touched his senses. She lay quietly in his arms, the rhythm of her breathing growing calmer. He had no way of stopping the one desire he felt; and so he said, "Judith," and when her face lifted he kissed her. Her lips were cool and firm and not afraid; and there was something in her that made him savagely happy—a quality that through the years would never grow less, something she could give to a man, yet never lose. She straightened and sat beside him again, not speaking. But he wasn't ashamed and he felt no need to apologize.

He said, quietly: "Sam's all right. There's still a trick or so I can try."

"And after that?"

"I don't know. I quit asking questions about tomorrow a long while ago."

She said gently: "You're a very wise man, Buck. But not wise enough to know why I should be crying now."

155

"Luck," he murmured, "comes even to the poorest of us. I had mine just now. It is a thing to remember beside many a campfire."

She rose swiftly and went back into the cave.

At noon of the following day Pokey crawled to the edge of the river and saw, diagonally across the stream, the face of the tunnel. Surratt stood there in the heavy sunlight with Judith Cameron, and the sight of the girl jerked up Pokey's eyebrows and left him slowly considering it. He had his rifle with him and when, half an hour later, Perrigo came out of the farther trees and dropped down the bluff to the tunnel, Pokey lifted his gun and had a clean chance at the little man. Pokey lined him up through the sights; he took up the trigger's slack and suspended his breath for the final pull. But he never made it. Instead, he lowered the gun and had a little talk with himself. He shook his head with some disgust and crawled back into the timber. After that he rode a mile down the river, crossed over and approached the hideout again. Putting his horse in the brush he squatted by the edge of that trail which led to the hideout, waiting with an inevitable patience.

When Perrigo came up to the tunnel, with Pokey's distant gun trained on him, he had completed a morning's swing through the hills. He crouched in front of Surratt and the girl, resting himself. Sweat ran freely along his very dark and very thin cheeks. "Plenty tracks around here," he said. "That fellow you saw last night in the meadow was within a hundred yards of this spot. A big bunch has been see-sawin' back and forth about a half-mile below. They keep cuttin' a higher trail each time. I saw men over on the pass road. The fords are pretty well covered. No chance of sneakin' over any bridges either. I think Head's workin' the country from the falls this way, piece at a time."

"Methodical," commented Surratt.

"One time I had my gun pointed on a fellow not more'n seventy feet off," grumbled Perrigo. "He was scoutin' alone." He looked at Judith. "One of your dad's men. He up here?"

"Bill Head sent for the men," said Judith bitterly. "Dad has no say in the matter."

"Your father," grunted Perrigo, "has been under the

156

Heads a good many years. He never had the claws and teeth to fight back. Where's Ferd?"

Surratt had started into the tunnel, but he wheeled when the question came. "He left here an hour ago, to hunt for you. Didn't see him?"

"No," said Perrigo. He considered that a long while. His face turned thin and noncommittal. He met Surratt's glance. "No," he repeated more slowly, "Ferd never went down that trail. His tracks don't show."

Judith knew what they were thinking. She said: "I have always thought Sam made a mistake using that man. He was nervous as a cat around here this morning." She stopped, then burst out: "You don't think he'd betray Sam?"

"Not Sam," countered Perrigo.

"Who, then?"

Perrigo put his finger out toward Surratt. He didn't say anything. He slapped a hand sharply across his thigh and stood up, going back to the trees on foot. He was traveling at a sort of crouched dogtrot when he vanished in the green undergrowth.

"There's another man I doubted," murmured Judith. "Somehow, I don't now."

They turned into the tunnel. The closeness of water made it damp and chilly in here, and the light was bad. Brann sat on the gravel with his coat collar turned up. His eyes were bloodshot from smoke and want of sleep. Ed was in another corner of the tunnel, dead to the world after putting in half the night patrolling. Torveen lay quietly underneath his blankets, but he grinned at sight of Judith.

"No chance of getting back to town before dark?" asked Brann.

"Hills are full of Head's men," countered Surratt. "You tired of waiting?"

"I left a full house on Neal Irish's poker table," grumbled Brann. "I——"

A far-off shot's echo stopped his talk. It came through the cave's dead air and turned them all. There was a second echo, and a third one, with a deliberate space of time between. Somebody deeper in the green slopes was signaling. The group held that attitude of waiting, constrained by the meaning of the sound.

"Gettin' nearer," observed Brann.

Judith looked at Torveen, a darkness across her fine gray eyes. "I hate to think of you being caught like a rat in a trap! What would happen if we went out and found Sheriff Ranier and surrendered to him?"

But Brann and Surratt and Torveen said, "No," almost in unison. The unanimity of their reactions surprised her. She looked at Surratt and found him humorlessly smiling. "Surrender isn't in the book of rules Bill Head carries, Judith."

"Ranier," grunted Brann, with the full shading of contempt, "is a weathervane."

Judith said nothing more, but her eyes glowed with a fresh anger, and her shoulders straightened and color came to her face. Surratt watched this, his faint smile turning sad. "Don't worry," he counseled her quietly. "There's one more deal left in the deck."

Torveen turned his face toward Brann. "Brann," he said, "look at those two people. There they are—the two finest friends I've ever had. By God, I'm happy for my luck—and I don't know what I'd do if I lost 'em. Don't they make a fine pair, Brann? Look at 'em!"

Brann said, "Uhuh." He had his glance on Surratt and the girl—a quick, keen glance—and dropped his eyes.

Surratt swung away, his question brusque. "What time is it?"

Brann looked at his watch: "Past two-thirty. Long day."

There was then the full rush of a shot's report, so near at hand that it rang against the rock walls. One shot and only one. Brann jerked himself upright; and Ed, sound asleep a moment before, sprang out of his blankets. Surratt was instantly on his way down the tunnel. He threw back a curt order, "Stay here," and halted at the edge of the sunlight a moment. But he thought he knew where that shot came from and ran up the side of the bluff and entered the trail. A horseman went smashing through the yonder brush. Perrigo's voice, beyond sight, was thin and fading; guided by its diminishing tone, Surratt plowed his way into the thicket. There was twenty yards off the trail, a small clearing. Coming upon it with a rush, he found Perrigo lying there, trying to support himself on an elbow. When he saw Surratt his elbow collapsed and he fell on his shoulder. "Watch out, Surratt!"

Surratt bent. "He's runnin'. Who was it?"

Perrigo began to cough in a slow, terrible way. Fear sprang into his black eyes and dilated them tremendously. He choked off the cough, little body racked by that effort. "I knew it would come like this someday."

"Bowie?"

Perrigo said faintly: "Him—no. Never mind. Damn Martin Head—he knew! He knew all the time! There's a terrible man to have against you."

Blood bubbled through a small round hole in Perrigo's chest. Perrigo lifted his head and saw that rent in his lungs and his hand reached up to cover it, like a gesture of decency. His lips stretched, they sagged at the corners; yet watching him, Surratt observed the fatalism and the grit at the bottom of Perrigo's nature come up to fight this mortal darkness into which he was slipping. Perrigo's voice kept ebbing, even while the desire to talk powerfully urged him. "Listen," he murmured, "I shot Les Head. It was why I mistrusted you. Thought you knew I'd done it. Surratt, keep watch over my girl."

"What?" said Surratt.

"Annette," murmured Perrigo. "That's my secret and Mrs. Carvel's. Annette don't know, but she's my girl. It was a mistake of long ago, and it has been on my mind a long while. She was a kid that grew up like a flower wantin' sun. She trusted men too much, and always wanted men to like her. I saw that coming up with Les Head, who was a dog and took what he could get. I have no regrets for puttin' him out of the way. It was why I did it—so he'd never hurt her."

He stopped a moment, bitterly holding himself alive. His voice afterwards was merely a suspiration of falling breath. "I have had her on my mind since she got to the age of attractin' men. By God, Surratt, I have hated all the breed of men, out of fear! It is why I disliked you. But it was a mistake, for I've watched you and found you an honest man. If you wasn't, you wouldn't be here fightin' Sam Torveen's fight. You take care of her for me, Surratt. I remember seein' her go to school when she was seven, with a red bow in her hair. Hell is a place that has no worries for me. I've had my hell watchin' a daughter I couldn't own. . . ."

Looking down at him, Surratt saw that he was dead.

He heard a sound then, small and scurrying; it struck the back of his neck, and pure reaction rolled him aside and around—thereby avoiding the bullet that scuffed up a thin furrow of soil where he had been. The rush of the shot filled the little clearing; and Ferd Bowie was there at the edge of it, his gun wheeling to catch Surratt's awkward shape on the ground. Surratt reached and seized the butt

159

of his revolver and snapped a quick shot. But it had been a chance aim and it went wide. Bowie ducked his head as that bullet's breath poured along on his cheek and then he whirled, as though his nerves and his courage could not hold him against Surratt's firing, and crashed out of sight in a low long dive. Surratt tried that area with a second bullet. He was on his feet, running against the brush. He heard Bowie cursing off there, behind the trees—and he stopped, faced by the risk of another ambush. Bowie had reached his horse. In a moment he was in the deep timber, racing away.

Chapter Sixteen

CORNERED

He looked back at Perrigo lying sprawled in that senseless, bottomless sleep, and for a moment he permitted himself to feel the tragedy of Perrigo's life, as Perrigo had felt it—the defeat and deep loneliness which so long had racked that small frame. Judged on the scales of human behavior this man had been bad and his snuffed-out life was no loss to the hills; yet he had died thinking of a little girl with a red bow in her hair walking under the sun, clutching at that memory with the regret common to all men, good and bad alike. For a moment Surratt understood this and for a moment he gave Perrigo his due; then he closed it out of his head and turned back to the cave, knowing then what his own duty was.

Judith and Brann and Ed were at the mouth of the cave. He said: "We've lost Perrigo."

Judith's eyes clung to him, wide and dark. But Brann didn't seem surprised. "What was those other shots?"

"That was Bowie having his say," murmured Surratt. "But he missed me—and he ran."

"The dog," murmured Ed, "will give us away."

"What time is it?"

"After three," said Brann.

"The shots have already given us away," reflected Surratt. "Anyhow, the fellow that got Perrigo knows we're around here. Crow Track will come over and beat up this section. It's four hours till dark. Brann, when can Sam be moved?"

"Tomorrow, maybe—but not under his own power."

Surratt turned into the tunnel. He had to stand a moment near Torveen before his eyes adjusted themselves to the semidarkness. Torveen's face, turning around to him, was strained and depressed.

"Somebody got Perrigo from the brush—and Bowie's run away."

"I heard the shootin'," sighed Torveen. He tried to lift himself—and fell back, breath thumping in and out of him. "I'd just as soon be dead as this!"

Surratt noticed the feebleness of the man then. Brann hadn't told them the whole truth concerning Torveen's condition. He said, "You hang tight," and picked up Torveen's gun belt. He thumbed half the cartridges from their loops and put them into his pocket.

"Kid," said Torveen, "we've played out our string. I think you better dust over the pass and be on your way."

Surratt grinned. "I've observed Bill Head to be a man who gets his ideas on the third bounce. It's the way we work this now. But you'll have to grit your teeth to it, Sam."

"What?"

Surratt turned back to the mouth of the tunnel. Ed had gone off somewhere, leaving the girl and Doc Brann here in the hard sunlight. The smell of the late day was resinous; the air clung to the ground, motionless and smoky and hot. There was, he observed, a fear in these two people. Brann's indifference couldn't hide it, and Judith Cameron's eyes were dark with what she thought. He said to Brann: "I can give you tonight—I think I can. But it is all I can give you."

"How'll we move him?" grumbled Brann. "He's weak as a dragged cat. The boy's hurt, you understand?"

"Let him take his choice of chances," said Surratt evenly. "There's little left to choose from. You've got tonight."

"Why?"

"Because I'm giving it to you," explained Surratt. "When dark comes you fix a way of moving him. Not farther up the hills, like Head might expect, but back down. It is around six miles, I'd guess, to Temple's house. How could Head think of him bein' there, that close to Morgantown?"

"No," said Brann, "I——"

But Surratt spoke with a real anger. "I thought you were a poker player!" He turned instantly away from them. Judith called his name. He didn't look back; he kept on, going up the bluff and into the brush where the horses were. Ed was there, standing without much purpose against his pony. Surratt swung into his saddle. "Ed," he said, "if you hear firin' after dark tonight, up in the north, that's your signal to get out of here." Judith was once more calling; he heard her running up the bluff. Turning his horse, he drove through the brush and reached the trail and galloped along it.

When he had gone two hundred yards he slid into the trees. There was a ridge rising in front of him, a piece of high ground separating this region from the pass road. He headed that way. Now and then, down some narrow vista, he got a quick glimpse of the sun, harsh and glittering in the west. The river was on his near right, sinking slowly into its deeper bed. Twenty minutes after leaving the hideout he came to a trail cutting across his route, a thin and winding alley through the forest twilight. Riders, he observed from the marks in the humus soil, had been this way during the afternoon. He crossed the trail and disappeared in the rising tangle of the ridge.

A mile from the scene of Perrigo's shooting, Pokey abandoned his brush riding and took the trail leading to the pass road. He had heard the subsequent firing—which was the swift duel between Surratt and Ferd Bowie—and he had been puzzled by it. Yet he felt himself safe, for Head riders were crossing and recrossing all this area with an increasing regularity, and his judgment told him none of Torveen's remaining party would venture after him. So he rode along at a casual gait, his little body humped over and his toes pointing outward, deep-sunk in his own strict reflections. There was a conscience in this wiry little man and an imagination, yet Perrigo's death affected him only remotely. For at bottom, Pokey was the henchman forever bound. Martin Head's word had been law with Pokey for twenty years and the knowledge of his exact obedience to that law was his pride. Martin Head had been injured by this Perrigo; therefore Perrigo was an enemy. Martin Head, terrible in his sense of right and wrong, had told Pokey to find and kill Perrigo; therefore Pokey went out to obey with a faithfulness that was almost oriental and a lack of compunction that was pure fatalism. To Pokey, Martin Head was God.

Bill Head, Pokey knew, had established a kind of headquarters on the pass road; that way Pokey drifted. But before he got there he swung to go up a little ridge whence he might have a view of the back trail. It was always his custom to keep his rear well guarded. From his vantage point he saw a group of men over on the pass road, less than a mile removed, with riders coming into the road at intervals and other parties leaving on fresh scouts. Having no love for Bill Head, Pokey remarked all this confusion with a critical eye; they were blotting out the scent with their ceaseless blundering. Afterwards his glance swung around and then he saw a horseman coming along the same trail he had used, apparently bound for Bill Head's location. He would have put the man out of his mind had it not been for the way in which that rider kept ducking off the trail at intervals. It was a nervousness that could belong to no Head rider. When the fellow got a little closer Pokey put his attention on the horse, which was plainer to his eye than the rider. There wasn't a horse in the country Pokey couldn't identify at a distance by its gait and color and height; and immediately he recognized Ferd Bowie's long-barreled pearl gelding.

Pokey's eyes winked carefully. He thought he understood what Bowie was up to, for Bowie had no standing among honorable men anywhere. Whereupon Pokey searched his mind for Old Martin Head's will in the matter and his own inclinations. He came to a prompt decision, cut down the ridge and stationed himself slightly to one side of the trail. When Bowie came around a farther bend Pokey moved into sight and stood quietly there.

At sight of Pokey, Bowie jerked back in his saddle. He was fifty feet away, and for a time Pokey thought the angular, gray-faced kid meant to bolt into the brush. He called out then.

"Where you goin, Ferd?"

"Pokey, I want to see you," said Bowie.

"Sure," said Pokey. "Only it's a poor place for you to be."

Bowie was cocked in his saddle, ready for trouble and suspecting it. But there was a stronger desire in his narrow head. That desire kept him from running. Pokey's hatbrim dropped against the low-thrown shafts of sunlight; nevertheless his glance clung to the least jerk of Ferd Bowie's high-strung muscles. He had no faith in the kid.

Bowie said: "I've had enough. I'm pullin' out of here."

"Turn and go the other way," suggested Pokey. "Or you'll get shot on sight."

"I can take care of myself. I want to make talk."

Pokey said nothing; the set of his face was sad and bland and unrevealing.

"You want to know where Surratt is?"

"Why you tellin'?"

"You want to know?" insisted Bowie. He looked around, his nervousness a growing thing. Then the long, pallid and savage face whipped disconcertingly back on Pokey. "Go up this trail three miles to the river bank. They're in that cave by the bend."

"You're sellin' out Sam Torveen?" murmured Pokey. "A handsome thing, Ferd. To sell out a man that fed and kept you. A handsome thing."

"Surratt's there." said Bowie, the name emerging from his throat in a hateful way.

Pokey's lips turned faintly at the corners. Little as he liked the kid, it was always his way to keep an open mind toward the sins and errors of men, to be slow in condemning them. But there was with him, as with all the riders in this Western country, an implicit adherence to one range commandment, the betrayal of which put a man past mercy or charity. Torveen had rested his faith in this kid, and now Ferd Bowie was betraying him. He said, with a softness that should have warned Bowie beyond a doubt: "Ferd, I'd hate to stand in your shoes at judgment seat."

Bowie bent forward in his saddle and stared across the interval with a consuming attention. "It comes to me, Pokey, you're Martin Head's man but no friend of Bill Head. Maybe I should have thought of that. Never mind. I'll find somebody who'll take my word to Bill."

"Sure," said Pokey. "Sure."

Silence came on in a tight. brittle way. Bowie wanted to get off the trail, but motion had become in the last ten seconds a risky thing. He was no fool and he saw how still Pokey remained and how wickedly calm Pokey's cheeks were. He pulled back on his reins and the pony stepped to the rear until it struck a clump of brush. Not daring to look about him to find a quick way of getting away from this spot, his nerves began to break. "Pokey," he called out angrily, "go on."

"Sure," said Pokey and wheeled his horse.

As he turned, his arm fell and rose with his gun and he put three bullets, one upon another, into that narrow swaying body down the trail without compunction and without pity. His third shot caught Bowie as the latter

165

made one vain, agony-driven effort to lift his gun. It was half risen when he died suddenly in the saddle, and fell out of it to the ground.

Pokey studied the lumpy shape of the kid a moment, hearing the echoes of this shooting roll and break and fade in the far corridors of the hills. He replaced the empty shells in his weapon with full loads and seated it in its holster; and trotted on toward the pass road.

When he came out upon the road he saw Bill Head and Hank Peyrolles standing close by, surrounded by a waiting group of riders. The crews of Head and Peyrolles and Cameron men were all mixed up here. Kersom and Kersom's hands seemed to be off on another scout.

"What was that shootin'?" demanded Head.

"Seemed like it was off yonder," remarked Pokey and vaguely smoothed his arm against the low, flashing sunlight.

"Where you been?"

"Just lookin'."

"See anything?"

"No," said Pokey. "Not a thing."

Bill Head's eyes considered Pokey without faith. Riders began to come out of the timber and collect here, brought back from their searching by the sound of the gunfire.

"I'll be going," suggested Pokey, turning his horse.

Bill Head stopped that with the bluntest possible command. "You stay here. I——"

He turned as though struck, his glance rising to the heights of the timber-clad ridge rising up on the road's south side. All the horses were pitching, and this group began to boil and run for the brush. Out of that high timber some man's long-range bullets began to arrive with a steady "spang," slanting into the road. They ripped up cloudy banners of dust; they made little dimpled whorls of dust. When they struck straight they had flat, snapping echoes; when they richocheted they whipped up a weird whining. This lead was landing above the riders, reaching no target; it kept hitting that same general spot, coming no closer. Pokey noticed that before he broke for shelter; noticed and considered it. All the riders were rushing into the thicket and Bill Head's voice started to crack around him like a whip. "Come over here! Get off that road!" The firing kept on, with the spaced regularity of a hammer driving down a nail. But it lifted from road to brush, the slugs spitting through leaf and cutting across tree bark. One horse let out a quick grunt and fell, throwing a Crow Track man forward on his face.

Peyrolles, by nature excitable, kept ducking and throwing up his hands. "By God, it's them! It's them, Bill! We got our cats up a tree!"

Head growled: "Shut up." He listened to the gunfire, his florid skin redder than it had been. A bullet left its breath on him in passing by; he moved without haste to the nearest tree and leaned behind it a moment, to continue his visual search of the heights of the ridge. He couldn't see well from his position, so he walked to the edge of the road and squatted down and thinly parted the thick sheaves of a hazel bush. He gestured at Peyrolles, who crawled cautiously over. "Watch," said Head. "You'll see smoke curling."

"Yes."

Bill Head walked back to his tree. He was of a sudden pleased and eager. "He can't cross this road without bein' seen. He can't run over to the river without bein' seen. Take your boys around that ridge and cut him off on that side."

"Him?"

"Surratt's doin' that," said Bill Head. "Everybody come here."

Pokey, aloof from this council, watched the group collect. Bill Head laid orders urgently about him. Peyrolles took his men and rode farther down the thicket, then went over the road at a rush. Bill Head ran to his horse as though anxious to have his fun. He had ten riders beside him when he broke through the brush and raced across the road to the yonder timber. The few men left behind moved away from Pokey toward the bridge, keeping to the shelter. Pokey remained indifferently in his saddle. He rolled himself a cigarette and lighted it, quietly listening to Head's hands crush on up the slope of the ridge. There was a calling over there. The shots of the hidden riflemen laid long, clear bars of sound across the still air and were silent for a while. All at once the sun dipped below the western line and its golden flash went out of the sky and a quick, pure-blue twilight ran through the alleys of this broken land. Pokey kept on smoking, plunged into his own obscure thoughts. Once he faintly smiled, which was rare for him.

On top of the ridge, less than half a mile away, Surratt

watched Peyrolles' column enter the trail which circled the ridge, and saw a second wave of riders afterwards cross the road and step into the timber directly below him. He knew the meaning of this maneuvering, but he remained awhile behind the bulwark of a deadfall. The sun was gone, with the quick powder blue of a timber country twilight flowing fast down these slopes. Head's fighters were crawling up through timber and thicket, well hidden, yet betrayed by the rattle of their progress. Now and then a voice lifted in that direction, its echo long floating in the soft air. The road below him was a pale-yellow streak turning sinuously downward toward Morgantown. Almost directly below stood the gray covered bridge crossing the river. A few hundred yards behind him the ridge dropped away to the water, but he already knew he could not find a footing down its stiff face. To reach the river he had either to descend to the bridge or retrace his path down the south side of the slope. The bridge route, he understood, was closed to him; for he saw the occasional stir of a man in the brush by the road, with one figure indistinctly appearing at intervals at the corner of the bridge itself. As for the other route—down the side of the ridge—he realized Peyrolles was rapidly sweeping around it to cut off his retreat.

That man at the corner of the bridge had raised some sort of a target. He began sending his shots up through the dimming air, dropping them wide of Surratt. The rattle of the climbing Head men was more distinct. He ducked away from the log, dropped down a small ravine and picked up his horse. In the saddle, he continued with the ravine, passing through satin-blue shadows spreading wider and deeper along all these secretive reaches. Somewhere a coyote lifted its wild wail to the high arch of infinity and something in that ancient call grimly reminded Surratt that he too was a member of that fraternity of the lost and the hopeless. But he had come here to stir up a steady firing, so that all Head's exploring men might be drawn back, so that the way would be clear for Sam Torveen's retreat. He seemed to be achieving his purpose.

The ravine became impassible, and he left it and swept leftward toward the river, still descending through the pines. In a quarter-hour darkness was definitive with a thin pale rind of a new moon slung low in the sky. Its faint glowing gave this darkness a vague silver luminosity treacherous to the eye, exaggerating distance and nearness alike. He had scarcely reached the bottom of the ridge when he made out Peyrolles' swift advancing.

The river was a slow murmur near by. He went that way, along a minute trail, and got to the graveled margin of the water. The far bank was a wall of shadow and the sluggishness of the river's running at this point warned him that it was a slack pool too deep for fording. Downstream, in the direction he meant to retreat, he saw a vague pillar rise high against the sky; and had a foreshadowed thought of trouble then. Leaving his horse in the brush he walked across the gravel until that pillar stood before his face. He laid his hand on it to discover the truth of his situation. The toe of the ridge dropped straight into the water. To pass it he had to swim around.

He stood here a little while, his mind searching fast for other ways of escape and finding none. To turn and go up the river's bank was to tow Head's men toward the tunnel. Otherwise he had no way of breaking through the cordon thrown around him except by putting away from shore, drifting down beneath the bridge and thus past the guard placed there. He had no liking for water and no skill with it, but this was the way it had to be. Cinching up his gun belt, he waded into the river. He was shoulder deep when the current lifted his feet and turned him along the smooth face of the cliff.

He rolled on his back to float, but the weight of his gun pulled him at once below the surface and instantly his fear of water became a thorough panic. He came up with his arms slashing enormous echoes through the night. He had been bumping along the edge of the cliff, but now that had drawn away from him and a quicker current threw him apparently into the center of the channel. He had, in this downbearing blackness, one hot and terrible moment; and then his sanity returned and he rolled with the current, quietly stroking.

They had lighted a fire on the road to make a barrier he could not pass. When he drifted below the toe of the ridge he saw a yellow, shuttering shaft of that light reach down and play a searchlight beam on the water's surface. Drifting toward this bright area, he let himself sink; when he came up again he was floating under the bridge, with the treading of some of Head's men plain in his ears. There was a grumbling of the current ahead, a lash of water against rocky shallows. Kicking his body around, he swam strongly for the bank. His boots touched bottom long after; when he finally walked out of the water he stood at the base of a low willow bank two hundred yards below the road and its fire.

He sat down and pulled off his boots and drained the water from them; and he remained here for a matter of minutes, ashamed of that little interval of dread he had experienced out in the current. Somebody on the yonder ridge sent three spaced shots across the darkness, the echoes long rolling through the hills. A voice kept calling. He got up then and climbed the bank. Groping through the trees, he came upon a trail and pursued it back toward the pass road; within twenty feet of the road he dropped to his knees. The fire was directly ahead of him, the shapes of men crouched in the brush illumined against it.

He saw no horses here. Therefore he swung away, sliding carefully from tree to tree. Near the road, seventy feet or so below the fire and in a little cleared patch between the pines, he found the horses. Nobody apparently guarded them, though in this blackness he could not be sure. Bill Head's voice kept calling along the ridge across the way —that sure bull-deep tone heavy and recognizable. Surratt walked into the little clearing swiftly and reached the nearest horse. He was up in the saddle; he was turning away, the horse uncertain and unsatisfied with its strange rider. But he hadn't moved five feet before a shapeless shadow sprang from the earth and stood directly underneath him. The man's voice sang out in an alarmed way:

"Wait—who's this?"

Surratt hauled the horse around and struck straight into the brush. He bent low, with his body turned and his gun lifting. He saw the man's revolver lick a purple streak across the dark; and then he fired at the streak and heard the sharp, astonished grunt of that man's breath. He slashed on through the brush and reached the road. All those hands by the fire were running straight down the road; and Head's voice grew enormous up on the hill. "What fool——!" The light of the fire reached vaguely out toward Surratt; he was dim in it, but still to be seen—and all the men had stopped their running. Fading on, Surratt rushed into the thicket again and heard the lead of their shots scurry and groan along the dust near by. He was out of that and beyond that when he came to the road once more. He kept to it now, racing downgrade for Morgantown. From the receding distance he made out Bill Head's booming yell rally up the crew.

Pokey, situated by the fire, saw Surratt vanish. Alone of the watchful group stationed here, he kept his place while the rest of them laced the night with their shots. Bill Head came smashing down the side of the ridge, howling at his men to follow. Pokey listened to all this, his little face taciturn against the light. Of a sudden he rose and dropped silently back to his horse. Forty minutes later he stood in the living room of the Head ranch, quietly reporting to Old Martin all that he had done.

When he had quite finished he looked away from Old Martin, for there was something so fierce, so blazing and so strange in the old cattleman's eyes that Pokey felt an unbearable shock.

"Pokey," said Old Martin, "get out the buckboard and drive me to Morgantown."

Chapter Seventeen

THE SUDDEN TURN

Two miles of steady running took Surratt beyond the sound of pursuit and it brought him to the edge of a vague side road reaching out of the southern broken land. He stopped, the racing recklessness in him settling down. He was at once raw and cold from his water-sogged clothing, but he listened to the rear for a few steady moments and heard nothing that indicated Bill Head was coming down. Considering that carefully, Surratt turned into the side road and followed it.

He knew little about this country and therefore had to fall back on his riding sense. He had gone, he supposed, two or three miles when he reached a stumpy clearing. The road simply disappeared, but Surratt swung to the east—in which direction the river lay—and explored the edges of the meadow until he found a break in the trees. This he took.

The going was slow and there was always the hint of stray Head riders to keep his senses honed sharp. Yet he thought he had succeeded in pulling all those exploring men over to the main road by his recent feint, and so he traveled with less caution. About an hour later he broke through solid brush and came upon the river. When he got his bearings he turned upstream, skirting the bluff of the river until he saw the mouth of the dry channel break through the silver-shot darkness. Here he halted and sent a quiet challenge forward.

He waited a long two minutes and heard no answer. Pushing down the bluff, he rode to the mouth of the tunnel. The smell of woodsmoke lay thinly in the air, but he could see no reflected glow of fire. He walked into the tunnel and turned its bend and faced pure blackness. He said: "Torveen," the echo of his voice striking the blank walls. He struck a match. Its glow threw a flickering beam

172

down upon an empty gravel floor; the charred circle of a dead fire lay on the gravel, and beside it the scooped-out spots where Torveen's bed had been. There wasn't anything here.

He left the tunnel immediately, satisfied they had retreated to Temple's ranch according to plan. And he turned that way with a slow satisfaction, drifting with the descending slope and crossing the meadow wherein, the night before, he and Judith had seen the Head rider posted. Beyond the meadow he entered the solid, black belt of pines. The trail was clear; he went along at a trot.

Water kept rolling down his skin, the night's slow wind turned him more and more cold, and his thoughts could find no breach in the wall Bill Head had put around Torveen. The bitter fact was, Torveen had been whipped. He had been driven off his ranch and could not return to it, and all that this night's riding had done was to give Torveen a temporary and fugitive safety. In Temple's place he could weather through his bullet wound; but when he was able to again ride there would be no safe road for him except the road that led across the pass to another land. Sam Torveen had shoved his chips to the middle of the table and made his bet. But Bill Head had drawn the better hand, leaving Torveen a ruined man. There was no way left to fight Bill Head, except by rousing the two-bit ranchers who believed, as Torveen believed, in free opportunity. But the weight of Head's riders kept them still; they had not come to Torveen's side.

For himself, Surratt acknowledged, it made no great difference. This was an episode that had neither more nor less meaning than any other. Beyond the pass lay another land, another day, another episode. But for Sam it meant the end of his fortune and his hope. And then, questing through this deep, dismal reach of pines, Surratt understood something else with an inexorable clarity. Torveen's faith was in him and he had no alternative but to face this trouble to the last end.

There was one way he had always known could be followed, which was the way an outcast might use—to ride by night, to shoot from ambush, to raid the big outfits at weak places, to strike and retreat and strike again, to throw this country into fear and confusion; to make men afraid of the daylight and leave them sleepless at night. It was a way of ruining the country. But it was not Surratt's way. He could not play that stealthy, prowling part. His

173

trail had to be open and his actions plain to all men. And, as he came through the trees and saw the dark outline of Billy Temple's house sitting in the sloping meadow below, he realized there was only one opening Bill Head had honestly left him, only one opening he could honestly take.

He had seen this coming. Whatever the results, whatever bearing it might have on his own fortunes or Sam Torveen's future, he had to accept the challenge of Bill Head's personal hatred. Bill Head had put him in the light of an outlaw and if he ran from it the thing would follow him like his own shadow the rest of his days. Moreover, he had in public named Bill Head yellow and Bill Head sought him now to answer that. He could not run from his words; he had to stand by them. It was once more the old, old pattern that never changed. There was a pride in men that terribly ruled them. Just or unjust, it governed them and gave to their lives a dignity they had to have.

He came softly across the meadow, sending his call against the lightless house. "Torveen." He waited there, feeling at once the emptiness of the place and not understanding it. A dog rushed forward from the house, snarling dismally at him. He called again, "Torveen," and rode on to the porch. He got down here, with the dog circling his feet. Crossing the porch, he stood by a closed door and tapped it and had no answer. He opened the door and saw a vague white square of paper sway loosely on the panel. When he called Torveen's name again, his voice ran dismally through the house; he knew definitely then that this place was deserted. He reached over and pulled the paper from the door and stepped inside to light a match. One word alone had been written on the paper: "Morgantown."

Whether it was for him or somebody else he didn't know. He whipped out the match and stood there, puzzled and thoughtful. There was warmth in this room that signified recent use; and a faint eye of light crept through a corner stove. He turned back to the porch and sat down to remove and drain his boots again. The dog crouched in the near-by dust, gutturally displeased. Surratt rose and went to the floor, to dig out of the panel the tack which had held the paper; he refixed the paper on the panel. Afterwards he went to his horse, swung up and left the yard. He was thinking now of Torveen, who had been in bad shape; maybe Brann had taken him to Morgantown as a last resort. At least he could think of no other meaning

174

the single word might convey, and so he swept down the plain road toward town.

He went at a slow canter, feeling the weariness of his horse; and it occurred to him then that he was weary too in a way that sleep could not help. The wind roved the pine tops, lifting up a steady, abrasive sound. It was, he judged, near eleven o'clock; and strangely his thoughts turned to Judith Cameron and her face was clear to him in the darkness, and the memory of her voice laid a soft and stirring and sad music in his mind. It was still with him, that melody, when he came out of the timber and found the lights of Morgantown below him.

All trouble, he recalled, struck at Morgantown from these hills—which would be therefore the quarter men watched. So he cut across the pass road, circled behind the buildings and came out at the lower end of the street. Paused, he scanned the street carefully.

But it was silent and almost empty. People were not sleeping—that he knew from the lights shining angularly out of shop and second-story windows. They were awake and waiting for the result of that quarreling up in the hills. This was Morgantown, a cockpit of cattle wars. Of the merchants and hangers-on here he had no fear, for they were like merchants the world over, keeping their opinions hidden from the partisans who rode so recklessly back and forth. It was Head's men he visually sought; and he saw none. A figure came through the saloon doors and turned upward along the board walk, passing the bank. Two men sat quietly on the porch of the White House. Somebody somewhere plunked casually at a guitar, and water spilled liquidly into a near-by drinking trough and made pleasant echoes. The smell of dust was in the slow wind. The door of the dressmaking shop stood open, a full lamplight streaming out.

He rode up the street, in the center of the street, and came abreast of the light and turned to catch the view of Annette Carvel standing inside. He was about to stop there when a voice came casually to him from the porch: "Surratt."

He rode over; and wet and hungry as he was his nerves began to whip up coolness and a restlessness. Old Martin Head sat there, blanketed in the dark, with Tom Bolderbuck beside him. It was Bolderbuck who had spoken, for he spoke again, the tip of his cigar throwing a faint glow

175

back upon the solid, enigmatic surface of his face. "Why?" said Bolderbuck.

"Torveen here?" said Surratt.

"No."

Old Martin Head's big torso tipped away from the chair. His head bent forward and Surratt felt all the tremendous power of that man's eyes strike against him, searching for weakness, searching for truth, searching for something. The saloon doors squealed behind Surratt. He threw a quick glance over there, to see Pokey coming across the dust. But Pokey recognized him and the shock of that threw the little man back on his heels, as though he had checked himself on the edge of some sharp drop. He remained thus frozen for a moment, letting Surratt's aroused attention have its way. Afterwards he drawled mildly: "That's all right," and walked a wide circle around Surratt and got to the hotel porch. He sat down, spreading his arms along his legs, so there could be no mistake about his intent.

"Surratt," said Bolderbuck evenly, "you——"

Old Martin Head interrupted with a curt, over-riding grunt. "Be quiet, Tom!"

Surratt flashed a long, careful look around him, rummaging all the shadows of doorway and alley. He was straight in the saddle and his shoulders were faintly swaying. This was a situation that keened him and brought up the latent rashness that so unquietly slept in him; and it was strange how ease came back and how pleasant the details of life became. He was faintly eager; he was faintly smiling. Old Martin sighed and relaxed against his chair when he observed that smile.

"Anything more to say, Tom?" suggested Surratt.

"No."

Surratt wheeled, crossing to the dressmaking shop. He got out of the saddle; he stood there by the horse a little while, depending on his questing senses to bring him such rumors of trouble as might be hidden in this sleepy town. But he had no warning. The stillness was an undisturbed stillness. He went on into the shop.

Annette Carvel had her back to the door. She heard him come and she turned, and all at once her face—so responsive to her moods—registered inexpressibly the swing of her emotions. The light of pleasure and relief was there and the way of her heart was there for him to see; but that was only for a moment. It fled before a strange, star-

176

tled fear. She said, throwing the words out with an expelled breath: "You shouldn't be here!"

"Annette," said a woman's voice. Turning, Buck discovered Mrs. Carvel in the doorway of another room.

"No, you shouldn't!" repeated Annette, almost in a cry.

"Who's in town?" asked Surratt quickly.

"Old Martin."

"Anybody else?"

"No," she murmured. "But they'll be back."

"Torveen—Brann? Miss Cameron? They're not here?"

"No. Where are they?"

He shook his head, listening to the fall of a horse's hoofs in the street. The horse stopped somewhere above the shop. There was no other sound just then. He had something in his mind and didn't know how best to say it, though he understood he had it to say. He looked at Mrs. Carvel; he took off his hat. He said quietly: "Nick Perrigo was killed this afternoon."

He was immediately to know what that news meant to her, for her lips came together and the straightness went out of her body. She put a hand against the door casing, lowering her head. Annette turned her curious eyes from Surratt to her mother. She said: "What is it?"

"In his fashion," reflected Surratt, "he was honest. I saw him die, and he died regrettin' many things."

Mrs. Carvel rose. She looked at Surratt in a way that hurt him and saddened him immeasurably. It was a sorry thing to stand before this woman and watch old tragedy rise in her eyes. It was there. But he kept thinking of Perrigo and of Perrigo's regret; and he felt bound to represent that little man truthfully. It turned him toward Annette. "He liked you. He said he remembered you best as a little girl wearin' a red bow in your hair."

"Me?" she said, deeply puzzled. "Me."

But Mrs. Carvel was near to crying. She said, "Thank you," in a muffled voice and walked back into the other room. Surratt's attentive ears kept registering the rise and fall of talk on the hotel porch. The run of time bothered him, and his nerves were stretched by a strain he felt and could not identify.

Annette Carvel murmured: "I don't understand."

He shook his head. "Never mind. Maybe it will help you to know that the glove found on Les Head's bunk meant nothing. You're loyal to your friends, Annette. It is a

177

strong light in a dark place. If you ever find a man you can put that loyalty on he'll be lucky."

She turned slowly away from him and walked to the end of the room. "Please, Buck," she said. "Please."

The sound of talk ceased, up by the hotel. There was a man moving idly past the dressmaking shop. These little impressions piled up and made a heavy weight on his nerves. He swung and went out of the shop, on out to his horse. The idling man was below him, under the porch awnings. Surratt turned to catch his foot in a stirrup, and his glance crossed to the hotel. He let the stirrup go and stood frozen there; he stepped away from the horse, into the middle of the street.

Bolderbuck and Old Martin still remained on the hotel porch. But a third man was standing before them now, his back swung on Surratt. Old Martin spoke, distinct enough for Surratt to hear:

"Turn around, Bill."

Bill Head said: "What?" but his great shoulders made a wheeling gesture and the ruddy, florid cheeks came about. He saw Surratt. The next moment he had crossed the walk in long strides. He came to a halt, out in the middle of Morgantown's dusty street, facing Surratt.

Chapter Eighteen

SO LONG!

Thus separated by an interval of thirty yards, they faced each other on Morgantown's street, with the store lamps shining softly upon them, with a fatal stillness falling around. Part of that stillness, Surratt understood, was the result of his senses slowly shutting out all unimportant details. He had been through this before and the story was the same now: everything faded except the shape of the man in front of him, and the energy of his body collected and seemed to pour into those few muscles he had to use. Bill Head was a magnified object down the street, the rise and fall of his chest and the faint shift of his shoulders magnified as well, and suddenly very important. He vaguely saw a horseman come into town and pause by the jail, and ride away. Around him, in the shadows of the board awnings, men's feet scraped a little, and then ceased to scrape. The smell of death was a thing that traveled fast. But his vision continued to narrow and his feeling of enormous solitude increased, and presently it was as though a black, high wall surrounded Bill Head and himself.

Bill Head called: "Surratt, what are you doing here?" But it wasn't in the tone of a question. It was the way a man would speak when lifted to unbearable heights of temper. He was a mauling man whose strength always had won its way. But here stood one who had whipped him in the Carson Ford saloon and had escaped the search of fifty riders, and the memory of that had its stinging, maddening way with him.

Surratt didn't answer; for talk was a useless thing now. He made a slim, straight shape in the mellow lamplight, with his arms hanging straight beside his wet clothes. His shoulders were thrown faintly forward and the weight of his body was a set, arranged weight.

Bill Head spoke again. "Surratt!" There was no purpose in that talk. It was only a vehement sound. His head tipped downward but his stare remained a fixed and calculating and wicked pressure against Surratt; and the ruddiness of his broad bold face was less than it had been. Surratt made no move. His purpose locked him viselike there. But then he saw Bill Head's lips faintly stir and stretch at the corners. It was a signal. It was a clear signal that Surratt had seen often before in other men waiting before him. And, seeing it, he reached for his gun and beat Head to the draw.

But it wasn't his shot that first shattered the silence.

He was lifting his gun for a deliberate aim when Bill Head began firing in a headlong way, throwing his lead in the same manner he threw his fists, a hot and thoughtless desire to destroy riding him uncontrollably. Dust sprayed up in front of Surratt; there was the breath of a bullet on his right cheek as it went by. These two reports were huge and thunderous in the town, slamming against the building walls. Surratt's eyes were pinned to that wide chest. He sent his bullet at it coolly—and sent no more, for his faith was that certain. Bill Head's arm stopped rising, his shoulders quit swinging; he froze in a queer, hunched posture and his face betrayed an unbelieving astonishment. A man somewhere in the shadows groaned at what he saw, and then Bill Head gave way at the knees and dropped awkwardly on his face. He was dead when he struck the ground. His hat rolled off his head; he lay that way, his face against the ground, his yellow hair shining with the dust.

For Surratt blackness rushed away and he was aware of all the dangers surrounding him. He made a complete wheeling circle, his gun raking all the shadows. There were townsmen crowding the walks, their faces dim and twisted by this scene. Annette Carvel was in the doorway of her shop, both hands clinging to the casing and a fright stamping a death's pallor on her graphic cheeks. Surratt threw his attention over to the White House porch. Pokey was on his feet, motionless. Bolderbuck had retreated to the hotel wall, where he remained in formidable quietness. Old Martin, in his chair, made no motion whatever.

Surratt walked that way and stood before the porch steps. Old Martin's eyes were hard to meet then, so bitter and blazing was the spirit rushing out of them. It was plain to Surratt at the moment that the man silently cried out for

180

a return of his own vigor, so that he might answer for his boy dead in the dust. But he sat there, gripping the arms of the chair, locked in a tumultuous hell—a fighter who could not fight and destroying himself from the thought.

Surratt shook his head. "It will do no good to say that I'm sorry. I came to this country without malice. I took the side of a man who befriended me. This is the end of that business, as is always the end. I cannot regret it now. Maybe——"

A sound up the street wheeled him around at once, and he discovered a column of horsemen entering the town. There was something lashed between the two leading horses, and after that he identified George Bernay and Blackjack Smith riding to either side of the burden the horses carried. It was a stretcher. He knew what it carried then, but he held his place. Doc Brann broke from the column and came on. He stopped before Bill Head's body; he looked at it. Afterwards his glance, turned to a grim brightness, jerked up to Surratt. He got off his horse and knelt down; his hand professionally touched the dead man's chest, soon coming away.

The column halted before the White House and broke to see what lay on the dusty street. George Bernay said: "Why, my God——!"

It was Sam Torveen who occupied the improvised stretcher lashed between the horses. He couldn't turn himself to see this, and his voice lifted weakly. "What's happened?"

Then Judith Cameron came from the rear of this group of men and paused to show Surratt a strange long glance, and rode rapidly down to the dressmaking shop. Another rider galloped out of the hills and was yelling when he struck the street. "They're comin' in!"

George Bernay's words jumped out of his throat. "Get Sam into the hotel!" He was down from his horse, unlashing the stretcher. Temple and Horsfall sprang out of their saddles, and the three of them took the stretcher and carried Torveen into the hotel. Small ruffles of steady sound broke away from the heights above Morgantown; and the yelling messenger charged along the dust and howled at Blackjack Smith, who sat so mountainously calm in his saddle.

"They're comin' in!"

Surratt had his careful look at the crowd. Blackjack and Blackjack's four men he knew. And Torveen's three par-

181

ticular friends he knew. But these others were strange to him. There were about twenty of them, all solemn and a little disturbed. Blackjack shifted his gross cheeks toward Surratt. He said briefly: "What you want to do?"

"Get down the street."

They heard him. They rode by and formed behind him, and he looked around to see how quietly they arranged themselves underneath the board awnings, and out across the street. He said evenly: "That's all right. Don't start any shooting until they do." For he knew who was coming; the smell of trouble was as clear to him as the odor of the disturbed dust curling up from the street.

Bernay and Billy Temple and Jud Horsfall came out of the White House on the run. They went up to their saddles and rode over to Surratt, turning beside him. George Bernay was a reckless man now; whitely grinning. He said: "These are my friends, Buck. They're also Sam Torveen's friends. Just a bunch of two-bit ranchers like me. I been ridin' ever since last night, to find 'em. We went up to the tunnel. You'd just left." He laughed outright. "Well —here's five horse thieves, twenty poor white trash, and a guy with a reward on his head. It's enough to make the angel Gabriel weep. Can we do it, Surratt?"

The question was suddenly high and thin. The man was game, but he wasn't sure. Surratt said softly: "We'll see," and watched Bill Head's men tip into Morgantown's street and ride fast forward.

Peyrolles and Dutch Kersom were leading the outfit; and both men discovered at once what faced them on the street. Peyrolles' arm shot high, to stop that rapid riding. They had gotten as far as the bank when they halted. Peyrolles bent in his saddle. He yelled excitedly: "If you boys want it, you can have it!"

Kersom said nothing. Sheriff Ranier worked his way forward through the riders and came abreast of Peyrolles. "Wait," he asked. "Wait a minute."

"Shut up!" yelled Peyrolles.

But Dutch Kersom suddenly pointed at Bill Head's body lying in the dust. It was a thing none of them had so far seen. Peyrolles stared down and his lantern jaw closed and his teeth snapped distinctly. Hughie Grant pushed forward, the coolest of the Head men. He put his arms across the saddle horn and had his look at Bill Head; nothing changed on his face. But he did something none of the rest of them had done. He lifted his hat in a way that was a gesture to the dead man and clapped it back on his head. His eyes threw a narrow glance across to Buck Surratt; he was quietly mad then. It was in his voice.

"You damn gunslinger, who asked you to come here?"

Surratt felt the high storm coming on. His men were shifting a little behind him; they were unsure, as was George Bernay. In front, the collected riders of the big outfits were slowly drifting, making a line wall to wall. Hughie Grant wheeled his horse onto the walk and wheeled again and faced Surratt at an angle. Peyrolles and Kersom both shifted away, sliding back into the mass of riders. Ranier rode up to the White House porch, to get out of the firing. In that space between these two factions was only Bill Head's prone body. The silence held on like this, screwing tighter, turning thin and thinner, becoming unendurable. Surratt swung his head toward the hotel porch, toward the obscure shape of Old Martin Head there. His talk was even and sad then, and very quiet.

"How many men do you want to die? This was your son's war and he's dead and that's the end of his pride. You can make this street a cemetery if it is your wish, but you'll settle nothing."

He had no answer from Old Martin. But Peyrolles, his excitability carrying him beyond thought, suddenly shouted: "Let the man have it!"

Old Martin's voice unexpectedly growled across the street with a strength and a taciturnity that stilled them all. "Peyrolles and Kersom—come here. I want you. Surratt, you come here."

Surratt walked across the dust. The other men were coming, but Old Martin Head stared at Surratt, the sore pride in him burning brightly. He said: "Push my chair into the hotel. I want Bolderbuck and I want Ranier. Bernay, come with us."

They all came along, the men Old Martin had named. They followed through the doorway. Surratt turned the wheel chair around; he stood near Old Martin, and he looked down at the man and saw the fire die out. Old Martin was speaking in a lost, defeated manner.

"I had three sons. One of them died for the South, a long time ago, and his memory is still fresh to me. It is all I have to remember, for my other boys were no good. They're gone and I'm a pretty old man and loneliness is a terrible thing. I've lived beyond my time. If I was a younger man, Surratt, I'd fight you for the joy of it—because fightin' was life to me, as fightin' is life to you now, though you do not recognize that thing in yourself. Few men do."

Peyrolles said angrily: "There's the man that killed your son, Martin."

"My son," said Old Martin quietly, "set the tune and he had to face the music out. The draw was even and Surratt stood his ground, as he had to do. I'd despised him if he hadn't. This is the way men have to act when the time for talkin' is all over. It is hard, but it is just. Now, Hank, we are going to make a decision here that will stand in my lifetime and yours. After that it does not matter. This is a young man's world and neither you nor me has a right to fence in all the water holes. So this is the way it is to be. Draw a line from Gray Bull peaks to the Cameron ridge. North of that line stays cattle; it stays cattle because we live over there and Dutch and Ab lives over there—and cattle is our life. South of that line sheep may come, and the young men may have their day. The fight is over."

Peyrolles' long jaws made a wicked, stubborn slant. "Not for me, Martin."

Old Martin rolled his shoulders. "I'm drawing my men out of this. Ab Cameron never wanted any of it. So where do you stand with your crew of ten and where does Dutch stand with his crew of nine? Surratt, you take those boys George Bernay brought you and ride over to Hank's house and burn it down. How'd you like that, Hank? The Head outfit will help you no more."

"I don't understand you," muttered Peyrolles dismally.

"Go out and tell everybody to go home," growled Old Martin.

Peyrolles turned his eyes toward Dutch Kersom, but Kersom was a studying shape in the background. He met Peyrolles' glance and merely lifted his shoulders. It angered Peyrolles immeasurably. He said: "Why don't you speak—you've got a tongue."

"I guess," said Kersom laconically, "we mind Martin."

Peyrolles ground his reluctant surrender between his teeth, "Let it be so," and shot his undimmed hostility at Surratt. "Stay on your side of that line," he added. He turned on his heels and walked out to the porch. All quiet in the room, they heard him speak irritably to the crews.

Old Martin looked about him to find Pokey quietly posted in a corner. "Get the buckboard. I'm going home."

Surratt's talk was soft, it was sad. "For all that's happened to you, for my part in it, I give you my regrets."

Old Martin shrugged his shoulders. "Things happen. It's the best any man can say. I should like to've had you for a son. Pokey—get me out of here."

Surratt swung and went across the lobby, George Bernay with him. They passed down a hall and stopped at a doorway. But Surratt didn't go in, for he saw Sam Torveen lying sound asleep on the bed, his arms flung out with the looseness of deep exhaustion. It made Surratt smile quietly to see that. "It was a chance—and it's all right now," he murmured. He went to the porch with George Bernay. Men were lifting Old Martin into a rig.

Bernay said: "So what now?"

Doc Brann came over the street. He stopped beside Surratt. "Go up to my office and pile into the bed there. You look like hell."

"For a fact," agreed Surratt. Weariness was like lead on his shoulders and he hadn't answered Bernay's question. He turned on the man, the smile remote and inscrutable. "Never be curious about tomorrow, George. It's bad enough when it comes." He left Bernay and crossed to the bank building. All the outfits were leaving Morgantown slowly; and Bill Head had been taken from the street, the spot where he had fallen ringed around by a group of curious men who eyed Surratt as he passed by. Before he turned up the bank stairway he saw Judith Cameron come from the dressmaking shop and meet Ab, who appeared on this street for the first time since the shooting. He went on up to Brann's room. There was a bottle of whisky sitting on the table, thoughtfully placed there. He helped himself, lifting the bottle to the corner of the room in a kind of salute to some thought in his mind; and had a long drink. Afterwards he peeled off his wet clothes and rolled up on the bed. He was thinking, as he fell asleep, of the trail he would be taking the next morning over the Gray Bull pass.

When he awoke he found Doc Brann sitting indolently in the room, obviously getting the full savor out of a morning cigar. Brann chuckled faintly and pointed at Surratt's clothes. "I dried 'em out. You'll find a razor and soap in the corner. Man, you been dead to the world." He fell silent then, but his eyes kept studying the tough, flat planes of Surratt's body and a long while afterward he added in a puzzled way: "I do not know where your power comes from. You're a deceptive man, Buck. The dynamite don't show."

Surratt shaved and made a smoke; and turned to look out of the window with an exploring glance. It was clear to Brann at the moment that Surratt's thoughts were gone from the room. Surratt put his hands into his pocket and rattled up some loose change. He said: "How's Sam?"

"All right," murmured Brann. "What you going to do now?"

But he knew the answer. Surratt had the way of a man who was finished with a chore. He stood before the window, uncertain and obviously restless—not knowing where to put the accumulating energy of his body. Brann read the regret in that smoky glance, and because he was a shrewd man he read something else as well. There was a quality in Surratt that Surratt himself never recognized—a flame that burned steady and clear and would not permit him to be satisfied with the ordinary rewards of life or the ordinary activities of men. Surratt thought he hated fighting. But this was self-delusion. For there was a hunger in him for some kind of attainment, for some kind of perfection, for some kind of final victory. It was like the dream of the prospector who sought the Mother Lode. And it put a terrific unrest in Surratt and would never let him be still; it made him fight, it took him into strange countries eagerly, it laid laughter on his face when trouble piled up and the end of all his searching seemed just beyond that trouble, and it brought out that deep wistfulness when, at last seeing no victory here, he rode on to another country. This, thought Brann, was the riddle of Buck Surratt. It made Brann quietly shake his head. He repeated his question: "What you going to do now?"

"I'm bound over the pass this morning," murmured Surratt. He looked around at Brann, faintly apologetic, faintly smiling. "The morning half of the trail is always pleasin' to the eye. A man can hope."

"One of the boys brought your horse down from the river," said Brann gruffly. "It's at the stable."

Somebody came up the stairs; and presently Pokey entered Brann's office. He nodded diffidently at Surratt. "Old Martin," he said, "would like to see you before you go. He's at the ranch."

"How," demanded Surratt with some wonder, "does he know I'm leaving?"

186

It made Brann shake his head again and say something that Surratt didn't understand. "Because," he remarked gently, "he knows you—like I know you."

"Pokey," said Surratt, "tell Old Martin I regret whatever hurt I've caused him. Tell him he's the sort of a man I'd like to ride for. And tell him so long for me." He turned suddenly from the room and went down to the street. He walked up to the stable and found a hand there. "Do me a favor," he asked the man. "Saddle up for me. I'll be soon back."

Fresh, long sunlight came out of the east. The morning was still cool and the rising, pine-banked slopes were a dark, summer's green. Dust and pine resin and the scent of leather and horseflesh—this made a keen blend to his nostrils. The world was fresh; and the restlessness, the undimmed hunger in him was livelier and more urgent than it had been. He crossed the yellow street, wherein Morgantown's people moved casually, and went into the hotel for his breakfast. There had been hell on that street the night before; but today it was a forgotten thing, which was the way life moved. The great moments and the brutal moments were like fire flares against a night sky. But then the flares died and the even run of plain things and plain hours came on. After he had finished breakfast he loitered, contrary to his custom, at the table a little while. He had a hard chore to do, and hated it.

But presently he got up and crossed the lobby to Torveen's room. The door was open and Judith Cameron and George Bernay stood inside. The talk quit instantly when he appeared there; it quit instantly and brought up his slow smile. "Talk of the devil and he's bound to come."

"Sure," said Torveen gruffly. There was a little color in his face. They had propped him up in the bed a few inches. Judith wheeled to a corner of the room, behind Surratt. She remained there, the sense of her presence very powerful to him. But he kept his glance on this strange Sam Torveen who looked irritably, cheerlessly back.

"Well," said Surratt.

"Sure," growled Torveen. "I know. You've had your fun and now you've rolled your blankets and in a minute you're long gone."

"Yes," said Surratt quietly. "I always was a fiddle-footed man." His grin turned strong and brilliant across the bronzed outline of his face. It destroyed the gentle gravity; it hid what his eyes might otherwise have said. "Put this down in the book, Sam. You're the first redheaded sheep-herder I ever knew."

"What'll I do for thankin' you?" muttered Torveen. And then George Bernay suddenly left the room.

"Never mind it, kid," suggested Surratt. "We've had our fun—which is enough."

Torveen showed a little curiosity. "One thing has puzzled me. This Blackjack Smith. Where did you know him before?"

"In my country, across the desert," smiled Surratt. "He was a rustler. We had our own private war—and then he left, and came here." He watched Torveen a moment. "Speaking of that, kid, what were you doin' down in Carson Ford that afternoon?"

"You were there?"

"In the back room, talkin' to Blackjack till you arrived."

"I wanted help from the man," explained Torveen. "I was in a frame of mind to dicker with even a rustler for a little help. But he didn't commit himself."

Surratt grinned. "He's in a jack pot now. He won't rustle off a friend, and he's made a lot of friends in this ruckus."

Judith said, behind him: "Buck."

It turned him around and it erased his grin. Looking at her now, he had no laughter in him. "Buck," she said carefully, "the glove was an accident. I'm telling you this because you never asked. It was a glove I long ago lost. Les always kept it in his pocket. You found it on him?"

"On the floor."

"It would be like him," she murmured. "He hated Bill and he knew Bill wanted me. I think he took the glove out of his pocket before he died and put it on the floor, where it would be seen. It was his manner of torturing his brother. of trying to make Bill believe he had a way with me Bill didn't have. That was Leslie always. I don't think he ever stopped to consider how that would hurt me. It was Bill he wanted to stab once more, as he had been doing all his life."

"I have never doubted you," said Surratt very quietly; and turned to Torveen. "Well, I wish you luck. The both of you. It has been my fortune to have good friends. I can say no more."

Torveen let out a long. ragged breath. He turned his eyes from Surratt to Judith in the background. When they came back to Surratt again they were full of shadow. His lips pressed thin and, until he spoke, the quietness of the room was deep and thick. "Some men," he said, a wonder in his voice, "were made to ride high and handsome and leave a trail behind that never dies out. How can a man forget you, kid?"

Surratt said, "So long, Sam," and swung around to leave this room rapidly. But he stopped in the hall, for Judith had followed. She closed the door and put her back against it, with her arms behind her; her face lifted toward him, with an expression below the strange darkness of her eyes he could not read, could not understand. He did not try to understand, knowing it would never help. Her presence, as always, stirred up a call in him that could not be answered—and turned the thought of tomorrow wholly empty. She was a treasure, he told himself, such as he might dream of but never possess; and he realized then that the memory of her standing so fair before him, so proud and reliant and so rich with the grace and fire of a woman, would be a light shining through the shadows wherever he went.

But he said nothing; he had his long look at her and bowed his head quietly and went across the lobby. He heard Sam Torveen calling out of the room in a strong, urgent way: "Judith, please come in here."

Surratt stopped a moment on the porch. Annette Carvel was there with George Bernay and he thought he saw something in the girl's eyes as she looked up at Bernay that was good for both these people. He smiled at her and took Bernay's hand, who seemed to want to speak. Surratt shook his head and went on across the dust to the stable. He climbed into the saddle and swung out, the urge to be on his way powerfully impelling him. People were on the street, and he saw Doc Brann look down from the second-story office window. Surratt lifted his hand toward Brann, and lifted it to the town—to all that it had meant to him—and grinned again. He said, "So long," and rode away.

When he reached the trees he was no longer smiling. The coolness was already gone from the day and he rode on through a murmuring, drowsy forest shade. He passed the side road into Torveen's place and remembered the events surrounding that ranch as though they had occurred long ago. He passed the trail into the sheep meadow and later the bridge under which he had drifted to escape Bill Head's trap. A little of that night's excitement came back to him—and then went away; for this was turning already into just another episode on his back trail, with its confusion and its excitement and its tragedy becoming even now indistinct. He had come into the country as a stranger and for a little while he had known its ways, and now he was a stranger riding out.

Still thinking about that he reached the heights of the pass road about ten o'clock and saw a flat plain running far off to the east, with the glitter of sunlight all along it and a heat haze rolling up on its far boundaries. He turned to have his last look at the green hills and then, shrugging his shoulders like a good gambler who had lost, he pushed onward, bound for the distant plains. The Gray Bull peaks threw a shoulder against the road here, and the road curved about it; and when he made the bend he saw Judith Cameron waiting there in her saddle.

Surratt stopped, twenty yards away. But Judith came up and she was smiling strangely at him, the shadows gone away from her splendid eyes. She said, with a gentleness that was like melody: "You are so wise, Buck. And so blind."

His reply was suddenly full of storm and anger. "I never knew where your heart was, Judith, but I know Sam's feelings very well. And I don't steal from my friends."

She slipped out of her saddle. She said: "Get down, Buck. Get down." Her lips were fresh and curved and red from her thinking. He got down and came up to her. All the desert below threw off a burning yellow light; the road ran across it, dwindling out into the remote distance. Judith's voice came over to him, like a demand.

"You are not looking at me. You're thinking of the trail and what lies beyond the next hill! Pull your head down and look at me!"

He said slowly: "You know what I am, Judith."

"Better than you do. And Sam knew better than both of us—and so he told me to follow you and find you." Her tone dropped to a remote whispering. "I should have done it, anyway. My dear, what are you looking for that makes you so restless, so sad?"

He was like a gambler, so stoically trained to bad fortune that he could not trust his change of luck. He reached out and took hold of her shoulders, full of doubt, darkly uncertain. "It is a hope," he said quietly, "I never permitted myself to have, Judith."

She said: "Why am I here then?"

He reached down and kissed her. The richness and fullness of that experience altogether unsettled him and set him back on his heels. Her smile was soft and shining and at once he saw that all her loyalty, reserved for some one man alone, came out of her gray eyes to him as a proud gift. It was a thing that entered him and quenched his hungers and made him suddenly understand what his long searching had been for. He knew then that was, for him, the end of the trail.